DAMAGE CONTROL

Also by Lisa Renee Jones

Hard Rules

DAMAGE CONTROL

A DIRTY MONEY NOVEL

LISA RENEE JONES

ST. MARTIN'S GRIFFIN
NEW YORK

DAMAGE CONTROL. Copyright © 2017 by Lisa Renee Jones. All rights reserved. Printed in the United States of America. For information, address St. Martin's Press, 175 Fifth Avenue, New York, N.Y. 10010.

www.stmartins.com

Designed by Omar Chapa

The Library of Congress Cataloging-in-Publication Data is available upon request.

ISBN 978-1-250-08383-8 (trade paperback)
ISBN 978-1-250-08387-6 (e-book)

Our books may be purchased in bulk for promotional, educational, or business use. Please contact your local bookseller or the Macmillan Corporate and Premium Sales Department at 1-800-221-7945, extension 5442, or by e-mail at MacmillanSpecialMarkets@macmillan.com.

First Edition: February 2017

10 9 8 7 6 5 4 3 2 1

Dear Readers,

I am so very excited to share *Damage Control* with you. If you haven't read *Hard Rules*, you need to read it before you read *Damage Control*, as we are going to be starting our story the moment after *Hard Rules* ends. And spoiler warning—I'm now going to recap *Hard Rules* for readers below.

We ended with Shane confronting Emily about her identity. He's long known she has a secret, but he wanted her to trust him and share it on her own. But thanks to Seth, Shane's right-hand man (The Fixer, who will get his own story!) Shane now knows she is not who she says she is, and his fear that she is either a federal agent or working for his family to set him up is in the forefront.

But how did they get to this point?

It all started with the wrong coffee. Emily picks up Shane's order by accident and drinks from it, and when he takes it back and drinks from it her lipstick ends up on his mouth. From there, a one-night stand evolves, and then passion, love, and friendship follow. Emily has become the one pure thing in Shane's life as he battles to save his family empire from their self-created corruption. He NEEDS her to be that person he trusts, who restores his faith in life and love. Will he lose that now? That's the real question. And if she has betrayed him, how do they recover? Can they recover?

Just a little more history, to refresh your memory about what Shane's facing:

If you remember, we learned that Shane was fast becoming one of the leading attorneys in the country when he left New York to return to Denver to save his family empire from the aforementioned corruption of their own doing. Brandon Enterprises has long been run by his father, Brandon Senior, and brother, Derek, who both walk the gray line, and Derek does so with less skill than his father. Shane pulls his brother, and the company, out of legal chaos while his father is diagnosed with terminal cancer.

Brandon Senior isn't one to repent, rather he is ready to kiss the devil hello, but only after he's pitted his sons against each other for control of the company, and a race to win the vote by the board of directors. It's a battle Shane reluctantly enters at first, as it means leaving all he's worked for in his law career behind, but he decides he wants to save his family name. He's going to win control of the company, but his brother feels he's earned the leadership role.

Shane buys a pharmaceutical company certain to produce enough revenue to offset any dirty money running through the company, but his brother wants that spotlight back. Derek makes a deal with a drug cartel, to run a new performance-enhancing drug (Sub-Zero), through Brandon Pharmaceuticals. And that drug leads to a high-profile baseball player's wife threatening to expose the ruse.

Now Shane is faced with a drug lord, a brother who might just be willing to kill him or Emily to win the head of the table, a father who is dying, and then let's not forget his mother. Is she with him or Derek? And what about Mike, the largest stockholder, who owns a professional basketball team? Could he become a problem?

So onward to that moment in the kitchen and Shane's declaration to Emily of "no more lies." It's time to find out who Emily really is!

I hope you enjoy and thank you so much for choosing to spend your time with one of my books!

Lisa

XOXO

CAST OF CHARACTERS

Emily Stevens (27)—Heroine in the series. She is Brandon Senior's newly appointed secretary. Learned after landing her new job that the one-night stand she had the night before is her boss's son, Shane Brandon. Emily has secrets, and she's running. But Shane will not let her run from him. During *Hard Rules*, the two had a lot of push and pull about their relationship, his family, and her secrets.

Shane Brandon (32)—Hero of the series. Shane Brandon is the black sheep of the family. The good one. The one willing to risk everything to play this game on the up-and-up and keep his brother from ruining the family empire, Brandon Enterprises, by getting in bed with the Martina family drug cartel. But Shane is treading on thin ice as he bring his legacy back from the brink of corruption. He is also dealing with Emily Stevens. A woman who breaks through his defenses and brings an innocence to his life that he can't have as a distraction. He wants and needs to protect her, possess her, and be worthy of her. She is already making him a better man and keeping him grounded. But she has secrets and could be the one to ultimately send his world crumbling harder than he ever anticipated.

Derek Brandon (37)—The older brother. While he's brilliant and good-looking, his greed for power drives him to make rash decisions. He and Shane were close as kids, but once they became adults and Shane joined Brandon Enterprises, that shifted. Everything became about who would control the empire. Derek has gotten the family corporation into bed with the Martina drug cartel, and Shane will do everything in his power to stop his brother.

Maggie Brandon—Shane and Derek's mother. Seemingly befriending Emily, yet we are uncertain about her ultimate motives concerning the current struggle between her sons for control over Brandon Enterprises. Married to David Brandon (Brandon Senior)

David Brandon—The head of Brandon Enterprises and the Brandon family. Father to Derek and Shane. Husband to Maggie. He is dying of cancer but wants to leave a legacy and hold on to control of Brandon Enterprises as long as possible. He's a bastard and pushes Shane and Derek in all the wrong ways. He is gruff, cold, and hard at every turn. He enjoys watching his sons battle for power. It entertains him.

Seth Cage (35)—Shane's right-hand man. Shane hired Seth away from their firm in New York to help clean up a mess for his family, and from there Seth remained on Shane's personal payroll, as well as taking up the role of head of security at Brandon Enterprises.

Jessica (29)—Shane's assistant. Ever the loyal employee, she followed him from New York and becomes friends with Emily as she starts to work as Brandon Senior's assistant. Jessica's job knows no bounds, as she helps Shane with everything from securing a new apartment to keeping an eye on Brandon Senior and Derek when Shane is not in the office and relaying any curious goings-on.

Eric Knight—A friend of Shane's from college who is a brilliant surgeon and has squeaky-clean morals. Eric is the doctor of the patient who was running her mouth about Brandon Pharmaceuticals (BP), part of Brandon Enterprises, being the distributor for an undetectable performance-enhancing drug that her Major League Baseball–player husband is taking. Eric brings this news to Shane, causing Shane to take action

Adrian Martina—The son of the Mexican cartel leader, Roberto Martina. Runs the U.S. side of the operations. He has some relationship with Derek Brandon, the extent of which is not fully known yet. Brother to Teresa Martina, who is sleeping with Derek.

Teresa Martina—Sister to Adrian. Sleeping with Derek. Bartender at Martina's Casa.

Randy—Security guard of the building where Brandon Enterprises offices are located. Emily and Shane have a conversation with him over her missing cell phone. Keeps Shane updated on David Brandon's activities.

Mike Rogers—Sits on the board of Brandon Enterprises. Holds 20 percent of their stock and owns a professional basketball team.

Key player in the hedge fund as well. Has a lot to lose if Brandon Enterprises were to shut down their investment division. His company, Rogers Athletics, is one of the proposed investments for the hedge fund. When Seth and Shane are trying to pull dirt on the board members in order to influence their votes for power of the company, Seth cannot find anything substantial on Mike.

Rick Stevens—Emily's brother. Is aware of her secrets and why she is hiding. He's very hard for Emily to get in touch with, and his silence and evasiveness make Emily nervous.

Lana Smith—A brilliant scientist and businessperson at Brandon Pharmaceuticals. She wants Shane and has caused him trouble in the past. She hid weed in his car and almost cost him his attendance at Harvard. She is still trying to get close to him now and caused a slight rift between him and Emily in *Hard Rules*.

Nick Snyder—Knows Seth from their CIA/FBI days. Saved Seth's life, and now Seth has brought him to Shane so Nick can help get to the bottom of the true involvement of the Martina Cartel in Brandon Enterprises. Confirms that the Brandon Enterprises trucking division is already distributing cocaine. Is going to help Shane and Seth figure out how to maneuver a takedown and extricate the company out of the hold of the Martina cartel.

DAMAGE CONTROL

CHAPTER ONE

SHANE

"No more lies," I repeat, my hands pressed to the counter behind Emily, my body caging her against my kitchen island, though it's her web of lies that is now her prison, and my personal hell. "I know you aren't who you say you are."

Panic flashes in her beautiful blue eyes that I'd once thought the window to innocence, while her palm flattens on my chest, as if preparing to push me away. "What are you talking about?" she demands, no doubt weighing how much trouble she's in, yet her voice is steady, her demeanor remarkably cool. The kind of cool that takes practice and skill. The kind of cool someone undercover exhibits.

"No more games, Emily. Or whatever the hell your name is. Seth had you investigated, and nothing about who you are quite manages to add up."

"Investigated," she repeats. "Right. Because why in the world wouldn't you investigate the woman in your bed?"

"Since the person you say you are doesn't exist, clearly for good reason."

"My secrets are mine. Mine to know. Mine to share. When I'm ready."

"When exactly were you going to be ready?"

Her fingers curl where they rest on my starched white shirt. "I never meant to lie to you," she says, another lie, and her voice is no longer steady, a tremble and a quake in its depths.

"But you *did* lie to me," I remind her, a lock of her long dark hair slipping over her face, a veil that will be no better a shield to protect her than more lies.

"I never even meant to go to dinner with you, let alone end up this close to you." She hesitates. "I thought we'd be the sum of that night. *One* night . . . The rest just happened."

"Ah yes. Dinner. The night the lies began."

"No," she says tightly. "My secrets didn't begin with you and they don't end with you. And I darn sure wasn't going to spill them to a stranger."

"I'm not a fucking stranger."

"You were," she reminds me. "You were a stranger when I told you who I am."

"I haven't been a stranger for a long time and we both know it. I want the truth."

"I can't," she says, her gaze falling to the buttons of my white collared shirt, the absence of my tie and jacket proof of how relaxed I'd been only fifteen minutes ago.

I cup her jaw with one hand and force her gaze to mine. "You will," I insist, the words darn near guttural, as emotions I don't want to name splinter through me.

"Let me go," she says, giving me a full-body push. "Move, Shane."

I don't even sway. "I'm not letting you go," I say, gripping the material of her navy blouse at her waist. "Who are you?"

"I can't tell you. That's it. There is no more, Shane."

"What are you after? Who hired you?"

"Right," she bites out. "I must be spying on you. Of course that's what you'd think." She shoves on my chest. "Move. Let me off this counter." After one more ineffectual shove, she glowers at me and declares, "This isn't about you or your fucked-up family, Shane."

"What do you expect me to think?"

"Just what you did. Which thinking back, is why I stayed. You were always too wrapped up in them to ever really see me. That made me safe."

I flinch with an accusation I do not want to be true. "I saw you. I thought I did."

"Clearly you didn't."

"You will not turn this on me. If this isn't about me, then what is it about? Who is it about?"

"Me. It's about me. Just me. Why does it have to be about you?"

I stare at her, searching her eyes, and damn it, I see torment and fear that I don't want to be about her betrayal. I want them to be about something else. Something I can fix, but I can't afford to be a fool. I release her, moving to the opposite side of the island, gripping the edges. I glance at the folder now lying between us, then at her. "Then explain the contents."

"I don't need to look," she says, refusing to look at it while the buttons on my shirt seem to have grown exceedingly interesting. "I already know everything there is to know about me."

"Don't you want to know what I know about you?"

She inhales and meets my stare, firming her voice. "This is just going to lead to questions I can't answer."

"Open the folder," I say, the steel in my voice and my will meant to send a clear message: I won't let her refuse.

She understands too. I see that in the way her jaw sets, the way her chest expands with a breath, which she holds. She opens the folder, flipping over a summary of her fake history, along with documents that show the many holes in her past. She has no yearbook photos. No driver's license before several years ago. I'd ruled out witness protection based on those stupid mistakes. If I hadn't exploited mistakes the Feds have made to save a few clients, including my brother and father, I wouldn't know they are far from flawless. But does she? Is she one of them?

Seconds tick by, becoming a full minute before she shuts the folder and looks at me, shoving hair behind her ear, then hugging herself. "You know I'm not who I say I am. I get that already."

"What's your name?"

"Emily."

"No games. Your real name."

"That person I was doesn't exist anymore."

I grab the envelope that is still in the center of the counter, removing the damning evidence of her betrayal inside. "Explain that," I say, plopping the highly confidential paperwork Seth found in her desk in front of her, the word "spying" ringing too damn true for comfort.

She glances down and immediately back to me. "Shane—"

"Who are you working for?" I demand, my voice low, tight, wrapped in barely contained anger, when nothing I do is ever "barely contained." She has pushed buttons I don't want pushed. She is a woman I let into my life and mind, who I trusted. Who I foolishly want to believe can explain all of this.

"I was collecting those documents for you," she says, giving me an answer I do not expect.

"You're going to have to do better than that, sweetheart."

"Have you even read them or did Seth just tell you they're damning so you believed him?"

"You tell me," I order. "About the papers. About everything."

"Your father is up to something with the hedge fund he's putting together. I pulled together the paperwork for you to look at."

"There's a lot more in those documents than information about that hedge fund."

"I was alone in the offices and I snuck into your father's office." She presses her hands to the counter and looks at me, really looks at me for the first time since I confronted her. "Shane," she says softly, a plea in her voice, a vulnerability in her eyes I'm not sure can be faked. "I know how this looks, but I swear to you that I did not betray you. This situation I'm in really isn't about you or your family."

I study her, trying to figure out why I want to believe her, when I have no reason to give her that trust at the point. "Then what's it about?" I demand.

"It's complicated," she says, another tremble to her voice.

I resist an insane urge to close the space between us, grab her, kiss her, and fucking tell her everything is going to be okay. "Tell me."

"I can't."

Rare, uncontained frustration rolls through me. "Damn it, Emily," I growl, scrubbing fingers through my dark hair, which will no doubt soon be gray. I then rest my hands back on the counter to face her head-on. "What the hell is your real name?"

"Emily," she repeats. "And this is going nowhere." She pushes off the island. "I'm sorry. I should have never gotten involved with you. I'm leaving and you won't see me again."

She walks in my direction because she has no choice. It's the only straight line to the door, and while I get that she is a caged animal trying to escape right now, that's not going to happen. "You aren't going anywhere until I get some answers," I say, shackling her arm before she passes, turning her to face me, letting her see the distrust burning in my eyes. "This isn't just about the two of us. This is about a company I pledged to protect."

"Check the hotel security footage," she says. "I was carrying a folder when I came here last night. Not that I can prove it had this information in it, but it did." She pulls against my hold, which I tighten. "Please let me go," she says, the plea laced with what almost sounds like regret, but then, what is real with her? What was ever real?

Seconds tick by, heavy like stone, and I stare at her, taking my time to reply, containing my simmering anger, but I let her see it. I let her feel the steel wire whipping here and there, and I don't give her a path to dodge it or even soften its blow. Finally, I release her, but before she can move, I've gripped the waist of her blouse again, dragging her to me, the impact of her soft curves against mine a little too right to be so damn wrong.

"Tell me," I demand, my tone roughened by the emotions I don't want to name or feel for that matter, nor do I want to be staring into her eyes, looking for whatever the hell I'm looking for that I won't find. Or maybe I will, and that's the problem. She doesn't want me to see it either, cutting her gaze to stare at my damn buttons again. "Look at me," I demand of her.

She inhales, a soft sound that I don't want to be sexy, but holy fuck, everything about this woman is sexy to me and that only pisses me off again. She lifts her chin, looking at me with those too blue eyes, and whispers, "I am sorry."

"Is that a confession?"

"It's an apology."

"For what?"

"Everything."

I don't like that answer. In fact, I hate that fucking answer, and I don't hate any more easily than I love. Worse, I'm pretty damn sure I'm headed to one or the other with this woman; maybe I've already reached both. My gaze lowers to her mouth, lingering there, mine ready to claim hers, to punish her. "I wonder," I say, my gaze finding hers, heat simmering low in my limbs, one part lust, another part fury, "how it is that I didn't taste your lies. I wonder if they'll taste differently now that I know they exist."

I lower my head, leaning into her to find out when she shoves my chest, and says, "No!" before twisting away from me, leaving me no option but to risk hurting her if I don't release her. I let her go; my idea of "punishment" is defined in many ways, and that includes her willing submission.

Emily wastes no time with her freedom, darting away from me and charging for the foyer. I stand there a moment, inhaling a calming breath and contemplating my next move and her potential departure. If I let her go, I find out where her panic leads her and to whom. But if that happens, will I ever find out how those lies really taste and why I've missed them? That's not an option, and I start walking, my long stride eating up the space she has put between us. I exit the kitchen to the foyer, just in time to see her slip her purse across her chest.

She glances up at me and dashes for the door, and I let her reach it, entrapping her from behind. Still, she reaches for the knob and I shove my hand on the wooden surface and hold it shut. She turns to find me almost on top of her, so close I could taste those lies right now, right in this moment. I could fuck her right here and now, the way she's been fucking me over and over for days.

"You're such an asshole," she hisses, surprising me with her attack. "Why can't you see that I'm protecting you?"

"Protecting me how?" I demand, all kinds of possibilities stirring in my mind. The Feds. The Martina cartel. My brother. "And from whom?" I add.

"Since protecting you meant not telling you what I have going on, I wouldn't be protecting you now if I told you. And what exactly is the difference in you pretending to fuck that woman to protect me and me keeping secrets to protect you?"

"You aren't who the hell you told me you are. That's the damn difference."

"Fucking someone else or me hiding my identity to protect you. Which is worse?"

"Since I didn't fuck another woman, but you did hide your identity, that answer is pretty damn clear."

"I could say about ten things to that, but then you'd just make some scathing remark I don't deserve. You didn't even ask me why I hid who I am. You just attacked me."

"This isn't a little thing."

"No," she says. "It's not. Not at all, but not for the reasons you assume."

"You're still trying to turn this one on me and it won't work. All you had to do was just say 'I can explain' and then do it. If you had, we'd be having a different conversation."

"Right," she says, "and starting the conversation with 'no more lies' is certainly the way to invite me to share my deepest, darkest secrets."

"I gave you every reason to trust me. Every reason to tell me what you chose not to tell me. You want delicate little questions? That's not me and it's sure as hell not me after I find out from someone else you've been lying to me and I have to question every moment I ever spent with you."

"We're done," she rasps out, delicately clearing her voice before adding, "We both know that, so let's not drag this out. Let me out of here."

I study her for several beats, reading uncertainty in her face that I want to understand, to taste on my tongue, a little too much. "Yes," I say tightly. "Let's get out of here before I strip you naked and fuck you, which I have no doubt we'll both enjoy, but I won't be sure who's seducing who. And I won't be that damn naked with you ever again."

"I told you why I did this, Shane," she murmurs, defeat in her voice.

"To protect me. Funny. My father loves to use that as an excuse."

"That was your excuse for being with that woman," she fires back, that fiery side of her I like too damn much returning.

"I wasn't fucking that woman and you know it."

"Do I? Because you're judging me by your family's actions, while their blood runs through your veins, not mine."

I press my fists on either side of the door by her head. "Being a bitch does not help you right now."

"Being an asshole just proves you're an asshole."

"Lying only makes you—"

"Honorable in ways you'll never understand," she blasts back.

"I'm *going* to understand," I assure her. "Sooner rather than later."

"I'd like to leave, sooner rather than later."

"We're going downstairs to the hotel restaurant to eat dinner."

She blanches. "What? No. I'm not having dinner with you."

"You will. The lies started with dinner, and so it's only appropriate they end with dinner."

"No—"

"And you'll do it because you owe me that damn much."

"What is dinner going to do but draw this out, Shane?"

"We're going to dinner," I insist, knowing she could try to run, but also knowing she's being followed, and that ultimately might be the only way I find out the truth of who, and what, she is really all about.

"What keeps me from leaving?"

"Nothing but you," I assure her.

"I'm going to leave."

"Then leave, Emily. I'll find out the answers from someone else, and be colored by their definitions. If that is how you want to end this, then it says a lot about who we are and what we are."

"Don't do that to me."

"I'm just being honest, a trait I value."

"If you knew what—"

"But I don't," I say, pushing off the door, damn ready to get her out of here before I really do strip her naked, and there'd be no coming back from how cold and hard I'd fuck her right now. And apparently I'm still just foolish enough to actually hold on to a hope that she really has an explanation for all of this that makes it possible. As if she wants to douse that idea, she quickly says, "Dinner won't change what I'm willing to tell you."

Displeased in about a hundred ways, I turn her to face the door, her back to my front, her lush backside nestled intimately against me. I arch around her, my lips at her ear, my hand flattening on her belly. "Much has already changed, Emily," I assure her. The floral scent of her perfume teases my nostrils with bittersweet memories of me wrapped in that smell, in this woman, whoever she is. "And so much more is about to."

"I was weak," she murmurs. "I should have ended this before you could feel the way you do right now."

"But you didn't," I say, not bothering to ask why. That answer is in the secrets she thinks she isn't going to tell me tonight.

She leans back into me, a subtle sway before she melts against me. "I tried," she whispers, her hands sliding to my thighs, and holy fuck, her touch is too damn right for her to be wrong. The idea jolts me and I step back, taking her with me to open the door, before I then set her away from me, and into the hallway. "It's time for that dinner and conversation."

She stumbles slightly and damn it, I want to right her footing. I want to save her, when I might be the one I need to be saved after this, after her. I watch her catch her balance and start walking, her pace even, when I have a feeling she wants to run; and even knowing Seth will have her followed, I don't want her to run. Reaching behind me, I shut the door, and in a few long strides, I catch up with her, but she doesn't look at me. I think it's fairly clear that she doesn't want to see the distrust in my eyes any more than I want to see the lies in hers. Once again, we're well matched, but for all of the wrong reasons.

We fall into step as we so often do, which is something I have never experienced with any other woman. But when I would normally reach for her, I do not, for the same reason I got us the hell out of the apartment. I don't need to fog my senses with the feelings this woman obviously delivers, when I didn't even believe that was possible. She wants to protect me? I'm protecting myself, and I'm not sure what bothers me more: The idea that she doesn't want my protection because she doesn't trust me or because she's my enemy.

In all of sixty seconds, we round the corner and stop at the elevator bank, neither of us looking at each other. I punch the call button while she hugs herself, a defensive stance that means little that I don't already know. She's guarded. She's always been guarded. I knew this. I knew she had some ghosts in her closet, but I thought they were things she wasn't ready to tell, not things she completely erased. The elevator dings almost instantly and I hold the door for her, not just because it's the gentlemanly thing to do but because I want to control every moment I'm with her tonight.

She steps inside the car, and while she is often bold and even confrontational, tonight she walks to the opposite side of the car, leaning on the wall, arms folded in front of her chest still. I join her inside, punching the lobby button, I rotate to face her, my hands on the railing of the wall behind me. Her long brown hair is sleek, her navy skirt and blouse simple but professional, though now I find myself wondering if her limitations are choice or circumstance. I wonder a lot of things I should have wondered sooner.

The elevator doors shut, sealing us inside a steel box with her lies and my questions. The car starts to move, and our gazes collide, the connection a punch in my chest I don't want her to have the power to deliver. But she does. I am vulnerable in ways I swore I never would be with a woman, or anyone for that matter, and I'd actually forgotten the lessons my family taught me years ago. What my mother warned me about with Emily. The people closest to you can hurt you the most. My jaw sets hard, my stare now sharp glass shards of accusation.

Apparently far from oblivious to that fact, Emily lifts her chin and declares, "I am not going to sit through dinner with you looking at me like that."

"How am I looking at you?"

"Like I'm one of the many people who you can't trust and who have betrayed you."

"Change my mind."

"So I'm right," she says, her voice cracking. "You do think I'm one of them."

"There are many things going on in my mind right now."

"I told you—"

"Don't tell me anything in this elevator."

"Right," she says tightly. "Because everyone in your family is watching everyone else, so it has cameras."

"You know me and my family well," I say dryly. "And yet I know far less about you than I want to know."

"I thought we weren't talking in the elevator?"

"I want to know more of you," I say, putting a double entendre to use. "And that's not something I mind anyone knowing."

"You know more than you think," she replied, thinking on her feet, and choosing her words to play to the same audience I am.

"And yet you still feel like a mystery to me," I reply, and it's in that moment the elevator slows and dings. Her gaze jerks toward the doors and I glance up and register that we are now on the fourth floor, rather than our destination. Not about to let a wall of human bodies give Emily a chance to escape, I close the distance between us, and by the time her gaze returns to me, I'm standing in front of her. She looks up at me, her lips parting in surprise, her gaze meeting mine, and there is no mistaking the flash of torment in her eyes that I want to understand.

The doors open and male voices sound, moving closer to us as they enter the car, crowding Emily and me, and in turn, forcing me to remove the step I've left between us, my hands bracketing her waist. She sucks in air with the contact, her hands wrapping my wrist, and I'm not sure if she's holding me in place, or wishing she could move me and escape. The doors shut to my right and the car jolts into action, while Emily sways forward, catching herself with a palm on my chest. Seeming to be stunned by what she's done, she tries to pull it away, but I cover her hand with mine, holding it to me. Her gaze seems to instinctively jerk from those spellbinding buttons to my face, offering me a glimpse of the confusion etched all over hers. She doesn't know if she wants to hold on to me or push me away. In that, we are one, but I am not comforted by her conflicting emotions. She's trapped by her own lies; what she does with the freedom I'm about to give her will speak volumes about who she is, and who we are together.

The car halts, and once again her gaze is averted, any answers I might find in it hidden. I'm hoping like hell she really does stay and that a table in the restaurant will offer her the security to tell me the truth, no matter how ugly it might be. I fight the urge to reach for her hand and hold on to her, instead stepping to the side and facing forward. She joins me, standing beside me to watch the doors open, as if ready to launch herself forward, and I remind myself that one way or another, I'm getting my answers, and despite my desire that she stay, letting her escape and following where she leads might be the easiest answer.

The two men with us exit, clearing our path, allowing us to walk into the corridor, and in that moment, I say to hell with making it easy for her to run. She lied to me. Leaving won't be easy. I reach around her waist and snag her hip, aligning our legs as we walk, preventing her escape. "Shane, I—"

"It's dinner," I say. "You'll have an audience to protect you."

She digs in her heels and stops, turning to face me, her hand landing on my chest again. "I don't need to be protected from you. You need to be protected from me."

Red flags go up all over again. "Do you know how many ways I could read that? Are you trying to warn me here or what?"

"No. Yes. No. Not from what you are thinking."

"What am I thinking?"

"You already told me you think I'm spying on you, and I'm not." She presses her hand to her face. "This is not working." She drops her hand and looks at me. "I have to go." Abruptly she pulls back from me, and being that we're in public I have to let her go, and we both know that.

She turns and takes a step, gasping and stopping dead in her tracks as my father steps directly in front of her. "Mr. Brandon."

Tall, with thinning gray hair, his custom blue suit hangs on his now frail, cancer-ridden body like it belongs to someone else, but there is nothing frail in the way his gaze lands on Emily.

"Emily," he states. "I didn't expect to see you here."

She grips her purse with a death hold, her spine going ramrod stiff, and a wave of protectiveness overcomes me that says much about my instincts with Emily and my father. I step to her side, close; my palm settling possessively on her lower back. "Why are you here, Father?" I ask, the demand short and clipped by design. I've told him to get his damn mistress out of the Four Seasons, considering I'm in the residential side of the building.

His gray eyes, still so much like mine, cut sharply to me. "I came to see you," he declares, reaching into his blue suit jacket and producing an envelope, which he offers me. "The deed to your apartment as requested. I've signed it over to you."

Aware he has a self-serving motive of some sort, I snatch the envelope from him, stick it in my pocket, and disinvite whatever conversation he hopes to have. "Go home to your wife."

"She's occupied," he says. "As she is far more often than you realize."

Holy fuck, I want to ask what that means, but I don't give him the satisfaction. "Do you blame her?"

His lips tighten, the only telltale sign that I've hit a nerve, but his reply is not what I expect. "No actually, I do not. I'm going upstairs to the apartment I still own, and will continue to own."

"That's not acceptable. I want you, and your plaything, out of my home."

"Well then, son, you'll be pleased to know that the doctors say you won't have to tolerate it for long. I'll be dead soon."

A tight hot knot forms in my chest, tension tightening my body, and Emily's fingers flex into my arm, her hip pressing ever so slightly into mine. "The dead-man-walking card doesn't work with me."

"We both know that's not true, son," he says. "If only it worked as well on your mother as it does you." Instead of using this as more bait, he leaves us to stew, ending the conversation. "I'll leave you to your evening." He flicks Emily a look. "We'll talk in the morning." He steps around us and starts walking, but I make no attempt to move, nor does Emily dart away, which she well could in this moment. I stand there. She stands there. And much to my irritation, he's right. He's hit the human side of me, my emotional side, which is reacting to the promise he will soon be dead. I inhale, working to contain rather than reject what I feel, which is too damn much. Because you can't control what you reject, and me having control is absolute survival for me, and perhaps my entire family. Perhaps Emily too.

My hand presses against Emily's back, intending to urge her forward, when I hear my father's voice again. "Son." I stop but I do not turn and he adds, "Come by the house Sunday night. Derek's coming. It's time we finish that chess game once and for all."

The air shifts and I know he is gone, leaving those words

hanging in the air as the taunt they are meant to be. Every family get-together, my brother and I continue a game that has stretched years, and my father is telling me it has to end soon, and one of us has to be the winner, or the board will go to a sudden death vote for control. And my father is the king manipulating the tournament that I hope like hell doesn't involve Emily. She's either in trouble or she is trouble, and somehow, this night isn't going to end without me finding out which one.

I could start walking again, but I don't. I wait and I do it for a reason. Emily wanted to leave. Let her go. I will find her. I will find her secrets.

"I'm staying," she says, linking her arm with mine.

A few minutes ago, I'd have asked her *why*, but now it doesn't matter. Now, my father has reminded me that anything, any answer, can be a form of manipulation. The only thing that counts from this point forward is the truth I need from Emily, no matter how I get it. Even if it means that I revert to my original inclination, take her back upstairs, tie her to the bed, and fuck her until I get my answers.

CHAPTER TWO

SHANE

I turn Emily and me around the corner and into the lobby, down the white-tiled path leading to Edge, the hotel restaurant. I don't speak. Emily doesn't speak. There is just her hand on my arm and the long row of tables to our left with cushioned chairs around them, busy with patrons. Those things and the damning silence. I don't fill that space with words, and neither does she, but then, unless her staying has come with a change of agenda, she still won't tell me what I want to know. My father isn't all that different. He won't tell me anything but he alludes and plays. He is the ultimate player playing the players, and will be all the way to his impending deathbed. And fuck me a hundred times over, I care that he is dying, despite all of these things. Like Emily makes me want to trust her when I have a family that has taught me not to trust.

I lead us left again, directly into the interior of the dimly lit bar, couches and tables framing our path, red drop lights dangling above them. My father's visit weighs on me as heavily as Emily's secrets. He's going to die, but most likely he'll end up bedridden first, and instead of letting us be a normal family that spends quality time together, and makes amends for past sins, my father is pushing me to take part in his.

We reach the rectangular glass and leather bar to my left, passing a row of stools, while Frank, one of Edge's managers, a stout muscle-head who I hit the weights with every once in a while, lifts a hand. I give him a nod, and we're finally at the entry to the dining room when Emily suddenly lets go of my arm.

I turn to face her and she says, "Shane . . ." She seems to want to say something more, but changes her mind, motioning toward the arched entryway to a bank of bathrooms. "I'll be right back." She doesn't wait for a reply, turning and rushing away, but not before I see the look of helplessness on her face that reaches inside me and touches the part of my soul that only she has visited. She's running scared and not from me, and while I can't afford to be stupid, the idea that she might be in danger is a hard blast of reality. I've known she had secrets she wasn't ready to share, but yet I just attacked her for that very thing. Had I asked questions instead, had I given her the chance to explain, maybe she wouldn't have withdrawn. She was right. I've let my family dictate my response to tonight's bombshell, when this woman is the only good thing in my life right now. I can't be wrong about that or her.

I reach in my pocket and at the same time flag down Rita, the twenty-something redheaded waitress who I, and every regular, know well. "Hey there, Shane," she says. "What's hot tonight? You or your father?"

I ignore what I know from our past exchanges is a joke about my father and his mistress. "Don't let anyone into the ladies' room for a few minutes," I instruct, palming her a hundred dollar bill.

"Are you kidding me?"

"Kidding isn't my thing," I say, already heading toward the bathroom, and I don't stop until I'm pushing open the door to the ladies' room and stepping inside.

"Shane," Emily gasps, as I enter and find her standing in an enclave with a sitting area and mirror.

I'm in front of her in an instant, pressing her against the wall, my legs framing hers. "Are we alone?"

"Damn it, Shane," she says pressing on my chest. "What are you doing?"

"*Are* we alone?"

"Yes but that could change any minute. You can't keep coming into women's bathrooms."

"I paid someone to ensure our privacy," I say, my hands bracketing her waist. "Why did you stay?"

"Why does it matter?" she repeats. "I'm here."

"It matters. I told myself it didn't, but it does. Why did you stay?"

"Shane—"

"Answer the question."

"Because your father gets to you like few others, and if you somehow connect us, even emotionally, you will come at me hard and fast. And you will not stop until it ends in trouble for one or both of us."

"What kind of trouble?"

"The kind you need to be able to deny." She balls her fists around my shirt. "Plausible deniability, Shane. I need you to let me go. Don't follow me. Don't do Internet searches on me. Already Seth could have gotten me attention I can't afford."

There is desperation in her, real fear that I do not believe could be about my family, and if it is, she is not operating of her own free will, and someone is going to pay. "Sweetheart," I say, softly covering her hands with mine. "You're safe. You're with me. You have to know that."

"Seth dug around in my background, Shane. I'm not safe here anymore and you won't be either, if I stay."

"Seth is an expert at being invisible. He didn't expose you and he can help you stay invisible."

"He thinks he's an expert. You don't know——" She stops herself. "And you can't."

"The biggest problem you have is not me or Seth. Whoever set up your fake identity left huge, gaping holes. Anyone with a keen eye can find that out and we can fix that."

"No." She shakes her head. "No, that can't be right. That's impossible."

"It's how we knew you aren't who you claim you are," I say, wondering whom she trusted this completely, but I don't push for that answer. I'm not going to push for any answers until I get her alone, where I now know I should have kept her. "It's how someone else will figure it out too. Let's go back upstairs and I'll show you."

"No. No, because you think if you get me back upstairs, I'll tell you everything, and I won't."

"Whoever you trusted to protect you isn't protecting you," I say. "Let me help you."

"I don't need you to be my hero."

"Well, I'm going to be, whether you like it or not."

A knock sounds on the door and I curse at the poorly timed interruption, before we hear, "There's a line for the bathroom, Shane." I grimace and call out, "One more minute," and refocus on Emily. "Whatever this is, we'll find a way out of it."

"I need you to——"

"Let you go? Sweetheart, you matter way too much to me for me to let that happen. That's why thinking you betrayed me gutted me. I'm not letting you go. Not a chance in hell."

"You can't afford to take a chance on me, Shane. You can't afford the risk that I represent, that you don't even understand."

I cup her face. "I'm taking care of you. End of conversation." I kiss her, a deep, gentle stroke of my tongue that I follow with another, and another, and then another, until she moans, her hand flattening on my chest, the other at my hip. And I can taste her fear, her guilt, but more so, I can taste her submission, not to me, but to us. To a bond neither of us expected or looked for, but it happened, and while it's indefinable, it is also undeniable.

Another knock sounds on the door, and a loud, "Shane, damn it!" as I tear my mouth from Emily's, stroking my thumb over her lip. "Whoever made you this afraid is going to be sorry," I vow, but I don't give her time to reply, caressing her hair behind her ear. "I don't want to embarrass you. Hide out in one of the stalls so you won't be embarrassed when the doors explode with women. I'll be outside waiting on you."

I start to move away and she grabs my arm. "Shane," she whispers. "You don't understand what you're dealing with."

I reach around her, cupping her backside and pulling her to me. "I've got you," I say, and her hand settles on my cheek.

"But who has you, Shane? That's what I'm worried about."

"You. More than you know." I kiss her, hard and fast this time, and then I walk away, opening the door and exiting the bathroom, really fucking pissed at myself for making this about me and my family, not her. Entering the hallway, I'm greeted with several glowering women and Rita, who pulls me to the archway and out of the path of the door.

"You now owe me," she hisses. "My boss was furious."

"He's my friend," I say. "I'll talk to him." I reach into my pocket and hand her an extra hundred. "A bonus."

She glances down at it and her eyes go wide, her glower fading to satisfaction. "I'll guard the door any time you like," she says, her lips curving. "But I'd rather be the woman that made you go in the ladies' room." She laughs, rushing away, while Seth steps in front of me in her place, and considering his tie is missing and his short blond hair looks in disarray, this can't be good.

"What's her story?"

"It's not about me or the company," I say. "For now, that's all I'm prepared to share."

"You're sure?"

"I am," I say.

"Well then, moving on to another problem. We need to talk about allegations made by your plastic surgeon pal."

He means Eric's patient's claim that our pharmaceutical brand is being used to package illegal drugs, and I have a good idea where this is headed, though the timing of the conversation is curious. "If you're telling me you want me to ask him for the patient's name—"

"I don't need a name. Eric said the patient was the estranged wife of a professional athlete and while he has numerous sports connections, only one patient fits that description exactly."

I should have known he'd already have the answer. "Who is it?"

"Do you know Brody Matthews?"

"Pro pitcher from Denver," I say. "Everyone in this city knows him and I've met the guy. I don't know where this is going, but I read people and I like this guy. He's another Eric. He walks a straight line and he doesn't cross it."

"Yeah well, this straight arrow suffered several injuries this past year, punched a fan tonight at a game, and is married to one of your pal Eric's patients. And I found this in his nightstand." Seth produces his phone from his pocket, and shows me a photo of a medicine bottle with our label on it, the drug name Ridel. The same one we've suspected is being used by my brother and the Martina cartel to run Sub-Zero through our facilities.

I hand Seth back his phone. "How the fuck did you get that?"

"What you don't know can't hurt you. Don't ask. Don't tell."

"Now you sound like Emily."

He arches a brow. "For some reason, I thought you indicated she was giving you answers?"

"She's in trouble and she doesn't want to drag me into it."

"That gets my vote."

"Yes, because leaving someone I care about to crash and burn on her own is who I am," I say, that remark of Emily's about being selfish still weighing on me. I have a brother in bed with a drug cartel. How safe am I really keeping her?

"Easy, man," Seth says. "I didn't realize this was as serious as it clearly is."

"Back to the pill bottle," I snap, crossing my arms in front of my chest.

He settles his hands on his hips under his jacket. "Unfortunately it was empty, but I have the bottle. Nick can get it tested for residue."

Nick being his ex-FBI buddy whose private security team I now employ. "I'm going to call Brody and invite him to dinner on the pretense of corporate sponsorship," I say. "If I can sit down with him, I can evaluate where his head is right now. Maybe I can even get him to talk."

"Brody isn't our problem," Seth says, "at least not immediately. It's his wife. She's running her mouth and getting noticed.

It's only so long before the FBI gets word of her claims and the Martina cartel as well. And for her, that could be lethal."

"She wants money," I say. "Give it to her. In payments with a confidentiality agreement that ensures she won't hold us captive for more."

"As in how much?"

"Start low and cap it at three hundred and fifty thousand, but you handle it. Not Nick or one of his people. I trust you. Not them."

"Understood," he says. "I'm actually meeting Nick here at the hotel to hand over the medicine bottle in fifteen minutes and then heading home, but we have people watching the hotel and her apartment." He eyes the bathroom area as an elderly woman exits the hallway. "Unless you need me to stay?"

"Go. I've got Emily handled."

He studies me for several beats, as if he wants to ask the questions about Emily that I can't answer, then inclines his chin and starts walking. My gaze goes to the bathroom, which Emily has yet to exit. Something feels off. I walk toward the bathroom and I'm at the archway, fully prepared to enter the bathroom again, when Rita catches my arm. "No," she snaps. "You are not going back in there no matter how much you pay me."

"Go inside and find Emily for me. Petite. Long brown hair. Blue eyes and she's wearing a navy skirt and blouse."

She glowers, but sighs and heads in that direction. I follow her to the door and wait, ready to just walk in myself. She has ten seconds and then I'm going in. One. Two. Three. Four. The door opens. "There's no one in here."

"Holy fuck."

"Wow," she says. "Shane Brandon's been blown off."

I ignore her, already walking toward the lobby, my phone in

my hand and Seth's auto-dial punched in. "Emily slipped past us. Tell me someone is following her."

"She hasn't come out the front door. I'm calling my men."

"Meet me at the front door."

EMILY

Still reeling from Shane's confrontation, which I'd foolishly convinced myself would never happen, I round the corner to enter the lobby now bustling with people, leaving Shane, along with a piece of my heart, behind in the bar. White tiles line my path to the front exit of the hotel Shane calls home, that I dared to believe I might be able to with him. But this is no yellow brick road, with an emerald palace waiting on me, and it never was. I should have left a long time ago, before I got this close to Shane, before someone like Seth thought I could be a problem. I can't believe a kiss and a promise from Shane almost made me forget how unfair the burden of my confessions would be to him. And how dangerous. Even knowing this, standing there in that bathroom, he'd made me believe he could take on every monster in my closet and win. To exit the bathroom and find him absorbed in an intense conversation with Seth had thrown much-needed water in my face. I don't have one monster to defeat. I have many, some of which are not just powerful, they're capable of destroying him, which means if I lead them to him, I'm the one destroying him.

I can't do that. I won't do that.

The sudden urge to turn and look behind me comes with the prickling of the hairs on the back of my neck and a sense of being followed or watched. It's all I can do not to at least peek over my shoulder, or quicken my pace, both of which will draw attention to me, which I can't afford. If Shane or someone else is pursuing me, nothing changes. I'm getting in a cab, even if it means making a scene. How I'll escape from there, I'll figure out later. I'm about to pass the hallway leading to the elevator bank, and my plan changes. It's a dangerous decision, and a good way to get trapped, but I cut right and down the hall, hoping for a true escape. All I need to do is get outside, and lost in the many nooks and crannies of downtown Denver. It's not a good plan, but it's my only option.

Reaching the cars, I punch the call button and hug myself, nervously watching for Shane or Seth or who knows who else to round that corner. Almost instantly, the doors to one of the two elevators open and I rush inside, facing the panel, about to punch the garage level, when a realization hits me: There's a camera in the elevator. My mind racing for yet another plan, I punch in the gym level, and hope that it will appear I am hiding there, which could buy me much needed time. Hugging myself again, I wait to be sealed inside, collapsing against the wall when no one stops my departure. Then I watch each floor tick by.

Finally, the doors open again, and I hold my breath, half expecting to be greeted on the other side, relieved when there is nothing but empty space. Exiting into the deserted hallway, and following the signs leading me to the gym, I spy the stairwell I feel certain won't have a camera. I could go into the gym and maybe get a change of clothes, but that seems like time I can't afford. Change of clothes. A daring idea hits me and I head for the stairwell. Even if the hallway is recorded, they'll expect me to go to the garage. I'm going where they won't expect me to go, and where I can change clothes. Shane's apartment.

Entering the narrow corridor, I seal myself inside, leaning against the door, nerves jumping around in my belly at the craziness I'm about to undertake, but I see no other option. Glancing toward the lower levels to confirm I'm alone, and then upward to do the same, I find the empty space quiet and empty, a taunt telling me this is what awaits me after my escape.

My cell phone begins to ring in my purse where it rests at my hip and I hope this means he's only now realized I'm missing. Maybe he'll think I've already slipped past Seth and his security team, who, after tonight's bombshell, I have no doubt are watching me. Worried about time, I start up the steps, unzipping my purse and glancing at Shane's number on the caller ID. Inhaling, I decline the call and then place my phone on vibrate before slipping it back inside my purse. I'll call Shane when I'm out of here, and detach myself from the assumptions he'll be making about me and his family, before I find a cheap hotel to hole up in where I can figure out what comes next.

Pushing onward, I jog up the next few levels, slowing at the ninth floor, but not stopping. By the time I reach the fifteenth floor, and my destination, my chest is heaving and I've ignored two more calls, no doubt from Shane. Cautiously, I crack open the door, glancing through the split to survey the hallway, then widen the gap to confirm my coast is clear. Exiting into the hallway, I don't walk. I run around the corner and down the hallway toward Shane's apartment, digging out my key as I go. Once I'm there, I don't second-guess myself. It's too late for that. I unlock the door, step into the foyer, and quickly shut myself inside. The familiar scent, all warm spice and masculinity, overwhelms me, twisting me in knots. An array of memories flickers through my mind, some intimate, some fun, while others are intense, emotional even, and I can't take it. This is gutting me.

Running across the pale bamboo floor, I cut left and up the wooden stairs leading to the second level and Shane's bedroom. It could have been my bedroom too had I continued to foolishly play

house, without considering these monsters of mine would surely
find our window and break it open. The frightening image of
Shane being ripped through broken glass has me shivering and
shaking. I blink back to the present and I'm standing at Shane's
door, gripping the frame. Nothing is going to happen to Shane. I
won't let it.

Shaking off the sense of foreboding trying to overtake me, I
dash into the dark bedroom, that masculine spicy scent of Shane's
is stronger here, encasing me. My gaze lands on the massive king-
sized bed that I've shared so very intimately with Shane. I jerk
my attention away and dash past the wall of windows to my left,
before cutting inside the bathroom. I flip on the light and the
sparkling white of the stunning bathroom with a sunken tub comes
into view. I set my purse on the counter and squat next to the bags
of gym clothing Shane had delivered for our run a few days back.
Rifling through the various items, I grab a pair of boyfriend-style
baggy black sweats, a black T-shirt, and tennis shoes. Quickly undressing, I pull on my selections and then hide everything I was
wearing inside the bags. Looking to hide anything that seems like
me, I slip my purse over my head and chest cross-body style, pull
a black hoodie over it, and zip up.

Preparing to leave, I tug the hood over my head and face the
mirror. Immediately upon focusing in on my image, I shove the
hood back down. No one wears a hood up inside a hotel. Pretty sure I
know where Shane keeps several beanies he wears when he runs,
I flip off the light and hurry into the bedroom and through the
inky shadows to the closet on the opposite side of the bed. Flipping on the light, I pause for several beats, my gaze flickering over
Shane's shirts and jackets. Some unidentified emotion pinches in
my chest. Refusing to name it or allow it to control me, I move to
the built-in dresser to the right and start pulling out drawers, man-

aging to find a black beanie that I quickly put on and then stuff my hair underneath.

My phone starts to buzz again, and with a new surge of adrenaline, I exit the closet and rush across the room, flying down the stairs, and I don't stop until I'm in the foyer, standing next to the coatrack, with one last thing to do before I leave. Certain Seth, who is ex-CIA and resourceful, will track my phone, I unzip my purse and remove the cell that he and Shane know about, but I keep my spare that I can use to call for help and to contact Shane. I stare at the three registered messages. I want to listen to them, the urge nearly unbearable, but that would require time and torment I can't spare. I turn the volume back on and shove the phone into my coat pocket, where Shane will think I left it earlier.

Task complete, I inhale and walk to the door, knowing once I open it, I will never return. That very idea is a knife slicing right through my heart, bleeding guilt. I yank open the door, almost expecting to see Shane, disappointed and relieved all at once when I do not. I start down the hallway and contemplate the stairs but I think that would be an easy way to get trapped. No. I have to be bold here and get on the elevator. I round the corner and punch the button, praying when it opens that Shane or Seth are not standing there.

Holding my breath, I watch the steel doors open and reveal an empty car. I step inside and this time, I punch the garage level, but then have second thoughts. Seth is smart. He'll be looking for me at the obvious escape route. I'm not dressed the way he expects, so I just have to be determined in my actions. I'll walk right out the front door. The elevator stops moving and once again, I hold my breath, waiting for the door to open. Waiting for Shane to appear. The steel doors part and a redheaded woman in ridiculously high heels rushes forward, ignoring my need to exit.

Once she's entered the car, I walk into the corridor, nearing the lobby and willing my heart to slow before it beats right out of my chest. I have to own this plan and the path I'm walking and I do. I cut right toward the exit, not left as I'd traveled with Shane, and I do not allow myself to look for him. I keep moving and it's not long until I'm exiting the hotel, cold air blasting me in the face and chilling my neck. I turn left, toward the 16th Street Mall area where there will be plenty of places to disappear. It's also toward my apartment, which I can't return to. I'm not sure where I'm going except away from Shane.

CHAPTER THREE

SHANE

Seth and his team search for Emily both inside and outside the property, while I check every spot in the hotel her access key and codes will get her, thinking she could be hiding out to throw off our search. After checking the restaurant and bathroom again, I end up in the gym, which seems like a possible hiding place, only to find it deserted at this nine o'clock hour, with no sign of Emily. Frustrated, I walk to the floor-to-ceiling windows wrapping the spacious facility, pressing my hand to the glass, my gaze sweeping the twinkling downtown lights, without truly seeing them for the fear clawing in my gut. I see again the panic, torment, and terror in Emily's eyes when we were in that bathroom. She told me the truth tonight. She didn't betray me, but she is in trouble, and I've let her escape to face it on her own.

My cell phone rings and I fish it from my pocket, answering Seth's call. "Tell me you have her."

"I was hoping you'd say you do. I pinged her cell phone. Shane, it's in your apartment."

"I'm on my way," I say, already striding through the gym. "I'll call you when I get there, but her coat is there. She could have left her phone as well, so don't assume she's not trying to slip past you." I end the call and exit to the hallway. While punching in my floor in the elevator car, I try to remember if Emily ever took her phone from her purse. I continue wracking my brain to no avail. By the time I've reached my apartment door, I've surmised that Emily had been on the balcony when Seth arrived with his bombshell about her. She could have set her phone down there, but she does have a key to get in too.

I enter the apartment and softly shut the door behind me, listening for any sound that tells me she is here. Seconds tick by like hours, but there is nothing. No sign of Emily. I consider calling out or searching the apartment, but something tells me that won't be productive. I retrieve my phone from my pocket and dial Emily, and grimace when her coat pocket rings. "Damn it. Damn it. Damn it."

I shove my phone back in my pocket and grab her jacket, removing her cell. Shoving aside the clawing sensation in my gut, I check her call log and messages. Both are blank except for my number, but if she cleared any calls, the right tech person can find them, and her, I hope.

My phone starts ringing, so I stick Emily's phone in my shirt pocket, and grab mine. I press my hand on the wall by the rack and lower my chin, that damn clawing sensation returning.

"She's not here."

"Shane."

At the sound of Emily's voice, I go still. "Where are you?"

"Somewhere you won't find me," she says, and there is no noise echoing her words; no wind that says she's outside, no voices that indicate she's in a public place in the hotel. "And that's how it has to stay."

I squeeze my eyes shut with the certainty that she not only means those words, but believes they will hold true. "Then why call me?"

"I needed you to know I didn't leave because I wanted to or because I'm guilty of being aligned with your family or your enemies. You have to trust your instincts to become the head of the Brandon empire, and I won't be the reason you misstep."

"I'm not doubting my instincts. I know you're running and I know someone is pulling your strings. I also know I can help you cut the ties."

"I don't need help. I need to explain."

"Explain in person."

"The night I met you," she says, going ahead anyway, "I didn't know we'd turn into what we did."

"What we are," I correct, amending her use of the past tense. "Which is why you should be here now."

"No," she says. "No. It's why I can't be there now, and now that I took away your ability to play hero, I can do just what you said. Explain things."

"I don't play at anything, most especially protecting you, me, or my company."

"I know that, Shane, but—"

"You don't know that or we wouldn't be talking on the phone right now. We'd be naked and—"

"You wouldn't know who was fucking who."

"That was—"

"Doubt," she says, "of me and your instincts. Don't tell me it wasn't. I can tell that you want to believe I didn't betray you, but you can't be sure I didn't. So I'm going to tell you everything I can tell you that is the absolute truth, without pulling you into this." She inhales and lets it out, still no background sounds to clue me into where she is, before she begins. "I'm blond. Seth's file won't say I took the LSAT, but I did. Seth's file will say my parents died in a plane crash, but that's not true. That night you were tormented by feeling love and hate for your father, I confessed the same, along with my father's suicide. That was real. My dad killed himself when I was thirteen, and my younger brother, who is also not in Seth's file, was eleven. And that suicide was the catalyst to the hell I'm in now."

She's blond. She has a brother. She was honest about her father and she has no plans to come back or be found, at least not now. Much like in a courtroom, I don't let myself feel anything about these things, but rather stay focused on fact-finding that will help me, and her, later. "Was your father in some sort of trouble when he died?"

"There was a scandal about his work, and that, along with his death, destroyed us all," she says. "I mean, my brother and I were too young to understand it then, but we knew what it did to our mother. Not to mention his suicide voided his life insurance, leaving us broke, struggling, and very alone."

Which tells me she has no other family. "And then something changed," I press, knowing somewhere in this story is the reason she likes Bentleys and knows expensive labels down to the estimated price.

"Only six months after my father died, a rich, good-looking man swept our mother off her feet, and he became her husband and the monster we knew as a stepfather and guardian to my brother when she died six years later. He's the root of all this hell I'm in, right after my father, who left us to fall into that man's life."

I don't miss the way she places no blame on her mother. "So the stepfather is a part of this hell you're in?"

"Oh yes." She swallows hard. "He's dead but it seems like he's trying to pull us into the grave with him."

I don't like how that sounds. "Tell me about your stepfather and why he was a monster."

"I don't know where to start."

"Anywhere you want. Say what comes to mind."

"He told us he worked as a consultant."

"What kind of consultant?"

"A computer analyst. He was 'solver of tech problems,' he used to say." She laughs without humor. "Who also owned two Porsche Carreras, while paying for our two-million-dollar house. Of course, neither me nor my brother knew the price tags for those until I hit high school and started putting two and two together."

"And what did you find?"

"I knew something with him wasn't right, but he hid his secrets well. That is, until he started teaching my brother to hack."

I arch a brow. "Hack?"

"Yes. Hack. As in criminal activity he involved my brother in when he was only fourteen. I was furious when I found out. Turns out, he'd hacked a database to prove it could be done, and then created a firewall to prevent it."

"After blackmailing those he'd hacked into paying for it."

"Yes," she concurs, "but like I said, I only know this because my brother got involved. He's still involved. And when I say involved, I mean, working for a clandestine operation capable of bringing down a small country if they decided to do it. I've tried to get him out for years, but he's addicted to the money and just the high of doing what he does."

"This doesn't tell me why you're hiding and on the run."

"I saw something I wish I hadn't seen."

"That makes you a liability," I conclude.

"Yes."

"So your brother half-assed you a fake persona and sent you on your way?"

"He didn't half-ass it," she insists, but there is doubt vibrating in her voice.

"Why don't you sound certain?"

"You just told me about the holes in my identity. I haven't had time to digest what it means but I can't believe my brother would risk my safety."

"He's who you talk to on the second phone."

"Yes. He's supposed to be fixing this mess."

"How?"

"I'm not telling you that. I've said all I can say."

Which isn't enough for me to find her if we disconnect this call. "I know the truth now. Come back or let me come to you."

"If knowing the truth erased the need for distance, I would have never left. These people will ruin you, Shane."

"The only enemy I can't fight is the one I don't know."

"There is no fight if they never know you."

"If you are in this fight, I'm in this fight."

"I have this handled. It will be over soon and until then, I need a favor."

"Anything as long as you ask me in person."

"In my apartment," she says, as if I haven't spoken. "In the top drawer of my bathroom vanity, there's a bracelet. It was my mother's and it's all I have left of her. Can you please hold it for me?"

"We'll get it together. I'll meet you at the apartment."

"We both know you'll stop me from leaving."

"Even if I wanted to get the bracelet, I don't have a key."

"I'll mail you a key to the apartment."

"I don't want you to fucking mail me a key. Bring it to me. Let me hold on to you, Emily. I'll protect you."

"Remember when I said I don't need a hero?"

"But do you want one?"

"Who doesn't want a hero?" She laughs. "Especially one like you."

"Then let me——"

"You don't need someone else to save from themselves. You have your brother. But thank you, Shane. For hearing me out. For being a friend. I know you will think this is crazy, since I lied to you, but you were fast becoming my best friend."

"Then *come back* to me."

"I hope I can one day. Good-bye, Shane." The line goes dead.

Cursing, I redial the number she'd called me on only to have it go direct to a voice mail that hasn't even been set up. That damn second cell I'd seen her with before, which obviously wasn't about a lost phone she'd replaced, but her brother and her secrets. Fuck. Fuck. Fuck! I don't believe she would have called me if she believed there was any way we could find her at this point. She's gone and I may never see her again. Worse, I let it happen. I dial Seth only to have his voice mail pick up too. I text him with the number Emily called me on and then try to call him again, with the same empty results.

Shoving my cell phone into my pocket, I lean on the wall, squeezing my eyes shut, my face lifted to the ceiling, and I replay every detail of the conversation I just had with her. No names. No locations. She was cautious, planned, and I weigh that realization, waiting for a sense of being played. But what reason would she have for doing that when she's already gone? Unless she's not? Unless she's still here and not sure she's getting away?

A knock sounds, and hoping for answers, I push off the wall, closing the small space between me and the door. I open it to find Seth. "I gave the number you texted me to Nick and his team."

"In other words," I say, not moving from the doorway, "you don't have her."

"There is no way she's left the hotel. We have every exit covered."

"Are you trying to convince me or yourself?"

"Nick—"

"Is charging us a small fortune to make sure we know what we need to know, when we need to know it, which clearly we do not."

His phone beeps with another message, and he reaches for it, while I turn away and start walking, leaving him to come or go, preferably go and find Emily. Rounding the corner, I bring the living area wrapped in floor-to-ceiling windows into view, the memories of making love to Emily on the balcony just beyond the glass ripping through me. I head toward the bamboo minibar to the right of the glass doors, passing behind the leather furnishings I'd inherited from my father when I took over this place. The idea that this is where he used to take his "other" women does nothing to help my mood. I'm just pulling the top off a decanter of stout Scottish whiskey, when I decide I need all-new everything. Preferably, I think as I fill my glass, furniture picked out with me by the woman who was sharing my bed until about an hour ago.

"What did Emily say when she called?"

At the sound of Seth's voice behind me, I down the contents of the glass and face him, hands on my hips, quickly giving him the rundown. By the time I've finished, he's standing in front of me, his arms folded over his chest, his look skeptical.

"No names," he says. "No location. No proof anything she said is valid, but if she's on the radar of an international hacking operation, we need to know who that is, in case they know who we are."

"We can handle them," I say. "She can't. But if we assume she is on their radar and we are too, we'd be in a better position if we knew where she was right now."

"She's in this hotel," he bites out at the same moment his cell phone beeps with a text. He digs it from his pocket, glancing at it, and then me. "Nick needs to see me downstairs."

"I smell a problem," I say dryly.

He shoves his phone back into his pocket. "Look, man. I'm as good at my job as you are in the courtroom, and you know it or you wouldn't have brought me with you from New York. I hired Nick because he's that good too. And I'm also your friend, which is why I know this woman sideswiped you. One minute you didn't give a shit about anyone. The next she was under your skin."

"And your point is?"

"Who we fuck can best fuck us. If she got out of here with the kind of coverage we have on her, she has skills that scream more than meets the eye, or matches her story."

"Being smart does not make her the enemy."

"But you have enemies, Shane, and not just your family. The Martina cartel will know that you stand between them and control of Brandon Enterprises."

"Points all well taken," I say. "Go find her."

"I will," he assures me. "Here or elsewhere." He turns and starts walking.

I stare after him, repeating his words in my head: *Who we fuck can best fuck us.* They're followed by those of my mother not so long ago, in reference to Emily: *Once someone is in your bed, they're dangerously close to you. Watch your back with that woman.* Again, I wait for doubt to rush over me. Instead there is a hole inside me that I can almost picture growing bigger, and in it are my father, and Emily. I need a favor, she'd said. It hits me then that Emily had no time to clean up her apartment. There might be information about her or her brother there. I'm also the person most likely to spot her on the street. Intending to change into running gear and head out by foot, I start walking, and I don't stop until I'm on the second level and in my dark bedroom. That's when I stop dead in my tracks at the sight of the light burning in the closet. The same light I always turn off.

The idea that Emily actually came here is ridiculous, but I find myself crossing to the closet and stopping in the doorway, the scent of sweet, floral perfume teasing my nostrils. She was here, and my gaze lands hard on a drawer that isn't quite shut. I cross to it and squat down, pulling it open, to reveal three of the four beanie hats I use for running. Holy fuck. She changed clothes. I abandon the closet and cross the bedroom, entering the bathroom to flip on the light, the same sweet scent touching my nose. I grab my phone from my pocket, punching in the auto-dial for Seth as I squat next to the bag by the cabinet and find the clothes she'd been wearing.

I'm already on my feet and entering the bedroom when Seth answers. "She was here," I say. "She changed clothes. She has on a beanie. Probably sweats and a hoodie."

"Holy shit," he says. "She's got balls."

"She's got brains," I correct, stepping into the closet and toe-ing off my shoes, already working on changing into running gear.

"Hold on," he says. "I'm with Nick. Let me have him get the word out."

He starts talking to Nick and by the time he turns his attention back to me I've pulled on sweats, a black T-shirt, and a hoodie. "Nick's getting the word out to the team," Seth says, "and I'm going to grab the security footage to the hotel and try to get a handle on when and how she left the building, if she did."

"She has," I say, grabbing my socks and shoes. "And I know her better than anyone. I'm changing into running clothes and hitting the streets. I'm going to jog in the direction of her apartment."

"And if she decides to come back to you? Then what?"

"She has a key that she's proven she's willing to use," I remind him.

"If she sees you, she might go underground."

"If she's not underground already, she wants me to find her. I'm leaving now."

I end the call, part of my conversation with Emily a grim repeat in my mind. *Where are you?* I'd asked. And her reply had been a confident: *Somewhere you won't find me.* Undeterred, I head for the door.

She's smart, but she's failed to understand that I don't lose. Not my cases. Not Brandon Enterprises. Not the woman who is either the best thing that ever happened to me or the worst.

CHAPTER FOUR

SHANE

It's cold and snowing when I step outside, close to twenty degrees
if I estimate right, which means there is no way Emily, who gets
chilled even on warmer nights, is going to be lingering outside. I
pull my hood over the top of my beanie and start walking, shoving my cold hands in my pockets, while scanning for Emily. She
said I'd never find her, which could mean she's already left the area.
In fact, knowing we wouldn't have yet found out she'd changed
clothes, the most likely move would have been to leave the area.

That means a cab, a bus, or a train, which I have no doubt
Seth will have covered, but then, he also thought Emily hadn't left
the hotel. Refusing to be defeated, I start jogging, covering the two
blocks that lead me to the always busy 16th Street Mall area where
the road is sealed to traffic, the sidewalks framing food booths and
lined with shops and restaurants. Any of which she could be hiding inside. I start walking, looking in windows and at the random
packs of people.

I cover four blocks, up and back, and despite the impossibility of this task, I know Emily more than any stranger looking for her. If she's in the neighborhood, I have the best shot of finding her. My cell beeps with a text message and I glance down to find a text picture of Emily from a security picture along with a message: *Emily leaving the hotel garage at exactly 8:52.* I glance at my watch, to find it's already nine forty-five. She's long gone. My phone rings with Seth's number, and I answer. "Tell me you have more than this photo."

"I don't," he says grimly. "But she'll have to use an ID to check into a hotel or travel. We just have to hope she didn't have another fake ID on her."

"She doesn't," I say with certainty. "I'm three blocks from her apartment. I'm going to go check it out. I'll call you if I find any clues there."

"I'll meet you there," he says, and I end the call, already starting to jog again, my mind going to her brother. Why would he do a half-ass job of setting up her identity? Even if he did it quickly, surely he'd have fixed it by now? My mind tracks back to the night I'd met her. She'd taken a call and been angry, playing it off as a maintenance issue at her apartment. Was that her brother? If not, who was it?

I blink and find myself covered in snow as I cross the parking lot to Emily's apartment, but once I'm at the door, the realization that I don't have a key hits me. I grab the frame on either side of me. "Damn it," I murmur, deciding I'll have to break the window.

"I've got it," I hear Seth say from behind me.

Pushing off the door frame, I turn to find him approaching, now wearing a trench coat. "You have a key?" I ask.

He stops beside me, and pulls out some sort of tool from his pocket. "Close enough." He inserts it into the lock and opens the door, but before he walks in, I grab his arm. Seth looks at me and nods his silent understanding, stepping aside. This is my woman and her personal space could contain my personal demons. I enter the apartment and tug down my hood, my heart sinking at the sight of an empty living room and kitchen.

I cross to the bedroom, the only other room in the apartment, and stop dead in my tracks in the frame of the open door. "Holy mother of Jesus," I mutter, staring at the blow-up bed in the corner, and not another piece of furniture in the room. How did I not know she was living like this? I cross to the bed—if you can even call it that—and squat down next to it, the sweet floral scent of Emily everywhere, while she is nowhere I can seem to find her.

"I take it you haven't seen this place before?" Seth asks from behind me.

I stand again and face him, hands on my hips. "If I had," I say, "she would have already been living with me." And while I have assumptions based on what I'm seeing here, I want to know what an ex-CIA operative thinks before I voice them. "What does this say to you about who and what she is?"

"My initial thoughts," he says, pausing as if in thought, before continuing with, "This could be a wounded-princess routine meant to manipulate you, but I'd have thought she'd have made sure you saw it before now, if that were the case."

"It's not been all that long ago that we met."

"Agreed, and I'm not saying that she didn't have a long game that she was playing, but it's doubtful at this point."

"Why?"

"I still think she would have made sure you saw this apartment, if it was part of a setup. But that said, this doesn't mean she told the truth on the phone, either."

"She's telling the truth," I say, no hesitation in my voice.

"I accept your judgment, because I know your judgment as good, but I submit to you that she might have been desperate, on the run, and in need of money and/or her new identity. Therefore, she was ripe for the picking for your family or another enemy to use as a weapon against you."

"Her brother set up her identity."

"She says," he argues. "Think about it, Shane. Who knows what she might tell you to keep you from finding out the truth, especially if she was threatened. Or maybe she regrets her choices and just doesn't want you to know what they were. Maybe she was promised money she desperately needs, and she loses the money she was promised if you find out. Maybe——"

"Enough," I snap. "I'm quite clear on the possibilities behind her actions but I've looked into her eyes, and you have not. Not like I have. She is running scared, but not from me." Uninterested in anything but facts, I cut off the conversation. "Let's search the apartment and get back on the streets." I cross the room and enter the bathroom, finding a few toiletries and nothing more. The picture I'm getting of her being alone, and now on the run, is cuttingly clear.

I yank open the middle drawer, and stare down at the velvet box inside the otherwise empty space. I reach for it and open the top, staring down at the delicate chain of a bracelet, Emily's words replaying in my mind: *It's all I have left of her.*

"Shane."

I shut the box and slip it inside my pocket, facing Seth.

"We located her."

A mix of relief and dread washes over me that I don't analyze or express. "Where?"

"At Union Square."

"The train station," I say in surprise, not because of the location, but rather the fact that she's still here. "She could have been long gone by now. Why linger there and risk us finding her?"

"She didn't," he says. "We found her leaving it, which leads to the question, why go there and leave, without taking a train?"

"She must have thought paying cash would avoid her having to show identification. She didn't want to be tracked."

"Which would be an easy conclusion, except for one hole in that theory. There's a big gap between when she left the hotel and when she left the train station. Surely she would have attempted to buy a ticket when she arrived, and left when she realized she needed identification."

I pull my phone from my pocket and glance at my call log. "She called me thirty minutes ago and there was no background noise. She wasn't in the train station, not even the bathroom. I'm guessing someplace close to it. In other words, she went there and something changed her mind. She's afraid of a group of hackers. It's reasonable to believe she thought she could pay cash and not show identification in order to buy her ticket."

"Or," he offers, "someone's been pulling her chains, and they may have stopped her departure."

"Or she decided she needed help after all, in which case, she'll show up back at my apartment. Where is she now?"

His cell phone rings, and he reaches for it, answering me. "She was walking toward the convention center," he says, taking his call, and then listening a moment before glancing at me. "Nick," he tells me. "General update. Nothing new. I'm going to search the kitchen while we talk."

I nod and he disappears into the other room while I consider the direction of Emily's path and the possibility it's not headed back to me. Inhaling a heavy breath, I turn away from the room and do a quick sweep of every drawer and cabinet, finding what few products she has are all generic, bargain brands, which drives home the reality of her empty apartment I wish like hell I'd known about. Walking to the closet, I find a small duffel bag and stuff everything I can find of Emily's inside. She's not coming back here. *Ever.*

With the bag on my shoulder, I exit the bathroom and walk to the side of the bed, grabbing a journal and a few other items she has sitting there, sticking them inside the bag. Zipping it up, I give the blow-up bed a grimace, and turn away. I can't look at that damn thing. No wonder she didn't want me here.

Entering the living area, I find Seth in the kitchen, opening and shutting drawers. "Anything?" I ask, leaning on the door frame.

He faces me and presses his hands on the counter. "She's been eating on paper plates and using plastic ware. She has no mail. No connection to another life. We aren't going to find answers here." His phone rings again and he answers, listening several minutes, before saying, "Yes. Do it."

"What was that?" I ask, walking to the bar that separates the living area from the kitchen where he stands facing me.

"She just entered the Hampton Inn by the Coliseum. Our man followed her inside, which brings us back to her ID and hackers. She can't travel, or rent a hotel room in her name, which we have to assume based on her actions thus far, she knows. In other words, she could be meeting someone."

"Or someone rented a room for her," I surmise, not liking where this is going.

"My thought exactly," he confirms. "But we have an opportunity here. People show their true colors when they don't know you're watching. What she does now will tell you who she is, far more than her true identity on paper ever could."

"More like who is controlling her."

"I'll head over there then," he says. "And I'll personally stay the night and let you know if anything happens."

"I'm going with you."

"You're the boss," he says. "But in my opinion, you're too close to this to get any closer."

"All the more reason I need my questions answered."

"I can answer them for you, and nothing may even happen tonight. Go home, Shane. I'll call you."

"One way or the other," I promise him, "something is going to happen tonight." I don't give him time to make his case further, already walking toward the door and exiting. The wind greets me, swiping my face and dusting me in snow flurries, the possibilities of where the next few hours could lead as icy as the droplets they become.

Seth joins me, pulling the door shut behind him, and my cell phone begins to ring. I reach for it, hoping like hell it's Emily, to find my ex-boss calling instead, no doubt trying to recruit me back to New York yet again. I decline the call and without the hesitation of the past. I have a mess here my family created that I have to clean up, once and for all this time, and lord help them if they're behind what's going on with Emily.

I glance up to find Seth already at the driver-side door of his car and I walk to my least favorite place—the passenger side. I don't like being the one taken on a ride, but then, that's a trait I share with the Brandon clan. The whole bunch of us prefer the driver's seat, which wouldn't be a problem if we all shared the same destination.

Seth clicks the locks, and I toss Emily's bag in the backseat before joining Seth in the front. He cranks the engine and the heat, placing us in reverse and then forward. "I need to know how you plan to handle any visitor she has," he says, pulling us onto the main road. "Because we have a chance to watch her and see her true colors."

"You said that already."

"And I'm saying it again," he says. "No matter who shows up to the hotel to meet her, we need to sit back and watch."

"Negative," I say. "If Emily has a guest that bears the Brandon name, the game is over. There's no reason to sit, watch, and wait."

"And if it's someone else?" he asks, already pulling us into a spot across from the hotel.

"We sit, watch, and wait."

His cell phone rings yet again and he kills the engine, grabbing his phone and eyeing the screen. "She checked into a room." He glances at me. "We're working to find out under what name." Another car pulls into the spot behind us, and a light flashes several times in the back window. "That's Nick," Seth adds. "I'll be right back." He opens his door and disappears, shutting me inside the car, alone.

I eye him in the rearview mirror, watching as he climbs into the black SUV behind us, and then turn my attention to the door, where people come and go, and I don't look away. Ten minutes pass, then fifteen, and Seth climbs back inside the car with me, an iPad in his hand. "She rented a room with cash using a fake name, but no identification. She convinced the manager she lost her wallet at the airport."

"And we know this how?"

"The man we had tailing her paid one of the girls at the front desk to get the details for him."

"At least we now know she didn't check in on someone else's account," I say, motioning to the iPad. "That has a purpose I assume."

"We have footage of Emily at the train station and then in the hotel, neither of which is eventful."

"I'll be the judge of that," I say, and even in the shadows of the car, I can see the thinning of his lips, but he swipes the iPad and brings the screen to life before handing it to me. I hit the play button on the video and find a ticket line at the train station at the same moment that Emily leaves the line, her hand pressed to her face, before she digs in her pocket and removes her phone. She dials it and seems to fret about no one answering. Three more times she dials before she rushes toward the exit. The feed cuts to her outside, in front of a drugstore not far from here. She's dialing her phone again. She paces. But what really gets me is when she squats down on the ground and leans against a wall, her hand back on her head. She's lost. She's scared. She's alone. It punches me in the gut and then twists. The feed shifts again to her going inside the hotel. Her walking to the check-in desk, and after a pleading conversation with the concierge, heading to the elevator bank, the doors closing her inside, and then the video goes black.

I look up at Seth. "Is this it?"

"Yes," he confirms. "Like I said. It's far from eventful."

For him. For Emily, I doubt it's so simple. It damn sure isn't for me. "What room number?"

"Shane—"

"Room number," I bite out, depositing the iPad next to me.

"Room 1211," he says, "and the garage is your most discreet entry point."

"Agreed," I say. "Make it happen."

He says nothing else, starting the engine and cutting us across the road, to the side of the hotel. His cell phone starts ringing. "Nick," he says, grabbing it once we pull into the garage. "No doubt, wondering what we're doing."

"Make sure that's it before I get out."

He answers the call and there is a clipped exchange, before Seth says, "I'll explain in a minute unless, there's a change you have to report." A brief pause and then he adds, "Just watch the door," and ends the call. "We're good," he tells me.

"Call me if I have a visitor on the way," I say. "Otherwise, I'll call when I have the answers we need." I exit the car without another word.

I can be a patient man. I can wait on my adversaries to make the wrong move, or say the wrong thing. But I do not believe Emily is my adversary, nor am I patient tonight. Whoever her enemy is, they are also mine. It's time for me to meet that enemy, along with the real woman who's been in my bed. But first, I'm going to remind her why she was in my bed in the first place.

EMILY

I force myself to sit on the side of the hotel bed, willing my heart to stop racing as I reach for the hotel phone again, hoping a public line protects me, but feeling I have no option but to take the risk. Six times I've called my brother. Six times since I reached this hotel room thirty minutes ago. That doesn't count the many attempts before I threw away the only phone I had left in a street trashcan. And just like all the times before, Rick doesn't answer. This time I don't bother leaving a message. I press my hands to my face. I've given up so much for that man even before this hell started, and this is what I get in return. Tears prick at my eyes and I reject them, furious at myself for being so weak. I stand up again. I don't have time to wallow in a pity party. I need to sleep and plan for tomorrow, in the opposite order. I remove my tennis shoes and hoodie and then walk across the small room to the desk against the wall, where I grab a pad of paper and a pen.

Returning to the bed, I climb on top, move the mass of pillows to lean on the headboard, and pull my knees to my chest. Pen perched, I start thinking about everything I have to do tomorrow, and how that list varies if I don't hear from my brother. No. I need to start with a—no matter what—list:

- Disposable phones
- Clothes
- Bank
- A place to stay

I pause. Should I leave town or stay here? Do I dare fly? What if the police are looking for me? I'm sure the hotel has a business center, but I'm afraid to Google my name to find out. What if I trigger attention I don't need? So, no. No flying. I write that down. Can I take a bus to another city? I add to my list:

- No flying. Research travel documentation needed for a bus.
- Research big cities nearby.

I have to be out of here by noon, and I need a change of clothes again. This isn't a fancy hotel, but surely they can direct me to a store that can deliver. I set my pad and pen aside and sit up, reaching for the phone at the same moment there's a knock on the door. My heart leaps into my throat. I go still. Completely, utterly still, not even daring to breathe. Another knock sounds and I wrap my fingers around the down comforter.

"Sweetheart."

The familiar rumble of Shane's deep, masculine voice sends a rush of adrenaline through me and delivers a jolt of too many emotions to name. "I know you're in there," he adds, his voice a seduction and a command, a skill he masters as well as he does me. "I'm going to need you to open the door."

I give a silent scream, and look skyward. All I went through tonight to keep him out of this, and he's found me. All the fear, the running, the panic I felt, and he is here and I am still struggling to save him from me. "Sweetheart," he repeats, the endearment doing the same funny thing to my stomach it always does. "I'm not leaving."

I climb off the bed and walk to the door, pressing my hand to the surface and for long seconds we are silent, him there, and me here, so close but so far away.

"Open up, sweetheart," he prods, his voice softer now, and somehow, I know he knows I'm right here, right in front of him, but divided by a door I both hate and need.

"You have to leave," I say. "Go, Shane. This is my business, not yours."

"You are my business," he replies. "And if I have to sleep in front of your door, I will. Eventually you'll have to come out."

"I could call security," I say, but I sound unresolved in that threat even to myself.

"And that would get attention you don't want."

Frustrated, confused, tormented, I raise my voice, giving a guttural, "You're such an asshole, Shane."

"If that's what holding on to you makes me, then you're right. I'm an asshole."

He's stubborn. So ridiculously stubborn and I have to make him leave. I push off the door and start pacing, trying to decide what to do. How do I make him go away? I could tell him I'm working for his family, but that would crush him and only make him demand answers. I could tell him I'm working for the Feds and he'd have to back off, but it's just another lie I don't want to tell.

"Emily."

At the sound of that name, that only one he has made bearable, I stop in place and face the door. He says nothing more, as if he knows what he's done. As if he knows that using this name, my new name, will shake me. And he probably does. He knows me in ways that defy a name on paper, in ways no other human being has ever truly known me. I walk back to the door. "Shane," I say. "Please go away."

"Would you go away if our circumstances were reversed?"

No. My answer is no, and therefore I have to open the door and step into the hallway. I have to give him some reason to let me go, and that idea guts me. Because that means being a bitch. Being mean. Leaving him thinking I'm the monster he feared when he first confronted me. I flip the steel lock slowly, softly, as not to alert him I'm about to exit, then inhale for courage. I open the door and in a blink, his hands are on my waist, and his big body is crowding mine, walking me inside the room. Another blink and the door slams behind him. Another and I'm against the door the way I was in his apartment, him in front of me, his powerful legs shackling mine, his spicy, deliciously perfect scent encasing me.

"You didn't really think I'd let you get away, did you?" he

says, a long dark lock of hair touching his brow, as if he's been running his hands through his hair, an act of uncontained emotion he rarely allows himself. But if his emotions are freer than normal, his control is still fully intact. He has it. I do not.

CHAPTER FIVE

EMILY

"You should have stayed away," I say, holding on to Shane's waist when I should be pushing him away.

He tangles rough fingers in my hair, giving my head a gentle tug, and forcing my gaze to his. "I won't stay away. Don't you see that? And even if I wanted to, which I don't, you're a drug to me. The only addiction, outside of success, I've ever had." He kisses me, a deep, intoxicating kiss, his tongue stroking, caressing, his hands under my T-shirt, warm on my bare skin. Sensations spiral through me—he spirals through me, this man who has become such a part of me in ways he can't understand, in ways I am not sure I understand. I moan with their impact, with the force that is this man consuming me, and I'm struggling to stay sane. In the moment, I shove at his chest, pulling away from his kiss.

"Shane, wait, I need—"

"We need," he says, and suddenly he is pulling my T-shirt over my head, tossing it aside, and his shirt follows. "It's not you anymore," he says, his hands back on my naked waist, branding me, seducing me. "It's not me anymore. It's us. It has been since the moment we shared that first cup of coffee. *Us*, Emily."

"Shane——" I try again, but I before I can say more he cups my face.

"No one was ever supposed to matter to me like this," he declares, and a moment later he is kissing me, his tongue doing a seductive slide against mine before he adds, "No one was supposed to taste this damn good." Before I know his intent, he's reached behind me, unhooked my bra, and dragged it down my arms. I flatten my hands on the hard wooden surface behind me, gasping with the contrast of the cold hotel air and the sizzling way his gaze strokes over my nipples. They tighten and knot and my breasts are heavy, my sex clenching. And now it's him flattening a hand on the door by my head, while his other palm scorches my hip all over again. "And no one," he adds, "was supposed to look this fucking good to me. So good I think about those rosy nipples in my mouth when I'm sitting at my desk."

A shiver runs down my spine and I tremble, but every remnant of fear I'd felt an hour ago is gone.

No. Not all of it. I fear this man in ways that are not about the secrets of my past. It's the way he seduces me and makes me forget everything else, even when I should remember. He is power. He is passion. Everything about him is too much. Too extreme. Too mighty. Too right and wrong at the same time. His hand slides between my shoulder blades and he molds me to him. "In case, I haven't been clear," he says, his voice a low rasp that manages to be both sandpaper and silk on my raw nerves. "I don't like the word 'can't,' so could I let you go? Yes. But I won't."

In this moment, I am most definitely consumed by this man. I don't want him to let me go, even though I know that makes me selfish. It makes me weak, but he is already kissing me again, and he tastes of all the things I crave. Power. Control. Passion. Shelter in a storm raging wildly around me. And those thing are drugs, he is a drug that has me moaning and leaning into him, while I barely resist the urge to touch him, to cling to him. But if I do not resist him now, I never will, and so I do touch him. I shove against his chest and struggle to tear my mouth away.

"You won't say 'can't,' but I will. I am. You have to let me go. This can't change that."

"It already has," he assures me, turning me to face the door, and pressing my hands to the wooden surface. "You just aren't admitting it yet, but you will. And right now, I have one goal. Reminding you how much you trust me." Before I can reply, he drags my sweats down, my panties following. In the next, his hand is on my backside, his teeth scraping the delicate flesh.

"I lied to you," I say, making a lame attempt to push him away. "That isn't trust."

"That was fear I'm going to erase." He seals that promise by wrapping my waist, lifting me and shoving aside the clothes pooling at my feet.

"Shane," I plead the instant I'm back on my feet, trying to get him to hear me out before I have no resolve left to argue.

His reply is to turn me to face him, my back resting against the door again. His hands are on my hips, those gray eyes of his dark, unreadable. "I'm right here," he promises. "With you, where I've been since the moment I met you. But what I said earlier is true. Everything has changed."

"Then why are you here?"

"I came for you," he declares. "I'm not leaving without you. Will you lie now and tell me you want me to?"

My chest tightens, eyes burning with the hint of betrayal I hear in his voice and my hands go to his arms. "I hated lying to you, Shane. Please know that. I thought this would end, I could confess."

He leans in, his lips at my ear. "Tell me you don't want me to stop," he commands. "Tell me what you really feel, not what you think you're supposed to feel."

"You know what I feel," I whisper.

"Say it."

There is a gravelly, tormented sound to his voice. I desperately need to answer, but if I say what he wants me to say, what I want to say, I will only ensure he won't let go of me when he has to let go. "No," I say firmly. "No. I won't."

He leans back and looks at me, his gray eyes sparking with flecks of blue I know to be anger. "Yes," he replies. "You will because I won't stop until you give me everything that is real. That is what I want and deserve. And so do you. But that is what we have to be from this point forward. Real. Absolute. Honest." He lowers himself to one knee, where his mouth presses to my belly, his tongue flickering over the sensitive flesh.

I pant and my lashes lower, because I know what is coming, what he will do next, and my willpower will soon evaporate, if it hasn't already. He wants what is real, but that is dark and blood-laden, and he doesn't deserve it. His hands caress up and down my hips, over my backside. His tongue flicks against me, sweeping into my belly button. I'm so very in this man's control but the thing is, that is when I feel the safest. That is when I feel like nothing else can touch me.

"Look at me," he orders, and as if I have no option, I do as he says. I look at him, and I find the smoldering heat of his desire and mine reflecting in his stare. And feel the connection I share with this man in every part of me. "I'm going to remind you how good we are together." He cups my sex. "I might not own you," he says, his thumb stroking my sex, and I feel each stroke in the tingling of my nipples. "But I own your pleasure. And more that we'll talk about after I make you come." He slips a finger inside me, then another. "More than once."

I try to grab his shoulders, but he is out of reach, forcing me to fist my hands by my sides, and endure the pleasure. Endure. Like this is hell when it's pretty much heaven. He lifts my leg to his shoulder, his lips pressing to my belly again, his free hand sliding up and down my thigh. And then it happens, that thing that I know will happen, and want to happen. His tongue finds my clit in a tease of a touch. Then another. And another, until he sucks me into his mouth, dragging deeply on the sensitive nub, while those two fingers are inside me. The world fades. There is just pleasure. Just Shane, who does indeed own my pleasure.

As if proving that point, his mouth lifts and his fingers stop moving. "Look at me," he orders again.

"You're killing me," I hiss, lifting my head to stare down at him.

"Do you want me to stop?"

"You already did."

"Do you want more?"

"Yes," I hiss, and knowing he will insist on more, I add, "Yes. Yes. Yes. I want more. Please stop teasing me."

"Whatever you say," he declares, his sexy, sometimes punishing mouth dangerously, wonderfully close to that sweet spot where I need and want him. "You're in charge."

"We both know that's not true," I manage, just in time to have his deep, rumble of laughter whisper against my clit, but he still denies me, giving me a darkly amused look. "Do you want control?"

"Not right now," I say. "Later I do."

His sexy, often punishing mouth quirks and then, to my

relief, there are no more questions. There is just a lick of his tongue, which is gone too soon. "Shane," I plead desperately.

The sexy laugh that follows tells me that my urgency pleases him, and thankfully, my reward for doing so is his mouth closing over me. His tongue and fingers stroking my sex a moment later. And oh God, the spiral of heat and pleasure is almost too much to bear. It overwhelms me and I can't think. I can only submit to this crazy, sexy, amazing man, and to the pleasure, so much pleasure. So very much and it's too much, too fast. I want to fight the ball of tension in my belly moving lower and lower, but it's powerful, fierce, and in a blink I stiffen, before my body spasms and pleasure rockets through me. A deep, low moan rips from my throat, a sound I barely know as my own, and time stands still. And then it's over, and my body feels like it's melting to the ground.

Shane lowers my leg and catches my hips, lifting me and carrying me across the room, setting me on top of the bed, his body arched above mine. And then he is kissing me, the saltiness of me on his lips, now on mine, before he tears his mouth from mine and declares, "I need to feel you wet and hot around me, and I need it right now. Skin to skin, the way I only let myself be with you."

He means no condom, because he trusts me with my birth control. And while it seems a small thing it is not. It's trust, he gives me. That's what he's telling me. He has, and does, trust me. And trust is a powerful, sexy thing. "Can you please hurry," I whisper, my body suddenly achy and empty, in a deep, burning way.

"Say it," he demands.

"I want you inside me. I *need* you inside me."

"Need," he repeats. "I like that word." He kisses me again, a deep passionate kiss that is over too soon. "I have on too many clothes."

He lifts off me and I ball my hand between my breasts, willing my racing heart to calm and trying to think, but he is already back. He is leaning over me, the thick ridge of his erection pressed against my sex, the heavy weight of him on top of me absolute perfection. And he stares down at me. I swear I can see what he wants from me in his eyes, and it's everything. He wants everything, and that should scare me, but right now, I want that too. Right now, I feel like it's possible. Seconds tick by, and questions and answers flow between us, and they all end in one place. How right we feel with each other. How connected.

He leans in, his lips at my ear. "Everything has changed," he says again, and I don't need to ask what he means, nor do I have time. He presses inside, filling me, stretching me, completing me in ways no other man has or ever could. He's different. We're different and the many ways that is true, are not all good.

"Shane," I whisper, burning with the need to hold him, not to lose him, and he responds, leaning back to look at me.

"I'm right here, and I'm not going anywhere, sweetheart, but you need to say the same thing. No more running. Not from me."

"I'm not."

"Say it."

"This isn't a fair time to—"

"Ask me if I give a fuck about fair right now. *Say it.*"

"I'm with you."

"You're staying."

"Yes. I'm staying, Shane, but you—"

He kisses me, and there are no more words. There is only passion. So much passion. It's like someone snapped their fingers and we exploded into want and need. His fingers are in my hair. Mine are in his. Our bodies are moving and swaying. And we don't start slow. We press our bodies together. We touch each other everywhere, anywhere. The feel of his taut muscle under my hands makes me want more. The feel of his cock driving into me makes me want him deeper. Harder. I think I say that. I do. I say it. I say it over and over. Except, I still feel like this is good-bye, like this is the only time I will ever touch him again.

Too soon, I feel the ache in my belly that I know is another orgasm, and I pant out, "Shane," trying to get him to slow down, but he answers with a deep thrust, and then another, and his tongue——his talented, demanding tongue——licks into my mouth, and I explode. I tumble over into the depths of pleasure, and my sex clenches around his shaft, and the sensation of him inside me, still pumping, still pushing, is almost too good to allow me to breathe. Then he is shuddering, a low, guttural growl escaping his lips, so raw and animalistic that it can only be described as pure sex.

When finally we collapse together, we don't speak or move. We hold each other, absorbing everything that has happened between us, but I do not feel anger from him. I don't feel accusation. I feel . . . us. I feel closer to him than I ever have and I don't know how that's possible. I lied to him.

He lifts his head, kissing my forehead in a tender act I feel as readily as I did that orgasm, but this time in my heart. "Stay still," he orders. "I'll get you a towel." He lifts off and out of me, and I can already feel the sticky warmth of his release, but there is so much more going on with me in this moment. I start to shiver, and I do not believe it's from the cold air blowing from somewhere in the room. I hug myself and images I've suppressed for weeks on end come at me. My father's casket. My mother's casket. And that night. The blood. So much blood. Nausea and panic overcome me, and I shoot to a sitting position, hunching forward.

Shane is there instantly, pressing the towel between my legs, and then his shirt is suddenly over my head, falling down to drape my body, a shelter that I want, but cannot have. A cold breeze blasts over us again, and he glowers in its direction. "Why the hell is the air on in the middle of the winter?" He stands and walks toward the thermostat in all his naked, leanly muscled glory, his backside a work of art. He is perfect, and not just his body. The way he controls everything around him. He is sex, power, and passion.

He adjusts the thermostat and grabs his pants, shoving his legs inside them before snatching up my sweats and bringing them to me. "Put these on so you can warm up."

I don't argue. Why would I? He's protecting me, and in this, I can actually accept the gesture. Reaching for my pants, I maneuver to pull them on and then he is on the bed in front of me again, and in his eyes, there is possession I should reject, but there is more. There is this sense of him feeling I am his to protect, to please, to hold on to, and somehow, that feels right and good. But I am wrong to feel this, to jeopardize his safety.

"No," I say, as if he has spoken those things, my hand settling on his chest, his heart thundering beneath my palm. "I can't pull you into this. It's wrong."

He covers my hand with his. "You aren't pulling me into anything. I'm here of my own free will."

"You have to have plausible deniability. You have to, Shane."

"Nothing that is spoken between you and I goes anywhere but you and I."

"If you were put on the stand that would change. You have a legal obligation. A code of honor."

"My code is to protect those I love and care about, even my family, who as you know, don't even deserve it."

"I'm not sure I deserve it."

"I am," he assures me. "And I should have found out the truth a long time ago."

"I didn't tell you because—"

"You didn't have to tell me. I should have seen your fear. I did see it, but I let it lead me to the wrong conclusions. I was so damn wrapped up in my family's war that I didn't let myself know what it meant."

"Let's keep it real, Shane. It meant I was lying to you. You will never trust me again. Not when everyone around you lies and cheats, and cuts each other's throats just to watch the other bleed."

"I'd bleed for you. That's what you don't seem to understand."

"I don't want you to bleed for me. That's what you don't seem to understand. That's the whole point. Damn it, Shane. This is as real as it gets. This is not about something you can fix."

"Tell me. Tell me and let me try."

"Murder. It's about murder."

CHAPTER SIX

SHANE

Murder. It's not a word I expected to hear from Emily's lips. That she has spoken it and that I am this surprised is a come-to-Jesus-moment for me, and not because of a murder I don't believe she committed. Not unless it was self-defense. It drives home how right Emily was about how the lies and deception of my family have shrouded everything else before me, including her.

"You're not saying anything," Emily says, her fingers curling on my chest beneath my hand. "I bet you're sorry you came after me now."

"What I'm sorry for," I say, "is not seeing how much you needed me."

"I don't understand you right now. I said the word 'murder.' How can you be this calm?"

"Overreacting doesn't solve anything."

"Damn it, Shane," she hisses, shifting to rest on her knees. "This isn't me inviting you to solve anything. It's me telling you why I kept you out of this. This isn't a problem you can fix. You can't fix this."

"I told you, 'can't' isn't in my vocabulary."

"It needs to be. Let me say this again. Murder, Shane. This is about murder and you have to distance yourself, something I should have done for you already."

I reach in my pocket and pull out my money clip to remove the hundred on top, before sticking it back in my pocket, then I grab her hand and press the bill against her palm. "That's a gift."

"I don't want your money."

"It's not my money now. It's yours. Now give it back to me and tell me I'm hired as your attorney."

She blanches. "No. No, that is not happening. You can't be my attorney. We practically live together."

"We do live together because you are never going back to that apartment."

"You already went to my apartment?"

"Yes. I did, and I saw how you were living. And from this point forward, my home is your home. You live with me now and not because of what I saw in that apartment. It's the natural next step for us."

"It's fast."

"But it was going to happen anyway. Hire me, so you can talk to me without worrying."

"No. There are ethical codes for attorneys. Your family might cross them, but you don't."

"Representing you is within those ethical codes as long as we were together before you hired me and I disclose that information under the necessary circumstances, which I will." I take the money back from her. "I accept the job."

"I didn't—"

"You did."

She shifts and pulls her knees to her chest under my shirt, successfully creating a barrier between me and her. "You aren't going to let this go, are you?"

My hand slides under the T-shirt to rest on her naked ankle. "Like I told you in the bar bathroom. Not a chance in hell. I'm in this with you now, which means it's time to give me real answers."

"You're stubborn."

"So are you but it's time to talk."

She inhales and lets it out. "You're right," she agrees. "I know you are, but I don't even know where to start and I don't think I want to see your face when you realize all the wrong moves I made. I think. I'm not even objective anymore about what happened and how I got into this."

"All the more reason to tell me." I wrap my arms around her calves and pull her closer. "Let's start simple. Were you here when you called me?"

"No. I was in a coffee shop beside the train station, in the bathroom. I knew I'd be on a train in a matter of minutes, and you wouldn't find me. Distance seemed the best way to keep you from finding me."

"But you didn't get on a train," I point out.

"I thought if I paid cash, I wouldn't have to show identification," she explains, confirming my assumption to be correct. "That wasn't the case, and I have enough respect for your resources to be sure you'd be waiting on me on the other side of the ride if I identified myself."

"I would have been," I confirm. "But staying here at this hotel wasn't putting distance between us. What changed?"

"I'd lost enough time that I knew you'd have the streets

covered. I needed a place to rest and think. I needed a plan I didn't have."

The certainty that someone, most likely her brother, has been directing her actions comes to my mind. "No one told you to come here?"

Her brow furrows. "Who would tell me to come here? What kind of question is that?" Her eyes go wide. "Do you think I'm supposed to be meeting someone?"

"Emily——"

"You do." Anger flashes in her eyes, and she tries to move away, but I tighten my grip around her legs.

"Emily," I try again.

"Let me go," she orders, pressing on my shoulders. "This is what I was talking about. Even if I tell you everything, you will never trust me."

"It's not like that. I admit that when you first came here, I thought you were meeting someone. Perhaps someone who was blackmailing you, but that isn't why I'm asking now. You call someone on that extra phone of yours, I assume to be your brother, and I need to know if he or someone else is involved."

"My brother is who I've been calling."

"No one else?"

She shakes her head. "No one else."

My questions are many, and I start with the most basic. "What's your real name?" She hesitates and I press. "You need——"

"I'm not that other person. I can't ever be her again."

"You can be her with me. Just me. Right here right now. What is——"

"Reagan Morgan," she blurts out.

"Reagan," I repeat, squeezing her legs. "Nice to meet you, Reagan."

"Emily," she corrects. "That's the name I have to keep if I'm going to stay safe."

"If you're staying Emily Stevens, then you need the holes in your identity fixed. Did you call your brother tonight?"

"Over and over," she says, and I don't miss how her fingers curl into her palms where they rest on her knees. "But as always, he's impossible to reach."

"Why is that?"

"He says he's fixing things, but he told me he'd fix things weeks ago. That's why I stayed with you. I thought this would be over, and then I could tell you everything. But it's not over and I'm starting to wonder if it ever will be. Honestly, I don't know how I thought it would ever be over."

"It will be," I say, cautiously moving toward the meat of her story, slowly gathering facts. "What's your brother's name?"

"Rick," I say. "Also Morgan."

"And your stepfather?"

"Cooper Wright."

"I need the name of the hacker group you're running from."

"I can't give that to you."

Again, I tighten my grip around her legs, but I soften my voice. "I can't protect us from an enemy I don't know. I won't see them coming and neither of us can know if they've found you or me. And if they haven't, they still might end up right here."

She pales. "They could already know who you are, and I let that happen." She doesn't give me time to reply. "The Geminis," she blurts out. "And they're powerful, Shane. Really, scary powerful."

I know her and she doesn't spook easily, but she's close to this. Maybe too close to see a solution, or a weakness, in what could be a two-bit hacking operation. "Why are they after you? What did you see?"

She presses her hands to her face. "Something bad. Really bad." She looks up at me. "I was in law school, Shane. Two years in and now I've thrown it away."

"Where?"

"The University of Texas, but I got accepted to Harvard."

Her eagerness to talk about my Harvard experience comes back to me. "Why didn't you attend?"

"I was worried about my brother. I just . . . I knew he was headed into trouble. He's not like me. He's impetuous. He's wild. He's into hot cars, hot women, and money. He's addicted to the money the Geminis represent to him. I think he's addicted to the danger."

"You can't save someone that doesn't want to be saved."

"In my mind I know that, but in my heart, he's my baby brother, and I've been protecting him since my mother checked out."

"Checked out?"

"She was different after my father's suicide and blind to any flaw that was my stepfather's. Therefore, with my brother working with him, learning a craft, she wanted to believe it was all legit. She all but pushed my brother into a life of crime."

"What did she do for a living?"

"She was an English professor, and it's the one thing she hung on to. Everything else was about my stepfather. He ordered her around. She almost seemed scared of him at times, but she was head over heels."

"How was it when he took over guardianship?"

"He barely spoke to me. He kept me around to satisfy my brother and I'm pretty sure he had my brother try to recruit me to work with him."

"But you refused."

"Of course I refused, but I darn sure took all the cash he threw at me as a method of parenting. I saved twenty thousand dollars for school that way."

I whistle. "That's a lot of cash to throw at a kid."

"That was nothing compared to what he gave my brother. And like I said. My brother likes the cash."

"Tell me how you got here."

"I hadn't been able to reach Rick for weeks and I was starting to fear he'd taken a job for the Geminis that had gone wrong. I went by his place and he wasn't there, and I was desperate enough to swing by my stepfather's."

"Your dead stepfather?"

"He wasn't dead until that night, Shane."

Murder. The word rips through my mind.

"No one was answering when I knocked, and I walked around to the back and the glass door was open. Making a long story short. My brother was there and my stepfather was dead. It was horrible, Shane. I've never seen anyone dead like that. There was blood. So much blood and his eyes . . ." She presses her hands to her face. "They were open."

I take her hand in mine. "I can't believe you've been holding this inside."

"Honestly, I didn't think about it. I couldn't or I'd lose it. I honestly don't know how I've blocked it out. I mean, how do you block out someone you lived with for years, lying in a puddle of his own blood? What kind of person can do that?"

"Don't do that to yourself," I say, resting my hand on top of her knees. "The mind is an amazing thing. It protects us. It compartmentalizes so we can stay sane. You've survived when many wouldn't have. You're stronger than I think you realize."

"I wasn't strong that night, or I might have made different

decisions. I was freaking out. Crying. Screaming. Losing my mind."

"Why did he kill him?"

"He claimed that he found out my stepfather stole money from him and the Geminis and made it look like my brother did it. They fought and came to blows, and my stepfather ended up with a statue in his head."

"So it was self-defense."

"He says it was."

I arch a brow. "That sounds like doubt."

"I don't know my brother anymore, and the past few weeks have really driven that point home. I mean, my first reaction was to go to the police. I wanted, no, I begged him to go to them, but he wouldn't."

"You said there was a murder. That doesn't sound like you think this was an accident."

"There was an obvious struggle. I believe they fought, but what kind of person bashes a man's head in, Shane?" She swallows hard and shuts her eyes a moment before she looks at me again. "It wasn't one bash to the head. Or maybe it was. Who am I to judge? I could barely look at him like that."

"If you think it was more than self-defense," I say, "I trust your instincts. What was his reasoning for not going to the police?"

"He said that Geminis don't turn in Geminis or they end up dead. And Geminis that steal from Geminis end up tortured and then dead. In my eyes, that was a reason for him to offer evidence against the Geminis in exchange for immunity."

"But he didn't agree."

"He told me he had to clean up the mess, prove his innocence. And if he failed, he said two things would happen: They'd make him watch me die and then they'd kill him. I told him I'd go to the police. I'm not a Gemini, but he said anyone who turned on them ended up dead."

"That's when he told you to run," I say, but I'm beginning to think he was just getting rid of a problem, thankfully without killing her.

"Yes," she confirms. "That's when he told me to run. He had me take a leave from school, made my new identification, and sent me on my way. He wouldn't even let me touch the money my mother left me that I have saved. He said it would look to the Geminis, and the police, like I was running. Which I am, but he made up some story about some trip to Africa to help the starving and sick. Booked my tickets, registered me."

"Let's hope he did a better job of that than he did on your identity." And as I'm suspicious by nature, and even more so about her brother, I ask, "How much money do you have in your account?"

"Two hundred thousand in three accounts. I'm paranoid. I didn't want it all in one place."

"And your brother has money too, right?"

"Oh yes. He's a millionaire, just like my stepfather. And if you're asking yourself why am I living like I am here in Denver, it's a good question. He keeps promising to send me my money, but he doesn't."

"What is his reasoning?"

"He says he's trying to find a way to send it to me without drawing attention, but he's sent me nothing. Not a dime. I left school because of him, and I can't even get to my own money. I was down to pennies when I got the job working for your father."

"Based on what you've told me about your stepfather, I now know why you handle my father so well."

"My brother and stepfather are different variations of your

father. All three are rich, arrogant jerks. He's actually a little too like my stepfather for comfort."

"They're both certainly poison to everyone around them. Do you have any idea if your stepfather has been found?"

"My brother told me he made it look like he left the country."

"We can find that out, and let's hope he did a better job of that than he did of creating your new identity. I'm going to get Seth to do some discreet digging and we'll have answers tomorrow." I stroke her hair behind her ear. "I want you to move in with me."

She catches my hand. "How, after all I've told you, can you think that having me in your life is a good idea? I don't want to be an obligation. I'm fine at my apartment."

"Sweetheart, there are a hundred ways I could help you and not invite you into my bed, or my life. I want you to live with me."

"Shane——"

I lean in and press my lips to hers, lingering there before I inch back and look at her. "Save whatever you're going to say for my bed that is now our bed, unless it's a request to get naked one more time before we leave." I lower my voice, confessing what I've felt, but haven't even admitted to myself. "I need you with me."

"You don't have to be my protector."

I think of my family, of the lines I've walked for them, of the lines, even now, I cross, and something about this woman reminds me why I can't be the Brandon my father wants me to be. "Maybe it's me who needs you to protect me."

"You? Who do you need protection from?

My lips quirk. "Usually my mother."

"I'd laugh, but I think we all need protection from your mother."

My mother's motives and actions burn in the back of my mind, but right now, it's Emily's mother that deserves attention. "Speaking of mothers," I say, reaching into my pocket and removing the velvet box, which I open for her.

She sucks in air and reaches out to touch the chain before glancing up at me. "Thank you, Shane."

"Why aren't you wearing it?"

"I never took it off before all of this happened. It seemed like something the police might detail on my wanted poster." She reaches up and tugs on her dark brown hair. "Right along with the blond hair I no longer have."

"You're really a blonde?"

"Yes. I am. Can you picture it?"

"I'll picture it when you change it back."

"I'm not sure I'm going to go back."

"We can buy a wig." I glance down at the velvet box. "Put the bracelet on."

"No," she says, resolutely shutting the box and taking it from me. "It's too much a part of the old me. I need to be the new me. That's how I survive." She speaks the words with the strength and bravado I expect from her, but underneath there is a vulnerability that says she's still scared. I want to tell her she doesn't have a reason to be.

My cell phone rings and I dig it out of my pocket, see Seth's number on the screen, and hit the answer button. "How are things there?" he asks, and I know him well enough to see this as the prelude to whatever he really called about.

"We're headed to the garage in five minutes," I say and, as if Emily takes my cue, she slides off the bed to start dressing. "Why?"

"There was a partial power outage at Brandon Pharmaceuticals," Seth says, "and it included the security cameras."

I don't react. Not with Emily sitting here watching me. I'm also aware that the assembly lines are shut down for the night, and that my cell phone can never be assured secure; I keep my question cautious. "Any activity?"

"They were back up before security could even alert us," he says. "And nothing appears out of line."

Translation: We know my brother has invited a drug cartel into our operation and we still have no clue how they're operating. "I'll talk to you when I get downstairs." I end the call and look up to find Emily standing by the door, her back to me, at the same moment as she pulls off my T-shirt, leaving me a view of her gorgeous naked skin, that has me thinking of her breasts. Inhaling, I remind myself I have problems to solve that won't happen in this room with Emily naked. But I will have her naked again tonight.

Standing, I shove my phone into my pocket. Emily whirls around to face me and tosses me my shirt. I catch it and put it on, the naturally sweet scent of her clinging to the cotton the way it does to my bed, which is now her bed. She is sweet, and yet somehow still tough as nails. It's a combination that works for me, but as I watch her shove that velvet box in her pocket, afraid to even embrace a tiny piece of her past, I am struck by a hard reality. She's escaping from one corrupt family to hide inside another. Mine.

EMILY

This time when Shane and I walk to the elevator, it's hand in hand, but he doesn't speak and I know him well enough to know he's troubled and I don't think it's about me. We enter the elevator and he punches the lobby level and then he's leaning against the wall and pulling me to him, and he is a hard body in all of the places

I am soft. Strong in ways that are not just sexy, but I admire that trait in him. And suddenly, I'm not thinking about my brother, or my name, or law school, but him. This man. His battles to save a company from a father who cannot be saved, and how I can help him survive and thrive.

"I have to take care of some business when we get to the apartment," he says. "But I'm thinking pizza, then a hot shower and a warm bed, both with you in them."

"You'll get no objection from me, but is there any chance we could swing by my apartment so I can grab a few things?"

"You and that empty apartment are done," he says. "Your stuff is in the car and a shopping trip is in your future. And"—he reaches into his pocket and hands me my cell phone—"I'm guessing you didn't accidentally leave that in your coat."

"No," I admit. "I was trying to throw you off."

"Coming to my apartment took balls."

"My secret weapon," I say. "I have a set of my own."

"I like that about you, except when it works against me." He molds me close. "Don't do that again."

"I won't," I promise.

"Maybe I'll just tie you to the bed to be sure."

"Will you be in bed with me?"

His lips curve. "That's the only way it makes sense."

The elevator dings and he takes my hand, leading me into the garage. We round the corner to find Seth a few feet away, wearing a trench coat and leaning against a black Mercedes. And while he normally has that lethal, hard air about him, which you'd expect from ex-CIA, tonight he's reading more like the Mafia, with me on the hit list.

"Can we hurry up and convince him I'm not the enemy before he shoots me or something?"

Shane laughs. "Look on the bright side. He'll shoot your enemies once he knows they exist too."

"No. He'll shoot your enemies."

"Your enemies are my enemies," he says, and fortunately Seth doesn't look at me as we reach the car. Or maybe it's unfortunately. I kind of get the impression he's calculating ways to tie me up and he's the wrong man for that job.

Shane opens the back door for me. "Give us just a minute," he says, and I gladly nod and slide into the car, the warm air surrounding me, exhaustion seeming to hit me like a blow. I slide low into the seat and close my eyes, heaviness overcoming me.

Shane and Seth's voices hum outside the car, random words reaching my ears. Brother. Stepfather. Texas. Law school. *Law school.* If I stay Emily, I've lost my credits, and I can't go back without risking discovery. God, that hurts, but I know it's true. I'm lingering on that painful thought when the word "Gemini" rumbles off the glass, spoken by Seth in just the right tone, at just the right spot outside, for me to hear him clearly now.

"I worked a case involving the Geminis," Seth goes on to say. "If they are after her, she's in trouble. And so are we if they find her."

I wonder if this is the moment when Shane regrets coming after me.

CHAPTER SEVEN

EMILY

I hold my breath, waiting on Shane's reply, which comes without hesitation. "Can you keep her off their radar?"

"I have questions I need answered before I can give you a conclusive reply."

They move toward the driver's door, and I frustratingly can't hear the rest of what they say. I'm about to just get out and ask when the doors open, and Shane slides in beside me, while Seth claims the driver's seat.

"What questions do you need answered?" I blurt out.

Seth eyes me in the rearview mirror and then he and Shane exchange a look, before Seth puts us in drive. Shane turns to me and takes my hand. "Obviously you heard that conversation."

"Enough to know the Geminis are as dangerous as I suspected and I need to disappear completely and I can't stay here and expose you."

"Does your brother know where you live or work?" Seth asks.

"No," I say. "He only knows I'm in Denver because he bought

my airline ticket. That and five thousand dollars and I was on my own."

"How long ago was that?" Seth asks.

"Two months ago," I reply.

Shane gives me a disbelieving look. "And he hasn't even asked how you're surviving?"

"He didn't ask," I confirm. "Our conversations were short and I didn't tell him I had a job because I was afraid he wouldn't send me my money."

"That certainly makes things less complicated," Seth says, and already we've traveled the short three blocks to the Four Seasons and are at the door.

"Seth is going to park and come upstairs," Shane says when the doorman opens the door.

Eager to get upstairs and get a plan together, I exit the car, and for once I'm thankful our favorite doorman Tai isn't around, because I really can't make small talk right now. Shane steps to my side, palming the man who'd gotten my door a bill, and then drapes his arm over my shoulder. "Deep breath, sweetheart. Things happen for a reason and that reason was to get our shields up and impermeable."

"Do you really think that's possible?"

"Yes. It's possible."

"God, I love how confident you are about everything," I say, and we round the corner toward the elevators. One of the cars dings and Shane and I step to the doors, waiting for them to open. When they do, they reveal Brandon Senior. I suck in air at the unexpected, and highly unlikely, second encounter in one night, but then everything about this evening has been trouble. He is different now. His tie is missing, his face is redder than normal, and I have the uncomfortable feeling he's just had sex, and yet, there is this dull throb of what I think might be pain, and perhaps the reason he's leaving, in the depths of his gray eyes.

"In for the evening?" he asks, looking between us.

"Mr. Brandon——" I begin, not even sure what explanation is going to come out of my mouth.

"In the morning," Shane says, his arm wrapping my waist, hand settling at my hip. "Goodnight, father."

Brandon Senior's eyes light, that dull throb banking as he looks at his son and says, "Goodnight, son."

Shane backs us up and around a bit and his father walks onward in the direction of the lobby. "Oh my God," I say, letting Shane lead me into the elevator, burying my face in my hands, and turn around as he finishes punching in our floor to face me. "He just looked at you like you'd scored the prize. Like you're the brother who got his secretary in bed, to use me for information."

He snags my hips and walks me to him, his back to the doors. "Which, of course, you know is not true."

"I do know, but that doesn't change how naked I feel right now." My fingers curl on his chest. "Really. Can this night end any time now?"

"Not for a while, I'm afraid, but when it does, it'll be us, in bed, preferably naked."

"Should we even be this close in an elevator? Or I guess we can, because it's kudos to Shane for fucking the secretary."

"Emily——"

"I know. I know it's not you, I promise. That look your father gave you just got to me. Icing on the cake, or more nails on a chalkboard, or someone smacking bubblegum over and over."

"My father and bubblegum smacking," he says, reaching up and covering my hands with his. "Those are two things I never thought I'd hear in the same sentence."

"I can't imagine what it was like to grow up with that man," I say, still fuming and feeling kind of dirty. "At least my father made me feel loved." I grimace. "Until he decided to desert me. Maybe that's why my brother is the way he is. He's selfish like my father."

"Don't give him that excuse. I sure as hell don't give it to Derek. We all choose who we want to be in life."

"We don't choose everything. Or maybe we do." The elevator dings and stops moving. "I could have stayed and faced this."

"I told you," he says, lacing the fingers of one of his hands with mine. "Trust your instincts." He leads me into the hallway.

"They told me to run."

"Then you needed to run."

At the expense of law school, I think, but I shove that thought aside before it starts shredding me to pieces all over again. "I'm pretty sure I'm fired," I say, as we reach his apartment.

"He won't fire you," he says. "He'll make you a player in our game. He'll taunt Derek about me winning over his secretary, not him."

We reach the door and he opens it, and his past warnings about Derek come to mind. "Isn't that trouble?" I ask, walking inside and turning to wait on him. "Won't he dig into my background?"

"We're going to clean up your background," he says, shutting the door and motioning me toward the archway leading to the kitchen. "Let's make coffee and talk."

"I'm too wired for coffee," I say, walking with him, both of us claiming a spot at the rectangular bamboo island, facing each other. A million seconds seem to pass, the implications of this night, and all we have been and could be, expanding and shifting between us.

"Shane," I whisper, because I do not even know what it is I want to say, just that I need to say it.

"Emily," he replies, his voice a low, velvety rasp. "Reagan. Whoever you are. I'm not deserting you."

"Maybe you should."

"Never. Things happen for a reason. I believe that, and you belong with me now."

"If that is true, then I believe I'm supposed to help you fight for the company and win. And it gives me a purpose I need right now. So if you're going to tell me I can't work for Brandon Enterprises—"

"I'm not."

I blink in surprise. "You're not?"

"No. I'm not, because I cannot have you in my life and hide you from my family, but you are above sitting at my father's door. Capable of so much more."

"I appreciate that, Shane, but it's where I belong now. It's where I can make a difference."

"Unfortunately, I have to let you win this battle at least for now, because we need to buy time to let Seth clean up your electronic records."

"Buy time how?"

"We need to let everyone think that I'm using you for a few more days. Just long enough for me to make a few strategic moves with Brandon Enterprises, and for Seth to fill in the holes in your background and assess what's going on with your brother." He leans on the counter. "I don't want you in the middle of my family's drama."

"It's your family, Shane. If I'm not a part of it, I'm not a part of your life. And I'm pretty sure my family drama tops yours."

"Don't count on that one." He runs his hand over the stubble shadowing his jaw and quickly changes the subject. "Just tell my father you were weak and ended up in bed with me again."

"But I'm living with you and everyone is following everyone else."

"We'll keep your apartment, but you'll stay here. They'll think I'm keeping you close to manipulate you."

"What about your brother? I know you said you're going to clean up my records, but what if hearing your father saw us together sparks new interest in me?"

"Knowing him, as long as you're nothing but a conquest to me in his eyes, he won't dig deeper. And by the time we let it be known you're more, there won't be anything to find." A knock sounds on the door, and Shane pushes off the counter. "That will be Seth." He walks away and I twist around to watch him, folding my arms in front of me, and wondering about his comment. I know there is trouble at Brandon Enterprises, but I handed him murder and hackers tonight. That's pretty hard to top.

Seth and Shane's voices sound, low rumbles I can't possibly make out, but there is this undercurrent to the conversation that is uncomfortably dark, and I'm concerned about whatever happened with the company while Shane was chasing me. Turning away, I walk out of the kitchen and go to the bar, staring down at the whiskey choices, and thinking I could use a little dumbing down right now to relive that night all over with Seth. There's a shift in the air and I turn to find Shane rounding the corner from the kitchen to join me, his hoodie gone, his T-shirt stretched across a hard, broad chest that is far more appealing than the conversation to come.

His stops in front of me, his hands settling on my waist. "You okay?"

"Are you?"

His eyes soften and warm. "Sweetheart, I've got you back. I'm fucking wonderful. And since you avoided my question, how about a drink?"

"I'd better wait until I talk to Seth. Where is he?"

"I'm here."

At the sound of Seth's voice, I glance left to find him at the archway that separates us from the kitchen, his trench coat and suit jacket gone, his starched white shirt rolled to the elbows. He holds up his iPad. "Ready to take notes."

Shane squeezes my hip and motions right. "Why don't we sit down?"

I glance at the fancy leather furniture and back at him. "I'd rather stand." I look at Seth, who is assessing me like I'm a criminal, and correct myself. "Never mind, let's sit." At least then he'll be at eye level.

We all make our way to the brown leather living area and Shane and I claim the couch, while Seth sits in the chair to my left, which is good. For a moment I revel in him not staring me in the face and then I realize that makes me seem guilty of something. I stand up and walk to the chair directly across from him, no longer sitting next to Shane.

Shane arches a brow.

"I'm on the witness stand, and I guess you are both judge and jury."

"No one is judging you, Emily," Shane says.

"I judge by data, not words," Seth adds, his expression unreadable.

"Since I'm telling the truth," I reply, "I'd say that statement is comforting, but I'm kind of terrified about what you'll find out. I know what happened the night I went into hiding. And more and more, I doubt what I thought I knew."

"Start with the basics," Seth says, asking me the same kinds of questions Shane had, but more of them. My name. My address. The address of my brother and stepfather. My parents' names. Every neighbor near the house. Every person I ever knew that worked with the Geminis, which was no one outside my stepfather and brother, but I'd heard names. He drills me, showing no emotion, for a good fifteen minutes, and one thing is certain: The man is stone cold. There is not even one tiny inflection in his voice.

"Now I need to know about that night," Seth says. "Every detail you remember."

"I told you what happened," I reply. "I got to my stepfather's house. He was dead. My brother was there. He refused to go to the police."

"You did," Seth agrees. "But I need you to replay it from the moment you got there."

I don't want to replay it, and push back at him. "How does that help?"

"When you slow down and relive things, you might remember something. A car parked across the street. A name written on a piece of paper. Anything that tells us who might have been there beside your brother."

"There was no one."

"Are you sure?" he presses.

"I am."

"Distress does not feed accuracy," he pushes back.

"Seth——" Shane starts, but I cut him off.

"It's fine, Shane." I look at him. "Thank you, but I'll try." I shut my eyes and inhale, forcing myself back to that night. I am there. I am living it again. *Desperate to confirm my brother was safe after two weeks of silence, I pull my silver Taurus into the driveway of my stepfather's two-story stucco mansion of a house, the lights aglow on the bottom level. He might be dodging my calls, but he's obviously home. He will have to tell me what's going on with Rick. I glance at the stack of books in the passenger seat—I should be home studying—and quickly reach for the door and get out.*

Motion detectors trigger lights and I walk up the drive and then make my way up the six steps leading to the front door. I ring the bell and wait. And wait some more. I ring it again and finally, I decide to go around back. I hurry down the steps and around the corner, more motion detectors setting my path aglow, until I'm at the back patio, where I find the door ajar. I walk toward it and . . .

My eyes pop open, that moment when I'd found my stepfather too near. "There is nothing new to tell. It was bloody. It was bad. My brother did it." I shut my eyes and think of the driveway, encased in trees, and then open them again. "No cars that I could see. The house isn't gated, but it's shrouded in trees."

"But your brother's car was there?" Seth asks.

My brow furrows. "No. Actually it wasn't."

"Did he park in the garage?"

"Not for a visit," I say. "Unless he moved back in and I didn't know it. Now, that I think about it, that's odd, and I don't even want to think about the suspicion that stirs in me. Despite all of this, I love my brother."

"I can see what you and Shane have in common," Seth says dryly. "Two brothers. Two problems."

A little too true to swallow right now. "How long will it take you to find out if my stepfather has been found?"

"I'll know a great deal by morning," he says. "And we'll get the holes in your record filled in by then as well."

"By morning?"

"You don't play around with the Geminis," he answers. "If that's who we're dealing with."

The comment rubs me wrong. "I didn't pull that name out of a hat."

He holds up his hands. "I didn't say you did."

"But you still don't trust me."

"I told you. I trust facts, not people."

"You don't trust me yet. Please just say it."

Shane moves to crouch on the ground in front of me, taking my hand, but I stay focused on Seth, who gives me my answer. "All right. I don't trust you yet."

I let out a breath. "Thank you."

He arches a brow. "Thank you?"

"For being honest. I like honesty right now. I like speaking it. I like hearing it." I turn to Shane. "I know you two need to talk about me and other things right now. I'm going to go upstairs."

"Before you go," Seth says, dragging both our attentions to him. "If your brother calls you, we need to have a plan as to what you should say to him."

"What should I say?"

"There's the real possibility that he knows where you work—"

I shake my head. "No. I didn't tell him."

"Your fake social security number will be in the IRS database."

"Right," I say, hating the dread that fills me. "So he can find me and connect me to Shane."

"The only way he's going to look up your social," Shane says, "is if he can't find you."

"Shane's right," Seth adds. "Tell him you got spooked and went to New Mexico. I'll handle getting your payroll changed to our shell company there."

I frown. "How will you explain that to HR?"

"We'll handle it through a technology back door."

I glance between them. "What company am I working for?"

"Drake Metals," Seth says. "But tell him the job doesn't start for a week, to give us time to set everything up."

"If he finally calls, I'll tell him, but I threw out my disposable phone."

Seth reaches into his pocket and hands me a new one. "Leave him a message now."

I nod and dial, hoping he answers, only to have the call go to voice mail. "Once again," I say, "I'm calling you. I'm in trouble, which you don't seem to care about. I'm leaving Denver. I'd like a little help here." I end the call, emotion balling in my chest, with both men staring at me.

"You have help now," Shane says softly, as if answering a question.

I look at him. "I know, but he's my brother."

"No one understands that statement more than me."

"If he calls," Seth says, dragging my attention back to him, "talk to him. Feed him the story about you leaving Denver. When the conversation ends, turn off the phone immediately and take the battery out. He can't track it if it's off and he can't turn it back on himself if the battery is out."

"Yes," I say. "Okay."

"We're pulling your payroll off the books," Seth continues. "That'll make it look like you've left if he checks up on your taxes and new social security number. And do not say anything to either of us in texts or on the phone that you don't want recorded or read. There are too many people rattling both of your cages to take that risk."

"Understood," I say, feeling sick to my stomach at the idea that my brother, the only person I thought I had in this world, could be dangerous to me and to Shane.

"I'm talking on any phone line about anything important to you or Shane or the company," he presses.

"Understood," I repeat, "and on that note, I'll go upstairs now."

Shane squeezes my hand and I face him again, finding concern in his gaze. "I'm tough, Shane. And I'm glad Seth doesn't trust easily. It actually makes me feel safer."

He gives a delayed nod, seeming to hesitate, but finally releases my hand. I turn and start walking, but I've made it to the side of Seth's chair when he says, "You're in good hands. I'm the best at what I do. Everyone Shane has working directly for him is the best."

"I know," I say. "It's Shane." I start walking again, and this time neither Shane nor Seth stop me. I pause at the bottom of the steps when my gaze catches on my bag sitting by the coatrack. I quickly divert, heft it over my shoulder, and head up the long row of stairs, the sound of Shane and Seth's voices reaching me, and it's not me they are talking about.

"No answer is unacceptable," Shane snaps. "I need to know what is going on inside BP. We aren't chasing our tails and playing shadow swords with my brother or Martina."

"What are you suggesting?" Seth asks, and as I reach the last step I want to linger and listen in, but eavesdropping is a kind of betrayal that Shane and I don't need between us. I'll tell him I overheard and ask what is happening.

Entering the bedroom, I flip on the light, and for a moment, I just stare at the spacious, masculine room, the giant bed draped in brown in the center. Shane's bed. My bed. Our bed. My lips curve and I cross the room, and entering the bathroom, I flip on the light to illuminate the sparkling white décor, before plopping my bag down on the counter. Unzipping it and craving structure and security, I take the liberty to claim parts of the sink, to set up my few makeup and hair-care products, the sight of them on Shane's counter next to his items feeling pretty surreal about now.

Task complete, I scoop up the shopping bags beside the bathtub, along with my duffel, and, a bit overloaded, struggle my way through the bedroom to the closet. Dumping it all at the door, I survey Shane's neatly organized closet, my stomach fluttering with the sight of his things, which will soon be next to my things. Well, the few things I have, which feels a little embarrassing right now, but somehow, not quite as hollow as it had just yesterday.

In all of this, I have found a man I care deeply for.

I walk forward and drag my hand down the row of neatly hung expensive suits, inhaling that raw masculine scent that is Shane everywhere around me, and considering where we were a few hours ago, it's surreal. I turn and press my hands to my hips, standing in the center of the closet. Glancing around me, I decide this is his space, his world, and it's best to allow him to invite me inside it in his own way. Still, I need to get my duffel out of the way and I pick a corner to neatly stack my clothing items and shoes. I do the same with the contents of the bags, then stuff the bags in the duffel. With some tiptoe action, I manage to shove the duffel on top of the empty shelf above.

Tasks complete and Shane's still downstairs, so I head to the bathroom, strip, and step into the shower. Warm water bordering on hot flows over me, and unbidden, my mind starts to drift to that night again, and I picture myself standing at the sliding glass door of my stepfather's house. *I reach for the handle, pulling it back, and it's like everything is in slow motion.*

The door fully opens. The sound of my stepfather's favorite Mozart compilation is playing in the background, the one I've come to hate, as it represents him. I dread seeing him because, of course, he will be arrogantly obnoxious. I inhale, and step into the kitchen.

I shake myself before I see the blood. Before I see my brother stand-ing there with red streaking his shirt and face.

The shower door opens and I yelp, only to be greeted by Shane's low, sexy laughter and his hard, naked body.

"You scared me," I reprimand him.

"I didn't mean to scare you," he says, folding me in his arms, and he is hard where I am soft, and strong in ways I wish I were not weak. He would face blood. "You're obviously jumpy, because no one else would be joining you in the shower, which, by the way, I liked coming upstairs to. But what's bothering you?"

I flatten my hand on his now damp chest. "That night. I hate thinking about that night and I hate that it rattles me so badly."

"You might not have liked your stepfather, but he was the man who helped raise you. There is a grieving process you have to endure at some point."

"I didn't like him. He cheated on my mother. He talked down to us. He dragged my brother into the Geminis, and that led to this. But then I think I'm blaming him for his own death. I feel guilty for that."

"I feel similar things about my father," he admits. "I hate him and I love him and I don't know how those two thing are possible to feel at the same time. Ironically, in this, I know Derek and I are the same. It's our only middle ground, but I can't find a way to make that bring us together. In fact, I can't bring us together and I'm done trying."

"Shane, he's still your brother. Are you sure?"

"I've tried. I'm done. It's war between me and Derek."

"I take it your problem tonight got bigger?"

"No. It's simply unsolved and unresolved, because at the root of it is the battle for power between myself and Derek, which I can't deny, to save this company and my family."

"Do you want to talk about it?"

He cups my face and presses me into the corner. "No," he says, his voice a low rasp. "I want to fuck." He kisses me then, a deep, demanding, tormented kiss, and before long he is inside me, pumping, thrusting, and I sense he is trying to drive away his demons, and mine with them. But long minutes later, when we are naked in bed, my back to his front, his big body draped around mine, I also sense that he isn't sleeping any more than I am. His demons and mine are alive and well, two poison kisses, which could too easily turn our sweet hello into a brutal good-bye.

CHAPTER EIGHT

SHANE

I wake at six in the morning, still naked, still holding onto Emily, not even remembering when I finally went to sleep. All I know is that for hours, I'd just held her, trying to figure out how to protect her from her brother and mine. And for a good long while, I think she did the same, until finally her deep breathing told me she rested, even if I could not. I inch back, trying not to wake her, and grab my phone from the nightstand, checking for a message from Seth with some kind of update. There isn't one, but then, he has to sleep. I know this, yet I struggle to contain the urge to text him now.

Sitting up, I run my hands through my hair and stand, taking my phone with me to the bathroom, and the hole in my stomach reminds me we never ordered that pizza. Emily is going to be starving when she wakes up. I shut the bathroom door and stare down at the few items she's set on the sink and it steals my breath. She is in my life now. Really in my life. My responsibility, though

Emily would disagree on that part, but I know of no other way than to take care of her, to protect her, and that is what is gutting me. How do I protect her when our families are basically two tornadoes about to sideswipe us at any moment, or worse, collide, with devastating results?

I push off the door and waste no time getting in the shower, and then out again, with two thoughts in mind. I have to contain Emily's situation. And I have to get rid of the Martina cartel before they are fully embedded in Brandon Enterprises, if it's not already too late. And I can't do it pussyfooting around, which is exactly what we're doing by toeing every spot Derek might be hiding the Martina involvement instead of stomping it out. Wrapping a towel around my waist, I inch the door open, finding Emily still asleep, the first glow of morning light illuminating her dark hair draped across the pillow. Seeing her like this, peaceful and sweet, punches me in the chest and stirs unfamiliar emotions. Crossing the bedroom, I step into the closet and shut the door, flipping on the light. That's when my gaze goes to Emily's tiny stack of clothes sitting on the floor, in a corner.

"Fuck," I whisper, deciding right now that this will be the last day I don't see a long row of her clothes in my closet. Interestingly enough, that idea is a good one: her clothes, next to mine. Her clothes in *our* closet. She is my woman now, and I have to protect her, something I have yet to ensure. The warmth I feel at her presence in my life becomes concern over her safety I need to be addressing now, not later.

Spurred into action with this thought, I dress in a gray pinstriped suit and a pale gray silk tie, and I open the door, light flooding my eyes. Emily is sitting on the bed, the blanket tucked under her arms, with her phone in her hand. "Did you hear from your brother?"

She sets the phone on the bed and twists around to look at me. "No call, but I was afraid maybe I missed one while sleeping." Her gaze sweeps over me, her eyes warm when they find mine, her hair adorable, all over the place. "I could really get used to waking up to you looking like that every day, Shane Brandon."

"And I could get used to waking up to you naked under the blankets," I say, my cock thickening with the knowledge that she's exactly that way now. "Which," I add, "means we may be late to work more often than not. And since this can't be one of those days, I'm going downstairs before I forget why." Her stomach gives a loud growl and I laugh. "Sounds like I need to feed you anyway."

"My stomach has told on me. I'm starving. How did we not eat last night?"

"We were hungry for other things," I remind her, thinking of the things I did to her before I let her sleep, and want to do to her now. "I'd better go take care of the business I got up to attend before I make you breakfast." I stand and start for the door, about to exit when I hear, "Shane."

I pause at the doorway and turn to look at her. "What am I going to say to your father?"

"You don't have to say anything. You can quit."

"What am I going to say to your father?" she repeats, clearly dismissing that idea.

"We'll talk about it when we're eating."

"Any word from Seth?"

"Not yet, but we'll know something today."

"I need a drink, but since I can't handle my booze, and it's far too early, can you make sure breakfast includes chocolate?"

"Chocolate," I confirm. "You got it."

Turning away, I head down the stairs, hating that I have to subject her to my father's games, when I really want to pull her out of Brandon Enterprises, which simply isn't happening right now. Aside from the fact that it won't protect her from my family as long as she's in my life, she's made it clear she'll fight me to stay, and at least I'll know she's in sight and safe. Or safer. And I admit to myself that I want her close. Selfishly, that light in the midst of a whole hell of a lot of darkness has been like a lifejacket I need more than I want to be true. But would I have taken our relationship up a notch this fast had Seth not made his discovery?

Reaching the kitchen, I flip on the light, making my way to the coffeemaker to get a cup brewing. It's then, staring at the drip, that I answer the question with a resounding no. I would not have, but not because I didn't want her here like every woman before her. It was about being sure I could keep her safe, so it's pretty fucking ironic that she's here now because her family might be just as dangerous as mine.

I grab my cup of coffee, sweeten it, and set it on the island counter. I drag a barstool up to the counter and sit down, opening my laptop, to quickly order breakfast. That done, I have three things I want to Google: the Geminis (though I won't, out of caution), the Martina family, and superstar pitcher Brody Matthews. I start with Adrian Martina, the man behind what might be Brody's demise, and mine too, for that matter, if I don't shut him out of Brandon Enterprises.

Twenty minutes later, I have a selection of pastries and egg-filled croissants waiting on Emily, and I'm not pleased with what I learned about Adrian. He's not the typical gangbanger stereotype you think of in jeans and bandana, with a gun in his back pocket and an impetuous spirit and trigger finger. He went to school in the States. Graduated from Brown University with honors. Dresses better than most of the people in my offices, and has legitimate investments here. And yet, he is regarded as the heir to

the Martina cartel, and right arm to his father, the acting kingpin. He's also thought to have killed at least a dozen people with
his own hands. And my brother is fucking his sister.

Scrubbing my freshly shaved jaw, I make another cup of coffee, pull another barstool into the kitchen for Emily, and then
reclaim mine. Now it's time to shift gears to Brody Matthews,
and a search brings up several articles that confirm he punched a
fan and then disappeared, both things that simply don't compute
with the man I've met. I dial Jessica, and she answers without a
hello, getting straight to the point. "Oh King. Oh Master, my
boss and leader. Why have you called me so early in the morning?" She firms her voice. "Seriously. Since you haven't called me
to bring you breakfast the entire year I've worked for you, what's
wrong?"

"I need you to get Brody Matthews's people on the phone and
get me a meeting. Tell them we want to offer him a seven-figure
sponsorship for a new yet-to-be-made-public product line."

"I'd be excited about meeting sir hotness himself, but are you
aware that he punched a fan and is now MIA? Not exactly a good
image for whatever project you haven't told me about."

"I have no intention of signing the man. I just need to talk
to him. Make it sound as lucrative as needs be, to get him out of
whatever hole he's in."

"Oh," she says. "Then this is trouble."

"I'm really sick of that damn word, but yes. It is."

"This has to do with Derek in some way, doesn't it?"

"Don't all things have to do with Derek?"

"I'm dialing now. I might be a little late to the office or might
not. I reserve that privilege, just in case I need it. I'm going to field
the calls before I finish getting ready."

"Understood."

We end the call and I look up to find Emily standing in the archway beside the bar, watching me, dressed in an emerald-green blouse and a simple black skirt, her dark hair a silky veil over her shoulders. She is stunning. "Everything okay?" she asks, walking toward me and rounding the counter to stand beside me.

I turn the barstool and walk her into me. "Nothing from Seth yet," I say, "but he and his men had to sleep." I lift my coffee in offering, her floral scent teasing my nostrils, and I decide I could wake up to that smell every day pretty damn easily.

She settles on the barstool beside me. "I wish I could think no news is good news," she says, "but no news is all I've had from my brother. And no news is what took me to my stepfather that night he died."

"Seth will have news," I promise. "And he'll have it today."

"I want answers and they make me nervous at the same time."

I offer her my coffee and she accepts it, taking a sip, her lips touching where my lips just were, our eyes locking and holding, a new intimacy between us, an understanding that we are more than we were even yesterday.

I cover her hand where it holds the cup and take a drink, the air crackling around us, and she actually sucks in a tiny breath. My lips quirk and I set the mug down on the table. "Hungry?"

"Is that even a question?"

I laugh and motion to the room service plates. "I meant food. For now."

"I know I was starving, but I don't think I can eat, after all."

"You have to eat," I say, removing the lids to the food.

Her eyes go wide at the sight of the pastries and she sighs. "Okay. I can eat." She grabs a small plate and I do the same.

We split a croissant, this idea of sharing my life with someone alien, but somehow with Emily it's right. "That paper my father gave me last night was the deed to the apartment."

"You got him to sell you the apartment?"

"No. I told him he was giving it to me."

She gapes. "And he did it?"

"It's all about knowing how to play his game."

"Does that mean you want to stay? Or use it for an investment property?"

"Stay. It's safe here. I know everyone. You'll be safe here."

"Don't stay because of me."

"We're staying because it's smart, but later, if you want to move, we can."

"Shane," she says, her voice cracking. "Don't make decisions for me when I could end up behind bars."

"Sweetheart, you have me for an attorney and you were afraid for your life. You aren't going to jail."

The doorbell rings and I push off the counter. "Seth and Jessica are the only two people who can get up here without notice. I'm betting on Seth."

"Oh God. What if it's bad news?"

I cup her face and kiss her. "Deep breath. There is nothing I can't fix here."

"Except the Geminis trying to kill us both."

The bell rings again, and I run my finger over her lips. "Stop looking for the apocalypse." I kiss her again and head for the door, but I silently relive my concerns over the Geminis threat, hoping for some kind of good news on that front.

I open the door and find Seth standing there, his black suit and tie and neatly trimmed blond hair as perfect as it always is, but his eyes are bloodshot. "I'd say good morning," I greet him, "but you look like shit. You need to sleep."

"I'll sleep when I know where we stand. I need to have Emily look at a couple of photos for me."

"Is there anything you're about to say that will scare the shit out of her?"

"If the absence of answers scares her, then yes."

I step back and silently invite him inside, already heading back to the kitchen. The door shuts behind me and I continue on to find Emily cleaning up our breakfast. I can see her hands trembling. And the only time she should tremble is from pleasure. I close the space between us as she sets our plates in the sink. I step to her side, aware of Seth joining us, and softly say, "He just wants you to look at some photos."

"No news?" she asks, and turns to face Seth. "Nothing on my brother?"

He steps to the opposite side of the island and Emily does the same, while I move to the end, to have both of them in my sights.

"What I can tell you right now," Seth replies, "is that there is no police report, missing person's report, or notable activity of either brother or stepfather with law enforcement. It does appear your stepfather left the country, which he did frequently, so this fits his profile."

"Only this time he's dead."

"Are you sure?" I ask.

"Quite sure," she assures me. "But where is the body? How did he hide it? I will always have this hanging over my head, afraid it will come back to me." She looks at me. "You will always have it hanging over your head, which is why I tried to leave."

"We'll find a way to pull you out of this," I assure her. "But if you're in it, we're in it."

"On the bright side," Seth adds, "your brother's done a much better job of covering up your stepfather's death than he did creating your documentation. And since the house was paid off last month, there is nothing like a lapsed mortgage payment to be a red flag to anyone. I also found the record of a lawn service that maintains the yard, leaving no fear the outside of the house will be unkempt, but—that was set up for years."

"I can't believe you even thought of that."

"I told you," I say. "Seth knows how to protect you."

She glances at Seth. "Do you trust me now?"

"Considering everything you told me checks out, I'm leaning toward yes. Right now, what I'm focused on is finding out how deep into the Geminis your brother and stepfather are."

"*Was*, for my stepfather," she amends. "He's dead. Anything you might be thinking differently is just not true. I saw the blood."

"Easy, sweetheart," I say, catching her gaze with mine. "We aren't suggesting he's alive, though it would be a good thing if he is."

"I know," she whispers. "But he's not."

"I need you to look at some photos for me," Seth says, sliding a folder in front of Emily. "They have the names on the back. Tell me if the face or name rings a bell."

She inhales and flips the folder open, setting one photo, and then another, to the side. "This man," she says, indicating a photo of a beefed-up military-looking man in his forties. "That's RJ. The name says Ryker Jones, but I know him as RJ. He visited the house once and I heard my brother and stepfather talk about him often. He's their boss. The other one that's labeled 'John Scott,' I know the name but not the face, and honestly, I don't even know why I know the name. Who are they?"

"John Scott is the founder of the Geminis," Seth informs us, "but anyone involved with the Geminis would say his name at some point, which makes me less concerned with him. Now, RJ is another story. We know he's close to Scott, and high up in the chain of command, as well as being an ex–Special Forces soldier in a top secret elite unit, where something went wrong. He did not leave the military on good terms. He's one of the best hackers on the planet."

"Out-of-character exaggeration?" Shane asks. "Or fact?"

"Fact," Seth states, moving on. "Another interesting detail. Neither Emily's stepfather Cooper Wright, or her brother Rick, are in any CIA or FBI records as persons of interest in connection to the Geminis, but then most of their operational staff are what we call ghost handlers."

"In other words," Emily says, "RJ's involvement is bad."

"Any Gemini involvement isn't good," Seth says, "but for all we know, your brother is still on good terms with them. I actually think you disappearing makes him, and you, look guilty of something, rather than the opposite."

"I thought the same," Shane adds. "He could have panicked, be it out of fear for his sister, or fear of the police."

"Wait. I look guilty? Is he still there? Does it look like I did something and ran?"

"I haven't located him," Seth says, "so I wouldn't jump to that conclusion. And you took a leave from school, but have you paid your rent?"

"My brother said he'd do that for me," she says. "But he also said he'd send me money." She presses her hand to her stomach. "I am not liking the gut feeling I'm getting."

I step to her side and wrap my arm around her waist. "Easy, sweetheart. Seth and I will get your rent and bills handled."

"Can't I just pay them out of my own account, if I haven't been evicted already? I mean it was just me taking money from here or taking a lump sum that's an issue right?"

"I need more time to develop a plan," Seth says, "but by this evening we'll have the holes in your background covered and we'll be able to decide how to proceed safely." He glances at his watch. "I have a meeting with Nick." He glances at me. "Right after I extend that offer we discussed last night," he says, obviously meaning paying off our pro ballplayer's wife. "If you still want to take that route?"

"I want you to drive right into it as cheaply as possible," I say, "and make it count."

"I always do," Seth assures me, while Emily interjects with, "Who's Nick?" thankfully leaving our insider conversation to stay inside.

"He's ex-FBI," I tell her. "And the owner of a private security firm I've contracted outside of Brandon Enterprises for this and many other things."

"And Nick and his team are all damn good," Seth adds. "They have a hacker they call GI Joe, whom they brought in on this last night, and I was damn glad. I worked with him on a CIA operation about six years ago. He's top Gemini caliber and he's a real asset right now." He glances at me. "Can you walk me to the elevator?"

"In other words you want to talk about me without me," Emily says. "I'll go get my purse."

"Emily—" I start.

"It's okay," she says. "I'm okay. Actually, really, I know more than I did and I think once I digest it all, I'll be even more okay."

"I'll meet you back here in five minutes."

She nods, rounding the island while Seth and I head to the door, stepping into the hallway. I pull the door shut, having no intention of walking to the elevator. Seth faces me. "Her bank account is being drained in weekly chunks, each time under the amount that requires reporting."

"What about his bank accounts?"

"They haven't been touched, but he hasn't had more than ten thousand in either of the two accounts in three months. Prior to that he had a chunk of change. We're working on what happened to it."

"Did he plan this, and move his money in advance?"

"That's where my head is on this. As far as his plan to protect Emily or throw her to the wolves, I need more information. I need a man on the ground in Austin to try to locate the brother."

"Make it happen," I say, and shift topics. "What about BP? Anything on last night's potential security breach?"

"Our men discreetly checked the building and found nothing, but as Emily said, I'm not liking what my gut is telling me."

"I've already trying to reach Brody's people."

"I'm meeting with Nick on all of the above."

"Go. Do. Get answers." He hesitates and I arch a brow.

"We don't know how well the Geminis know this woman. She lived with two members for years. We don't know how much of a liability she represents to them." He reaches into his pocket and hands me a thumb drive. "That's information on the Geminis you need to know. I know I've said this before but I'm saying it again: They're dangerous." I accept the drive and he adds, "If she knows how dangerous they are, and she left to protect you, she's a brave-ass bitch."

"Sounds like you trust her."

"Leaning that way," he repeats stubbornly.

"Lean harder and find a way to protect her. She matters to me."

He nods and turns, while I do the same, entering the apartment and shutting the door. Emily is not yet present, and I walk to the kitchen and put on my suit jacket before loading my computer into my briefcase. By the time I'm back in the foyer, she's standing there in her coat, ready to go. "He still doesn't trust me."

"Why do you say that?" I ask, slipping on my coat to downplay Seth's concerns, which I know won't last.

" 'Leaning that way,' " she says, repeating what he'd said about trusting her. "I was attached to the Geminis for a decade plus. He's doing his job."

Shifting my briefcase on my shoulder I face her, finding her oddly at ease. "You don't seem upset."

"I am upset. I'm scared. I hate my brother put me in this position. But the good news is that I have a full stomach or I might just plain flip out. I should really warn you that I'm unstable when unfed. Maybe I should take food to your father. Maybe that's the key to soothing the beast."

"Unless it's raw meat," I say, "don't bother." And I tell myself that I'm playing along with this façade of flippancy because it's obviously her way of coping, a way of being strong. But silence is better than a comfort rooted in a lie.

Emily and I end up stopping the elevator four times on the way to the ground level and finally step out into the garage. "There are a few negatives to this living arrangement," I say, as we walk toward the car.

"The pluses outweigh the negatives," she says. "Room service. Security. Location."

I click the button to unlock the Bentley, and the lights flash. At the same moment, a black Cadillac Escalade pulls out of a parking spot and drives just past us, then stops. Unease rolls down my spine and I stop walking, turning to look over my shoulder. Still, it sits there. "That's weird," Emily comments. "Why is it just sitting there?"

I have no idea why but I know in my gut who is waiting for me in that hundred-thousand-dollar SUV. I take Emily's hand and palm her the keys. "Go to the office. I'll meet you there."

"What? Why? Shane——"

"I need you to do this and not ask questions. Text me after you meet with my father, and tell me you're okay. But don't say or text anything you don't want hacked or listened in on."

"Okay I will, but I can't drive your Bentley. I'll walk. What if you need it?"

"I have a spare key. I'll pick it up at the office." I firm my voice. "Take the car. Go now."

She inhales and then nods. "Yes. Okay." And then as if she senses the danger I know exists right now, she adds, "Be careful, Shane." She turns and walks to the car and gets in. Only when she starts the engine do I turn back around and walk to the vehicle. When I reach the back window, it rolls down, exposing a man in his thirties with dark wavy hair and dark eyes. He leans forward; I know him from photos.

"Adrian Martina," I say, making it clear I know I am talking to the second in the Martina cartel, and the man my brother has brought to my doorstep.

"Shane Brandon," he replies. "It's time we talk, don't you think?" He pops open the door and I show no hesitation getting in. Fear doesn't win. And I'm going to win.

I climb into the double backseat, sitting across from him, and shut the door. Adrian hits the button to raise the window that seals us away from the driver. He is refined in every way, his suit a glossy pale blue that practically gleams money.

Our eyes meet, and in his I feel the push for control, the hunger for power and money he already possesses but wants more of. The things that draw him to my brother, but also put them at odds, as they want the same things. "I understand we're practically family."

I arch a brow. "How exactly is that?"

"You don't know your brother and my sister are dating?"

"Dating doesn't constitute family."

"I understand that might change." I don't react, though I silently vow to cage my brother before he marries us to a cartel. "Mexicans take family to heart. It's serious. It's business."

"My business is not your business."

"Your brother's business is my business," he counters.

"If my brother controlled Brandon Enterprises, that would be true, but he doesn't. Just as you don't control your family operation."

"Our fathers," he says. "Both ready to retire." His lips quirk slightly. "In their own ways."

The inference that mine will soon die is without question, and is meant to gain a reaction I don't give him. "Since when is your father ready to retire?"

"Whether he does or does not, I am heir to all that is his, but you, my new friend, we both know, cannot say the same."

"Don't believe everything my brother tells you. He'll land you in jail."

"Yes. About that. I understand you have Feds sniffing around."

"And the irony of that is that it's unrelated to whatever arrangement you've made with my brother, but not unrelated to him. He bribed an inspector to get drug approval." Surprise flickers in his eyes. "He didn't tell you," I say, jumping on this. "Or he didn't tell you the truth. But then why would he want you to know that he's done something to assure the Feds are all over us."

"Surely you can clean it up."

"Had I not cleaned up a mess with the Feds my brother created a year ago, you'd be right." I lean in and rest my elbows on my knees. "There's a reason no other operation such as yours has infiltrated the legit market. It's swarming with Feds. Get out before my brother hands you, and me, to them on a silver platter."

"I don't want out. I want you in."

"That will never happen." I open the door and get out, and he rolls the window down to glance at me.

"The Feds will find nothing wrong inside your operations. You have my word. And I am a man of my word." The window closes.

I am a man of my word, as well, I think as the SUV drives away, and when I said his business is not my business, I meant it. I turn to find the Bentley gone as I expect it to be, and while Emily has driven it away, she is still consuming my thoughts and in my life in a way that means I have more on the line than ever. I head toward the elevator and start walking, removing my phone as I do to key in Seth's number. He doesn't answer.

"I'm at my apartment, alone. Meet me here. We have a mammoth-sized fucking situation I can't talk about on the phone." I end the call, but the problem keeps growing.

By the time I'm back inside my apartment, my mind is replaying Martina's words. *The Feds will find nothing wrong inside your operations.* I head to the kitchen and start a cup of coffee, trying to convince myself that Martina is using our labels, but not our facility, and that security breach last night was just a glitch. I reach for my coffee, and start doctoring it my way, while I replay Adrian's statement again. Damn it to hell. He said "operations," as in plural, and a man like him does not make slips of the tongue. I lean on the counter. We know for a fact that the transportation division in Boulder is moving drugs, which means Adrian's message is he cleaned up the evidence, at least for now. I'm not comforted, not even slightly.

My gaze lifts and catches on the folder Seth had found in Emily's desk, and I sit down on the barstool I'd claimed earlier and start reading. Emily said she felt like something was off in the paperwork, and that premise always has legs when it comes to my father. And one of the reasons my father likes hedge funds is how under regulated they are. How easily the manager of the fund— him in this case—can manipulate the money. It's gray water that leads to a black hole that seems to be opening up on all sides of this company and my family, with Emily along for the ride. Because I have no doubt Martina chose to approach me when I was with her for a reason. It was a threat. The entire meeting was one big not-so-subtle threat.

CHAPTER NINE

EMILY

I pull the Bentley into Shane's reserved parking spot in the private garage of the high-rise Brandon Enterprises calls home and kill the engine, having taken no joy in driving it. Not when whatever happened back there was trouble. I open the door and grab my purse, settling it on my shoulder, and step out of the car. Pausing, I check my coat pocket and my phone just to be sure my brother hasn't called. And he hasn't. After the desperate messages I left him, he hasn't called and I have to be angry, otherwise I'll start thinking of him lying in a puddle of blood. No matter what, that would destroy me.

Disappointed, I shove it back in my pocket, and shut the car, locking the doors. "Holy Rocky Balboa, are you driving the Bentley?" I turn to find Jessica rushing toward me, her spiky blond hair a tad lighter today, her black pantsuit stylish and sleek. "How did you convince him to let you drive it?" she asks, falling into step with me as we head toward the elevator. "He won't let me drive it."

"He shoved the keys at me and told me to take it. There was some man in a black SUV who showed up in the private part of the Four Seasons parking garage." I punch the call button for the elevator and it opens right away. "Do you know who that was?"

"I have no idea," she says as we step into the car, "but most likely one of Seth's people working for Shane. Have you ever driven the Bentley before?"

"Forget the Bentley," I snap.

"I have a point here, honey, sweetie, cranky. If you've never driven it and he shoved the keys at you—that tells you how much he wanted you away from that meeting."

"Sorry. I didn't mean to snap. I've never driven the Bentley before."

"Then whoever it was is a problem."

The doors open and we enter the lobby, heading toward the main elevator. "I'm really worried about this war he has with his brother."

"There's a lot to be worried about," she says as we reach the elevator bank. She punches the button herself this time.

I glower at her and the car opens, thankfully empty. "Thanks for making me feel better," I say, as she keys in the twenty-fifth floor.

"Honey, I'm not Dr. Phil and I don't pretend to be. I'm more Judge Judy. Right to the point."

"And kind of judgmental," I add, thinking of her lecturing me about hurting Shane sometime back, as if I would do so on purpose.

"Just a little," she replies, holding up two fingers, and apparently completely unapologetic, which is actually fine. It's her knowing herself and owning it. It's honest, like Seth last night. I'm seeing a trend. I'm the only one in his life close to him that's lied to him. No matter my reasons, that's going to take time to completely erase. I refocus on Jessica.

"What can I do to help him?"

She holds up her hands. "Me pushing you to dive into troubled waters will get me in hot water."

"I'm serious. He has to win, Jessica. We both have to do what we can to help him. What does he need most to win this war?"

"What he needs most is to be back in New York practicing law. He loved it."

"And yet he's here," I say, realizing now that we have even more in common than I thought. We're both here. We're both not practicing law. And that choice was made for both of us by our families. No wonder we connected so quickly.

"Yes. He's here and he's not going anywhere, so you're right. He has to win."

"Which means I have to keep my job at his father's door today."

"Why today? Is Senior more of an ass than normal?" She cringes. "I occasionally feel sorry for saying things like that since he's dying, but then he does something new and freshly brutal and I say it again."

"He saw Shane and I together last night getting off the private elevators at the Four Seasons. It's pretty obvious I'd only be there for one reason."

"So you now look like the office slut and Shane is the brother who banged the woman in front of his father's door."

"Can you not be you at this very moment and say stuff like that?"

"Judge Judy, honey. You're now part of the game. You won't get fired."

"That's exactly what Shane said and if that's true, I can still use my position to help Shane. Brandon Senior is doing something weird with the hedge fund he's putting together and I don't know enough about this type of thing to figure it out."

"What are you thinking?"

"Mike. The one who owns the professional basketball team and who is a huge stockholder. I don't know if he knows it's dirty, but I think *he* is, and that means he'd be on Derek's team, not Shane's."

"Are you sure? Because I really wanted that man to be the father of my children."

"I'm not sure. Maybe he doesn't know what Senior is up to, but they have been communicating often. Jessica, what if Brandon Senior isn't really letting Shane have a shot at the company? What if this game has already ended?"

"A stacked deck maybe, but Senior knows Shane is savvy. You know this, Emily. Nothing is done until it's done." The elevator dings. "But you do need to share your concerns about Mike with Shane."

"I will," I say as we step into the lobby, my gaze catching on the Brandon Enterprises logo on the wall, the lion emblem reminding me of Shane's tattoo: a lion, which represents his father, with an eagle with spread wings representing Shane, perched on the lion's head. He confessed getting it one night when he was drunk. Knowing him better now, Shane doing anything while drunk and driven by emotion doesn't fit him, and I wonder what was in his head that night. What had pushed him to a place he doesn't go?

"Did you hear me?" Jessica asks.

"What?" I say, blinking her back into view and realizing I'm standing and staring at the wall, not walking.

"I have to go. I've got something to handle for Shane."

"Yes," I say, wondering if that something has to do with ball-player Brody Matthews, which seemed to distress Shane this morning. "Sorry," I add, when she's still looking at me expectantly. "Go ahead."

"Good luck with Senior," she says, hurrying away.

Luck isn't likely to help me with Brandon Senior, I think, walking toward the door with no real plan as to what I'm doing. Remembering everything I did last night, it seems the controlled, planned, calculated person I was not so long ago with the name Reagan is gone. Entering the lobby I wave to the receptionist, and oh the irony of her chomping on bubblegum after my comment about such behavior resembling Brandon Senior.

I stop at her desk. "Is Senior in yet?"

She chomps, then answers with, "He was here when I got here," before chomping some more, and I can't take it.

"You might not want to chomp that gum while on the phone. I hear Senior dislikes it."

She pales. "Oh. Yes. That was bad of me on the phones. Thank you." She turns to the trashcan, and I start down the hallway to the left, which leads to the alcove and my desk. It guards Senior's office, but no one is here to guard me this morning. Clearly, he's feeling rather spry today to be here so early, which really isn't in my favor.

Rounding the corner, I find my desk looking as neat as when I left it last night, while Senior's door is thankfully closed. Letting out a sigh of relief at the momentary reprieve that gives me a chance to prepare for the storm ahead, I walk to my desk and sit down. I stick my purse inside my desk, then remove both of my phones and stick them in my top drawer. That's when the door behind me opens, and I instinctively stand, expecting Brandon Senior, but instead, his wife walks out.

"Emily," she greets me, and always stylish, her shoulder-length dark hair is a dramatic contrast to the pale pink dress she's paired with sleek knee-high boots.

"Hello, Mrs. Brandon," I reply, wondering how she can be Shane's mother when she looks like she's forty-five years old at the most.

"Maggie, please," she says, stopping in front of me. "You're making me feel old. And we're friends now."

"Maggie," I repeat, not sure what to make of her now or ever.

"We have so much to talk about," she says, and I'm pretty sure the spicy scent I smell is her husband's cologne, though it's not at all familiar. "How about another lunch? Would tomorrow work?"

I'm not sure if this means I still have a job and I'm invited into the game, or if she doesn't know I'm possibly about to be fired. "Yes," I say. "Great. As long as I don't have anything work related to stop me."

She gives me an all-knowing smile. "I'll make sure you are free. I'll meet you here at one. See you then." She walks away and my intercom buzzes.

"In my office, Ms. Stevens."

I grimace, certain that bubblegum chick told on me and is not to be trusted. Hardly anyone in this place can be trusted it seems, which is all the more reason Shane needs me here.

"Ms. Stevens?" I hear again.

"On my way," I say, heading to the door, when it hits me that maybe leaving my phone behind when my brother could call isn't such a great idea, though I don't know what I'd do if he chose right now to finally contact me. Still . . . Turning around, I grab it from my desk, place it on vibrate, and then stick it under my blouse in the band of my pantyhose beneath my skirt. With a calming breath, I return to Brandon Senior's door, and open it.

Entering it, I find him sitting behind his massive half-moon-shaped wooden desk, his fingers steepled on the sleek wooden surface, but rather than looking at me, he is sitting with his head is tilted downward, his eyes shut, and oddly, I'm pretty sure he doesn't know I'm here.

"Mr. Brandon?" I ask, and his head jerks up, his eyes fluttering a moment before they focus on me. Good gosh, is he in pain?

"Shut the door," he orders, and there is a hint of rasp to his voice, and for a few moments, I forget the manipulator he is and see a dying man who is also Shane's father.

I do as I'm told, sealing us inside together, and he motions toward the high-backed leather visitor's chair I would have claimed anyway, but that is part of control to him, the tendency to dictate the actions of others. My stepfather was this type of person. In some ways Shane is as well, and I don't really know why it doesn't bother me with Brandon Senior the way it does others in most cases, but not now. Right now, Senior is still that dying man.

Crossing the room, I sit down in front of him. "Hi," I say, because "good morning" really doesn't seem appropriate considering how red his cheeks are at a closer view. He's having a bad cancer day and trying to hide it. I'm sure of it.

"Ms. Stevens," he says. "This conversation is going to revolve around conflicting words and actions."

"Obviously we're speaking of last night."

"Obviously. Words and actions. Your dots do not connect."

My mind races, and I wonder why I haven't practiced answers to these questions. "I know I told you he was using me . . ."

"Yes. You did."

I quickly decide to be as honest as possible. "I consider myself a strong person, but your son. He's a weakness."

"In other words, you will continue to end up in his bed."

"It's not . . . yes."

He studies me with hard bloodshot eyes. "You're aware my sons are battling for control of the company."

"I am."

"Then I assume your loyalty is to Shane."

"Yes," I say. "It is."

More of his intense scrutiny follows. "You're dismissed, Ms. Stevens."

My heart sinks. "I can still do my job. I can—"

"Which is why I said you're dismissed. Go get to work."

Apparently, it's confirmed. I'm not fired. I'm off so easily, I'm stunned. "That's all?" I ask. "Nothing else about me and Shane?"

"You didn't lie about where your loyalty lies, and therefore, I know where you stand. That's more than I can say for most sitting outside my door or in any chair in the building. Now get to work." He reaches for his phone.

Confused by him letting me off without at least tormenting me a little bit, I stand and cross the office. "Close the door behind you," he calls out as I exit to my work space, and once again, I do as commanded.

My phone in my desk vibrates, and I hurry forward, expecting Shane. Sitting down, I open the drawer and answer. "Hello."

"Did you wreck the Bentley?"

I smile at Shane's deep voice, amazed at how it manages to do funny things to my belly no matter how many times I hear it. "I did not wreck the Bentley but I did make Jessica extremely jealous." I'm also relieved everything seems to be okay, when I had a bad feeling about that SUV that seemed to show things were not.

"See?" he says. "You had nothing to worry about. Did you love driving it as much as you knew you would?"

"More," I admit, lowering my voice. "But I was worried about you. Who was that person?"

"No one I ever want you to know." He changes the subject, which evidently isn't meant for the phone. "How badly did my father jab you this morning?"

"Honestly? It was uneventful. I'm still employed."

"Well the only surprising part to you still being employed is the uneventful part." He does another change of topic. "I have a situation to handle, including a couple of meetings. I'm going to be gone most of the day. If you need to reach me, and I don't answer, text me and I'll call you as soon as I can."

"I can't imagine anything urgent," I say. "It's not like I'm going to get that phone call I've been waiting on and even if I do, I'm pretty sure it will be uneventful as well."

"Uneventful is not a bad thing." He hesitates. "Emily."

"Yes?"

"The apartment smells like you now."

I blink in surprise and my belly flutters. "Is that good?"

"Distracting," he says, clearly indicating he's at the apartment. "But I like it. I'll talk to you soon."

He ends the call and my intercom buzzes. "Come back in here, Ms. Stevens."

Okay. Maybe this is where uneventful turns eventful. I stand and walk into the office, to find him staring down at a document. "Door open is fine," he says, without glancing up.

Hoping that's a sign this is nothing big, I cross to his desk and stand in front of it. He doesn't look up and I start to sit. "No need to get comfortable," he says, finally giving me his attention, those gray eyes more bloodshot now than minutes before. "There's a team of bankers coming in to meet me at four o'clock. I'll need refreshments and I'll e-mail you the presentation material I want put together and bound before they arrive. And it's time for a board meeting. Set it up for next Wednesday. You'll find the respective company heads in your Rolodex. Tell them it's not optional and that you can attend to appropriate travel arrangements, if necessary. And get Harvey Fitzgerald on the phone." He goes silent and we stare at each other until he glowers and says, "Now, Ms. Stevens."

"Right. Yes. Of course." I turn and rush for the door, about to exit when he says, "Ms. Stevens."

I face him. "Your first phone call will be to Fitzgerald, not my son to spread my business. This arrangement only amuses me until it no longer amuses me. Understand?"

"Yes. Of course. Fitzgerald."

I rotate and he says, "Shut the door."

I shut the door and walk to my desk, not giving myself time to think of the implications of a board meeting, for fear I'll end up booted, and be of no help to Shane in the future. Dragging the Rolodex to me, I find the contact I need for Brandon Senior and in two minutes have transferred his call to him. My mind turns to Shane and that black Escalade, the ominous feeling still weighing heavily. And what about the bankers and the board meeting? Something is going on, and I desperately want to talk to Shane about it all, but I dare not until we're face-to-face. I mean, was that what Brandon Senior just implied? I could use my second phone, but can my brother hack it since I left him messages from it? What if he can, or did, track my call to Shane? My God. What is happening to my life?

Brandon Senior buzzes my desk. "My son is not in. Where is he?"

"I don't know," I say, which is actually true.

"Find out. I need a contract for Fitzgerald he had to approve, and yes, Ms. Stevens, you can tell him I called a board meeting. That will most certainly get his attention."

Bingo. I dial Shane and he doesn't answer. I text him: *Your father is looking for you. He's calling a board meeting for Wednesday. He says he needs a Fitzgerald contract.*

He replies right away: *Jessica has the contract.*

Yikes. I text: *Sorry. I should have checked with her.*

He answers: *Never apologize for texting me.*

I hesitate, wanting to tell him about the bankers, and he says nothing about the board meeting. I buzz Senior. "I'm going to get the contract from Jessica."

"Make it fast."

Standing, I make sure both of my phones are in my waistband. Crossing my work space and then the lobby, I enter the hallway leading to both of the Brandon brothers' offices. Passing several offices, I reach the fork at the end, to find Derek's secretary sitting in front of a sealed office. She doesn't look at me and I don't look at her. I cut left to bring Jessica's desk into view, and I walk straight to her.

"I need the Fitzgerald contract. Shane says you have it."

She offers me an envelope. "Did you talk to him? Because he won't take my calls and I need to reach him."

"I, ah . . ."

She purses her lips. "You did. He has me doing something important. Call him for me."

"I can't do that. You know I can't, not if he's not taking your calls."

She makes a sound resembling a growl. "Fine. I'll handle it."

I soften my voice. "Senior is having a meeting at four o'clock with a group of bankers. I'm going to leave a copy of the names and documents for the meeting in the copy center for you."

She gives a negative shake. "They all work for the company. Leave it at security."

"Got it, and Shane doesn't know about that meeting. Please don't tell him on the phone."

"I am always as discreet as a wife with a sex toy she doesn't want her husband to find out about."

I shake my head and actually laugh. "You are a crazy person."

"Who made you laugh. Glad to see you're still around. I'll handle the situation."

"Thank you." I turn and start walking toward Derek's office again when I have a flashback to the other night before I went to Shane's apartment, and those terrifying moments trying to get into his office, afraid I'd be caught. I turn down the hallway, and my stomach knots. The security guard who didn't really work here. I can't believe I haven't told Shane and Seth. They have so much going on. I should just reconfirm the security guard isn't real. Maybe the guard I talked to the first time was confused. I return to my desk and consider dialing downstairs, but think better of it. I need to do everything I can in person.

I need food for the meeting and to visit the copy center, also on the lobby level. I'll stop by security when I'm there. Pulling up my e-mail, I find Brandon Senior's message, and open it. There are six guests on the list and an attached document. A lightbulb goes off. The document will tell me what this meeting is about. I open it and start scrolling. There's hedge fund data, profit reports, and data that doesn't make clear his intent. Do bankers deal with hedge funds? Aren't they separate? I press my fingers to my temples. I really need to study up on this stuff. I slip a data stick in my computer, load the document, and then buzz Senior.

"Yes, Ms. Stevens?"

"I'm going downstairs to make your copies and order refreshments. Can I bring you anything?"

He hacks several times and then croaks out. "Yourself back to your desk setting up my board meeting."

"Hot tea with honey coming up," I say, letting go of the button.

Hurrying forward, I travel the hallway, exiting through the lobby to the elevator. The car arrives quickly and I spend the ride replaying the encounter with the security guard: *I've just finished with the final documents, gathering all my paperwork, when I hear, "It's late to be working alone, isn't it?"*

I jolt at the male voice, whirling around to find a dark-haired security guard I've never seen before standing in the doorway. "What are you doing here?" I demand, his big body, and the empty office, hitting all of my many raw nerves.

"I saw the light on and thought something was amiss."

"Just catching up on my work."

"I see that," he says, eyeing the stack of files I've created, and with what strikes me as more interest than an outsider should have.

"Thanks for checking on me," I say, shutting the file I have open and scooping up the entire stack of files. "I'm fine. I'm going to leave soon."

"I know you think you are," he says, "but that's when people make mistakes."

My throat goes dry with what seems to be a hidden meaning. "Mistakes?"

"They let their guard down and forget to stay alert. Case in point, we've had a few strange reports in the building this week, which one wouldn't expect with our level of security. You said you're leaving soon. Why don't you let me walk you downstairs?"

"Oh no," I say, kicking myself for giving him that opening, and growing more uncomfortable by the moment. "Thank you, but 'soon' for me translates to the next hour or so."

He studies me for several more of those creepy-filled moments in which I contemplate the heel of my shoe as a weapon, before he finally gives a quick nod and says, "Be careful on your way down." He disappears out of the door, and I have no idea what possesses me, considering he creeps me out, but I dart forward, catching him as he's about to exit the office.

"Excuse me," I call out.

He faces me, and I ask, "What strange happenings?"

"For tenant privacy reasons, I'm not at liberty to say."

"I understand. What's your name?"

"Randy," he says.

"Randy," I repeat. "Thank you, again."

I blink back to the present with the ding of the doors, and whisper, "But there was no Randy that fit that man's description working that night." Unless someone was confused, I remind myself. One of my law professors always said to double-, and even triple-check, critical details. I need to find out before I overreact and hand this to Shane and Seth on top of everything else. Exiting the car, I dash for the copy center, drop off the data, and head to the coffee shop, where the owner, Karen, a forty-something redhead with an overwhelming personality, is behind the register.

"You're a regular now, aren't you, honey?"

"I am," I say, and I have this odd sense of being in the eye of this storm that feels ridiculously right, a sense of this being where I am meant to be. "I work for Brandon Senior." Her eyes light and it takes me fifteen minutes to get past her infatuation with my boss to get my order of pastries, cookies, and coffees, and then I leave with Senior's hot tea and honey. I've just stepped into the lobby when my cell phone rings, the ringtone that signals my brother is calling.

I walk back into the coffee shop, claiming a seat at a wooden table huddled between free-standing product displays, freeing my hands and removing the phone from my waistband. The number is blocked, but it always is the first time I call him from a new phone. I punch the answer button.

"Finally you call me," I hiss softly. "I've needed you."

"I've been juggling a few problems here, in case you didn't remember. RJ's been trying to reach Cooper."

RJ. The one Seth called the best hacker on planet Earth, and high up in the Geminis.

"I took a job Cooper was supposed to do and made it look like he disappeared while he was doing it."

I inhale and let it out. "Does that mean I can come home now?"

"RJ hasn't even figured out Cooper is missing yet, so no. You cannot."

"Does this mean you can send me money now?"

"I'm not back in the country yet. When I return, I'll arrange it."

I don't believe him anymore, and suddenly I embrace the plan to convince him I'm somewhere I'm not. I *want* to protect myself from my own brother. "I left Denver. I got a job offer in New Mexico. It pays well, which is good news because I need my money."

"And I need to go."

"Of course you do."

"Leave me your new address when you get to New Mexico. Bye, sis." He hangs up and I grind my teeth, immediately turning my phone off and then turning it over to remove the battery. I stick both pieces in my waistband, my mind replaying the call. He didn't ask how I'm getting to New Mexico or where I'm going to work. He didn't ask how my money was holding up or how I'm holding up. He didn't ask what motivated me to leave or how I got a job in another state. Irritatingly, my eyes prickle, when my brother does not deserve my tears. I shut that down, refusing to mourn a relationship that clearly was lost a long time ago. I consider calling Shane, but I'm pretty sure that hearing his voice will turn the prickling into tears, and neither of us need me to be that weak right now. Besides, I really have nothing to tell him aside from the RJ remarks, and those still aren't much. Or maybe they are. I don't know. They certainly aren't urgent and if I find out details about the security guard, I can tell him everything at once.

Standing, I replace the tea with a fresh one, fielding more questions I don't want to answer from Karen while my mind is on my brother. I almost think he just wants me to go away. I've lost law school and I can't touch my money. He doesn't care and the writing is on the wall.

I've lost the battle to save my brother. I've most likely lost law school, thanks to the Gemini connection I can never escape, but I am not losing my money too. And I'm still working for Brandon Senior's office where I can do my part to ensure Shane doesn't lose Brandon Enterprises.

My mission to help Shane renewed, I head to the security booth in the front of the building, remembering the night I'd met Shane as I approach the long glossy desk. I'd lost my phone. He'd interjected and insisted the guard check the lost and found, against evening hour's policy, promising to watch the desk for him.

The guard rushes away, leaving me stunned at his quick de-

parture while Shane rests an arm on the counter and faces me. "You ran away today."

My eyes go wide. "That's the way to get right to the point. And for your information, I had someplace to be."

"You didn't even take your coffee with you."

"I didn't have time to drink it," I say quickly, no stranger to thinking on my feet.

"You ran," he repeats.

"You're kind of intimidating," I counter.

Amusement lights his gray eyes. "You aren't intimidated by me."

"Are you saying you are intimidating to others?" I challenge.

"To some I am, but not to you."

"You base this assessment on what, exactly?"

"Anyone intimidated wouldn't be brave enough to say they are." He closes the distance between us, the scent of him, autumn leaves and spice, teasing my nostrils. "Are you intimidated now?" he asks, the heat in his eyes blisteringly hot.

"No," I say, suddenly warm all over, when lately, everything has made me cold. "I'm not intimated."

But I was so very drawn to him, I think, reaching the desk, where I find a female guard I've never seen before.

"Hi," I say. "I work for Brandon Enterprises. I was here late two nights ago and a very nice guard helped me. His name was Randy. Big bulky muscular guy with dark hair." I consider a moment. "Late thirties maybe? I wanted to tell his supervisor how much I appreciated it."

Her brow furrows. "We have a Randy, but he looks nothing like that. Actually, I don't know of anyone here that fits that description."

"Maybe I'm remembering his name wrong."

"We still have no one that fits that description. The two guys that were on that night were Randy and Josh, but he is twenty-five, blond, and good-looking."

That's one more guard than I saw the other night, but it doesn't help me much. My formerly knotted stomach is now downright sick. "It must have been a Brandon Enterprises employee. Thanks anyway." I turn away and start for the elevator. It could have been a Brandon employee. Seth will know. It has to be a Brandon employee. Right? I mean, who else could it have been?

CHAPTER TEN

SHANE

By the time I manage to get Seth on the phone, he's already sitting outside the house of Brody Matthews's estranged wife, preparing to negotiate her silence. Ready to remove at least one noose from my neck, I instruct him to finish the job and meet me at my apartment, sans Nick, an ex-Fed who will no doubt pressure me to go to them for help when he hears about Martina, regardless of the price to the company. It's a detail that has me uneasy about his employment, but hiring someone else always represents the potential of betrayal, which I won't even consider risking. In the meantime, I busy myself reading through the documents Emily put together for me from my father's office. Aside from the hedge fund data, which has a few potential red flags, my real point of interest is my father's file on our largest stockholder, Mike Rogers.

When I'd agreed to save the company last year, I'd initially thought owning a professional basketball team and having a public image to protect gave Mike reason to support my efforts to clean up the company, and I'd done everything to win his faith and keep him with us. And then he'd gone cold on me.

Looking for that reason, I open his file, and turn on my computer to start comparing years of financial data, setting every other thought aside and losing myself in the investigative process. Time passes, and I down another cup of coffee before the doorbell rings. Eyeing my watch, I see it's already near noon. Pushing to my feet, I stand and head to the door, hoping like hell Seth has contained at least one of our problems. I open it and he seems to know what I'm looking for, because he announces, "Brody's wife took the payoff."

I give him a nod and motion him inside.

"Emily's rent was paid on time," he adds, following me to the kitchen, "which means her brother is, at least, keeping her off the radar, an indication he's not throwing her to the wolves."

"He already threw her to the wolves back in Texas," I say, reclaiming my barstool. "The risk of the Geminis coming after her will always exist. She can't return to the past, or law school, and I'm the person who is going to have to tell her that."

"She's smart," he says, claiming the spot directly across from me. "She already knows."

"Knowing it and accepting it are two different things." I change the subject. "How much did Brody's wife cost me?"

"Three hundred, and she agreed to leave the country."

"Three hundred thousand dollars, and her moving expenses, all to cover up my brother's mistakes. I'm living a year ago all over again, and then some. Adrian Martina showed up in the parking lot as Emily and I were leaving this morning. That's why I sent her to the office ahead of me." In normal Seth style, his reaction is a nonreaction, completely indiscernible, and I give him a rundown of the entire story.

"Showing up with Emily by your side," he remarks, when I'm done speaking, "that wasn't a coincidence. He's aware she's close to you."

"And the irony of that," I say, "is that he didn't have to follow me, or watch me, to find out. My brother could have told him."

"I'm sure he did," he concludes. "Derek made them promises or Martina wouldn't be in your operation. There have been bumps, which means Derek needs a fall guy, because I promise you, he doesn't want the wrath of the Martina cartel."

"And I'm the fall guy." It's this part of the equation I've spent the morning blocking with numbers and research and no one understands how Emily must feel with her own brother's betrayal better than me.

"Adrian Martina handed it to you, all right," Seth concurs. "That whole 'you're practically family' thing. That was a mind game, a way of telling you that through your brother, you're in this now. You can't get out."

"I'm not in."

"You're in, Shane, and you don't just walk away from the Martina cartel. There would be a price." He studies me a moment. "Nick—"

"No," I bite out.

"He has friends at the Feds."

"I said no. We are not going to the Feds. That would destroy the company I'm trying to save."

"There's no reason it has to go public."

"We've had this conversation. Leaks happen all the time. Are you going to tell me they don't?"

"Dead people happen all the time with Martina too. That's my concern. You are the only thing standing between Martina and Brandon Enterprises."

"Adrian is second to his father. He doesn't have the final say."

"Roberto Martina is well known to be a brutal killer."

"Exactly," I say, having read up on the man the moment I'd heard of their involvement with Derek. "That's my point. Roberto bragged about killing Adrian's brother for costing him money."

"Because he betrayed him."

"Failure to a man like Roberto is betrayal. We need to convince Adrian we're the kind of fire he can't put out. I planted the seed. I told him there is a reason cartels stay away from legit operations. We are watched like hawks. That's where you get Nick and his men, to make that seem like reality."

He studies me for several drawn-out moments. "It's a long shot."

"That we're going to make work."

"I'll talk to Nick. We'll come up with a way to spook him."

"Do nothing until I approve it. Moving on." I tap the paperwork in front of me. "Have you studied these documents?"

"I made copies. I haven't had time to analyze them."

"I've been comparing the transactions for Mike Rogers in this folder to the company database. One in four don't match up. He's too smart, and too involved with my father, to be a victim."

"We've always thought your father was helping him hide money."

"We also thought he had too much to lose to ultimately stand with Derek, but the man owns a professional basketball team and Martina is marketing to professional athletes. I can't ignore where that's leading me."

"While I agree," Seth says. "He's also filthy rich and well insulated. We have nothing to prove he's dirty."

"We don't have time for 'well insulated' to be the only answer you give me. He's a twenty percent stock holder, the vote that hands the company to Derek." My lips thin. "My father called a board meeting for Wednesday, after requesting a family dinner meeting on Sunday."

"Where do you think that's headed?"

"He may not have a choice," I say, the words acid on my tongue. "Not if he wants to be around for it. The bylaws require the board have sixty days' notice. He told me last night he's not going to be around long."

"He has to be afraid you'll cause trouble at the meeting."

"I assume that is why Sunday night is happening." I tap the folder again. "The hedge fund. And our transportation division, which I assume is a placeholder for someone else he's hiding. I don't believe for a minute that this is legit. It's my father's last hurrah, and he has nothing to lose."

"And Mike's involved. We find out what it's about and we have our leverage on him we can use for the vote."

"And clean up this damn company once and for all." My cell phone beeps with a text and I glance down to read a message from Jessica: *Stop blowing me off.* I glance at Seth. "Jessica is trying to reach Brody's people. Any news on him?"

"Still missing. Nick's folks are nosing around. I'll come back here, once I have a full update." I nod and he stares at me. "Say what it is you want to say," I press, "but if it involves the Feds—"

"The best way to find out what's happening with that hedge fund is to squeeze those involved. Are you prepared to do that?"

A month ago, I would have asked him to define squeeze, but a month ago Adrian Martina wasn't inviting me for a morning chat, with Emily living in my home. "Get me what I need on Mike."

He gives me a sharp incline of his chin and turns for the door.

I hit auto-dial on my phone and call Jessica. "It's about time," she greets me. "I'm in the lobby about to come up."

In other words, there are things she doesn't feel she can say on the phone. It's an epidemic today. "You know the code and the door is open," I say, ending the call, standing and walking to the refrigerator and grabbing a protein shake, which I pop open and guzzle.

The door opens and Jessica's heels click on the floor before she appears in the kitchen, sans coat, and eyes the paperwork I have spread all over the island. "You really should tell your secretary when you plan a work-from-home day," she says, setting her purse and a file on the counter.

"I didn't plan to work from home."

"Considering you gave Emily the Bentley, I figured as much, but I didn't know. I thought maybe it was a ploy for breathing room."

"From my family, not Emily. What was urgent enough to bring you here?"

She slides the folder toward me. "Your father's having a meeting with six bankers at four o'clock in the conference room."

"Is he requesting my presence?"

"No," she says. "We only know about it because of Emily."

I indicate the folder. "And this is?"

"Emily snuck me the handouts for the meeting."

"Let me guess," I say dryly, "the documents are generalized and tell us nothing about what this meeting is about."

"Correct. They give a company overview, including a non-specific financial picture. I figured this was just some of his normal hedge fund activity, but I also know you have concerns about the transactions he hides and don't want him bringing on debt and problems you have to handle."

"If there was anything he didn't want me to see or hear, he wouldn't have given the documents to Emily, who he now knows I'm seeing."

"Yes, about that. I heard he saw you together last night."

It's a prompt for details I don't offer. "And as a response to that encounter, this meeting materializes. This is his way of testing Emily, to see if he can trust her."

She narrows her eyes on me. "Aren't you worried he's going to make a habit of this?"

"Emily handles my father better than I do. And speaking of Emily. She moved here for a job that fell through and brought very little with her. Order her anything and everything you think she needs and have it delivered here. And whatever you do, don't tell her. She'll move out before I get her fully moved in."

Her lips part and she starts to speak and then stops, then starts again. "She's moving in?"

"She already did."

"Oh," she says, and she looks like she might turn blue from holding back whatever she isn't saying.

I arch a brow. "Since when do you bite your tongue with me?"

"I have whiplash. You were going to make her quit her job to protect her from your family. You even pushed her away and broke off contact. Now, she's sitting at your father's door with your blessing and living in your house. What changed?"

"My mind," I say, not about to tell her the details of Emily's past. "Buy her what she needs. Have it delivered here and work with Tai to ensure it's not all sitting out in the open when she gets home."

"In other words," she says. "Bite my tongue again."

"Nailed my thoughts exactly."

Her lips purse. "Fine. Can I look at what she has already?"

"Nothing. Start from scratch. Buy her everything she might need."

"Everything? As in clothes, shoes, makeup, and purses? Purses are expensive."

"Whatever she needs."

"Don't you think she might want to pick some of it out herself?"

"I'm sure she would, but it will be a long time before Emily freely spends my money and I'm not leaving her with nothing waiting for that day to come. Use my Black Card."

"The no-credit-limit card. Okay, well I'll get some of my favorite sales ladies to help me make this happen today. Tell me again why we never dated?"

"Because you like your men submissive and I like my women with less snark."

"I do not like my men submissive, but I get it. We'd kill each other." She settles her purse back on her shoulder when her phone rings. She digs it from her purse and glances at the number. "Brody's manager." She answers and has a short exchange before covering the phone. "He has time this evening or in the morning."

"I'm glad he has time to talk about seven figures," I say. "But his time isn't the time I need. It's Brody's."

"They haven't been able to reach him."

Not the answer I'd hoped for, but at least his estranged wife is handled. "Tell them I have time when Brody has time."

She nods and has a short exchange before ending the call. "They're trying to reach him. Are you going to tell me what that's about?"

"No."

"Okay. I'll ask again later. Do you need a ride to the office?"

"I'll meet you there."

"All right then." She turns and heads for the hallway, but pauses, and turns to face me. "I like Emily."

"Then we have that in common."

"I once told Emily that if she hurts you, I'd hurt her, but now I know she's devoted to you. And now I'm going to say this to you: Don't hurt her and don't let your family hurt her." She doesn't wait for an answer. She walks away, her footsteps sounding until the door opens and closes. I sit there a moment, staring after her, my gaze landing on the paperwork she'd brought me from Emily. I pull it toward me but I don't open it. My father tested Emily today, and she failed him, but came through for me. She protected me and I am protecting her, but it doesn't stop Jessica's words from clawing at my mind: *Don't let your family hurt her.* My family that connected the dots between us and the Martina cartel. Between Emily and Adrian Martina.

CHAPTER ELEVEN

EMILY

It's nearly one o'clock, and I'm juggling travel arrangements, phone calls, and questions I can't answer about the board meeting, when Jessica sets a slice of pizza from the joint downstairs in front of me. "Eat."

"I don't have time."

"Make time. My orders."

"Is Shane here?" I ask, as both the security guard and the call from my brother still nag at me.

"He's going to be soon."

"Can you tell him I need to talk to him?"

"Of course."

"What about Seth? Is he here?"

"I have no idea. That man checks in with no one but Shane. Why? What in the world do you need Seth for?"

My intercom buzzes and Brandon Senior barks, "Get Fitzgerald back on the line."

"Right away," I say, refocusing on Jessica. "Thanks for the pizza and I'm back to work."

She leans on the desk. "Do you need me to find Shane or Seth for you?"

"No," I say. "It's nothing important." I hope. I think. "I can talk to Shane this evening."

"Everything's okay?"

"Yes. Fine. Please don't bother them." My brow furrows. "Why are you being so motherly? It doesn't suit you."

"Motherly?" She pushes off the desk, a frown on her face. "I have never been motherly. I am not that old. Eat your damn pizza." She turns and walks away, and I laugh, grabbing the phone to get Fitzgerald on the line, but not before deciding I'll have to delve into Jessica's mothering syndrome over lunch sometime soon.

Another few calls and I finally stuff a bite of pizza in my mouth, and at that very moment, Derek walks around the corner, an older version of Shane in a black suit paired with a red tie. He's standing over me before I can blink and swallow, watching as I choke and reach for a bottle of water, never saying a word, and I hate that he will think he's rattled me. I hate it so much. Finally, I'm no longer struggling and find my voice.

"Sorry. I swallowed wrong."

"Tell him I'm here."

I pick up the phone and buzz Brandon Senior. "Derek is here," I say.

"I don't have time for his nonsense right now. Get rid of him." He hacks in my ear for several seconds. "Get me more of that damn tea you're always shoving down my throat."

"Right away," I say, quite enjoying the opportunity to send Derek away. I hang up and say, "It's a bad time. He's about to be in a big meeting."

"Is that what he said to you?"

I paraphrase, though nothing would make me happier than to repeat Senior's exact words. "He said it's not a good time."

His eyes glint hard, lingering on me and he abruptly moves. Before I know what is happening, he's opening his father's door. The door shuts again, but not before Senior's angry spewing of profanity reaches my ears. I sigh, resigned to the chastising I will get over this, like I can control Derek. I need to go get the man his tea. I stand up and stick both of my phones back in my waistband, and head for the lobby.

A thought hits me. I dial Jessica. "Can I get Seth's phone number?"

"Seth again? What's wrong?"

"Nothing is wrong," I repeat, removing my phone from my waistband. "And I'm in a hurry. Senior wants tea, and considering Derek just barged into his office after he told me to get rid of him, I want to be back here when whatever is happening in there is over."

"How very Derek of Derek. It's not even like it's unexpected. It's just him, but I get it. Senior will blame you for the way he made his son. Here's Seth's number. Are you ready?"

I pull up a new contact on my phone. "Ready." She gives me the number and I key it into my contacts. "Thanks."

"Emily—"

"Mother Jessica. It's nothing. I promise."

She sighs. "Fine. How about bringing me a coffee so I have an excuse to nag you again?"

"What do you want?"

"Vanilla latte, nonfat."

"You got it."

We end the call, and I head through the lobby, and make my

way to the elevator. Once inside, I dial Seth, not even sure he'll answer, but he does.

"Emily. What's wrong?"

"Nothing is wrong," I say, "and I hope you don't mind Jessica giving me your number."

"I should have given it to you myself. Did you get that call we talked about?"

"Yes, I did and——"

"I'll be there in ten to fifteen minutes. I'll find you."

"Yes, I——" He ends the call and I murmur, "I just want to know about the security guard," to the empty space, sticking my phone back in my waistband.

That man is not full of charm, but I'm not easily ruffled and he's smart and hard in ways I can see work for the role he has by Shane's side. Which is what, exactly? Head of security? More like the ultimate fixer of all things broken? Yes. He's the fixer, all right. The man who seals the cracks that might appear in Shane's armor, while Shane himself fights to hold together the pieces of a family too broken to mend. It's a problem I understand all too well, and unbidden, my eyes shut, and I flash back to my stepfather lying in a puddle of his own blood, my brother standing in the kitchen covered in that same blood, and my brother's words play in my head: *What the fuck are you doing here?*

The car jolts and I inhale with my return to the present, but this time it's not fear that I feel over the blood and death. My brother had been angry. I've remembered that often, but never until now do I remember it being at me. I exit the elevator with the sense that there was more to that night than I have wanted to face, but I can't think about this now.

Shoving aside thoughts of a night that has forever changed my life, I cross the lobby and enter the coffee shop, relieved when a college-age kid is behind the counter instead of the chatty owner, which will allow me more time for Seth before I have to head back upstairs. I place the order for Brandon Senior and Jessica, and make my way to the end of the bar to wait for the order, my mind taunting me with my brother's words again. *What the fuck are you doing here?* And this time I dare to ask the question I've suppressed all this time. Was my stepfather's death self-defense, or a planned murder?

The drinks appear and I'm reaching for them when suddenly Shane is standing in front of me, lifting one of them to his lips, that spicy male scent of him suddenly enveloping me, and driving away everything but him.

"Wait," I say as he lifts the cup and then pulls a face that only he could make strikingly sexy.

"What the hell did I just drink?"

I laugh, amazed at how easily the rest of my worries have faded. "That was your father's tea."

He reaches for the other coffee, and takes a sip. "Now what did I just drink?" he asks, setting the cup down.

"Jessica's coffee."

He laughs, one of those deep, sexy laughs of his that ignites a fire in me and yet somehow soothes all the jagged pieces of my soul these past few years have created. "Not what I had in mind," he says, leaning in close to me, his shoulder pressed to mine, his hand settling on my hip. "I was expecting a little taste of you," he murmurs, his breath a warm fan on my neck. "I have a proposition for you tonight."

He has officially and easily seduced me, and for just a moment or two or three, all my worries fade from black to a cool rosy hue. "Why not now?" I ask, and even to my own ears, my voice has a raspy, affected quality.

He inches back to look at me, those gray eyes of his aglow with flecks of warm amber. "Now sounds really damn good, sweetheart, but I prefer our private conversations to be without an audience."

"Is something wrong with the drinks?" the girl behind the counter asks.

Shane strokes a lock of hair behind my ear, seeming to resist the interruption. "Tonight," he says softly, releasing me to turn to the counter. "The drinks are fine," he replies, and with the absence of his touch, just that easily, too easily, my mind begins to race with random thoughts. My brother's call. The security guard. The Geminis. His father's meeting. Shane turns back to me. "I reordered the drinks and had them made extra hot." His eyes narrow on me and suddenly, his hands are on my waist, and he's backing me up, stopping only when I'm against a wall, behind a big corner display. "What's wrong?"

"Nothing is wrong," I say, "but I've been waiting to see you in person to tell you that my brother called."

His fingers flex at my waist. "When?"

"A few hours ago, but—"

"Why didn't you call me and tell me you needed to see me?" he demands, his voice low but fierce.

"It was uneventful and I knew you had things going on."

"If you have something big happen, you call me. Screw everything else. This could be about your safety."

"It's not. Not this time."

Seth appears by our side. "Okay. What did I miss?"

Shane releases me, his brows furrowed. "What did I miss? Why are you here?"

"Emily called me and Jessica told me where to find her."

Shane hones in on me. "I thought you said your brother's call wasn't urgent?"

"I didn't call Seth about my brother."

"What about your brother?" Seth demands.

Testosterone suffocates me. "You two are making me claustrophobic. From the beginning: My brother called and we spoke for all of about three minutes. I told him I was leaving for New Mexico and he didn't even ask how I was going to get there. I brought up money, and he all but hung up on me."

"Nothing else?" Seth asks.

"He said he's been MIA because he took a job outside the country in Cooper's place, but made it look like Cooper took it himself."

"Cooper is your stepfather," Shane verifies.

"Yes," I confirm. "And he made it look like Cooper disappeared while doing the job."

"The good news here," Seth says, "is this plan of his seems smart and it won't connect you to any of this."

"Right," I say. "Yes. I hadn't thought of that."

Seth gives me a probing look. "You don't sound relieved."

"The only way I'll be relieved is to find out they're looking for me and I can't be found. Something we can't test until they actually put me on their radar."

"This plan of your brother's bought us time to seal any leaks leading to you," Shane states, giving me some positive to hang on to. "This is good news."

Seth doesn't give me time to revel in Shane's welcomed reminder, getting right back to business. "Did you turn the phone off and remove the battery like I told you?"

"The minute I hung up," I confirm, removing the two pieces from my waistband, and he quickly takes them from me.

"And you called me why?" he asks, sticking to his direct way of communication I'm getting used to with this man.

"I remembered something that happened the night I was here alone making copies of Brandon Senior's files. It's probably nothing, but a man claiming to be a guard checked on me."

"What man?" Shane asks.

"He wasn't wearing a uniform and he gave me a weird vibe. On my way out that night, I checked with the desk downstairs and they didn't know who I was talking about. Same story today. No one with the building security knows who he is. I assume he's one of Seth's men, but I just wanted to confirm."

"What was his name?" Seth asks.

"Randy."

"Are you sure that's his name?" Shane presses.

"Yes," I confirm. "I repeated it to him. It was Randy. Maybe it was a nickname?"

"What did he look like?" Seth asks.

"Tall with dark hair, early forties, I think, and muscular."

"What nationality?" Shane asks.

I consider a moment, thinking back. "I don't know, but he might have had a slight accent."

Neither Shane nor Seth look at each other, nor do their expressions change, but there is a subtle thickening in the air that tells me this news does not please them. "Emily and I need to talk," Shane says to Seth.

Seth gives a quick nod, and walks away, while Shane leans forward, one hand pressed to the wall just above my head, his big body a barricade creating our little private spot. "What's the real reason you didn't call me?"

I am momentarily stunned. "What?"

"You are savvy enough to give me a coded message by phone

or text, and I know you know that I would want to hear this news. Why didn't you do one of those things?"

"I needed some time to convince myself not to cry over a brother who doesn't deserve my tears and had I heard your voice, I would have."

Understanding fills his eyes. "The anger comes next, and long after, acceptance."

"Are you at acceptance?"

"Every time I think I am, I get angry again."

"Maybe they aren't exclusive."

"Maybe they aren't, but anger is dangerous. Something perhaps my brother—and yours—needs to remember." Shadows flicker in his eyes and are gone before they're fully realized, but I still recognize them. I know them as ghosts of what once was, turned to monsters. "Call me next time. Give me the peace of mind to know you're out of imminent danger."

"Yes. I will. I'm sorry."

"Don't be sorry." He runs a finger down my cheek. "Be safe. Come on." He pushes off the wall. "Let's head upstairs."

I nod and we walk to the counter where he hands me his father's drink and he takes Jessica's, then we start a silent walk through the building lobby, his shadows, and perhaps mine as well, still between us. We've just reached the elevator and stepped inside when he turns to face me, breaking the silence. "My father will either cancel that meeting or miraculously move it to another location."

"But he had me order food and supplies."

"Because he's a master game player. He would never dangle something in my face he didn't want me to know about. He's too smart for that. He was either testing you or taunting me, looking for a reaction I'm not giving him."

Looking for a reaction. "He got one from your brother. Just before I came downstairs, Derek showed up at my desk and demanded to see your father, who proceeded to tell me to get rid of him."

Shane's lips quirk. "And Derek stormed into my father's office."

"Yes. Exactly."

"Like I said. My father is a master game player and my brother is far more predictable than he knows."

"I guess that's a good thing for you."

"It's sure to be a bad thing."

"Who was that this morning, Shane?"

"Someone who doesn't believe in keeping business in the office," he says. "But it gave me an excuse to spend the morning studying a certain folder filled with paperwork."

"And?"

"And it was interesting reading. I'll tell you about it tonight." The elevator opens and we step into the hallway, walking toward the door and entering the lobby, where we pause. "I may have to leave for a meeting but I'll be back to pick you up." He softens his voice. "We leave together. Okay?"

"Yes," I say and his eyes linger on mine a moment before he walks away, but I don't move. I stare after him, and while the idea of leaving with him is a good one, I can't get past the idea that he's acting as my bodyguard, any more than I can the tension in the air when I'd told him and Seth about Randy.

Inhaling, I focus on the receptionist, who is looking at me like I've just grown two heads. No. She's looking at me like I just had sex with Shane in the lobby. Straightening my spine, I ignore her and start down the hallway, and I have this strong sense that nothing about my past, or my present, is exactly how it seems.

SHANE

I leave Emily in the lobby of Brandon Enterprises, my stride long as I travel the hallway, tension radiating down my spine with the implications of the unknown security guard whose presence holds dangerous implications. And my mood is too damn dark to find Derek at the end of my path, propped in his doorway, looking ready for a confrontation. At this very moment, I have a very uncharacteristic urge to beat his fucking face in. I pass him by, cutting left toward my office, but he isn't going to take a hint.

"Shane," he says, willing me to turn, but now is not the time. I do not have all my ammunition in place, nor do I have the temperament nor the patience to play the manipulation game, that beating him requires in any form that is not literal. I keep moving, setting Jessica's coffee on her desk without looking at her before entering my office, shutting the door behind me, and crossing to my window where I press my fist against the surface.

I inhale a breath of uncommon rage, which I managed to contain on the elevator ride up, but anger is a beast inside me, created by the beast that is my brother's greed. The intercom buzzes, and Jessica says, "Seth."

"Send him in," I reply, and almost instantly the door opens behind me.

Pushing off the glass, I turn to find Seth already joining me and shutting the door behind him. I walk forward and press my fist against my desk this time. Seth stops directly in front of me.

"Yes," he says, as if I've asked a question, "I'm thinking what you're thinking. It's one of Martina's men."

"On our secure floor, which means we have yet another hacker, or my brother let him in here."

"That would be correct."

"Do you and your team have a plan to convince Adrian Martina to get the fuck out of my company?"

"We have ideas we aren't ready to present yet."

"Get ready and then come back."

His jaw tenses but he says nothing more before he leaves. I turn back to the window, staring out at the city without really seeing it, Jessica's words once again in my mind: *Don't let your family hurt her.* I won't let them hurt her. I turn to my desk and grab the back of my chair. I can't wait on someone else to fix this. I *won't* wait on someone else to fix this and if someone's going to get hurt before this is over, it won't be Emily.

CHAPTER TWELVE

EMILY

Come three thirty, I'm in the conference room on the opposite side of our offices, preparing for the meeting that seems to still be happening. The food, a selection of cookies and pastries, has been delivered and is displayed at the end of the long glossy table, large enough for twelve, and I've set up the information packets at seven different locations. Everything is ready to go, and I'm about to head to the lobby to check on our guests when Brandon Senior appears in the doorway. I'm struck immediately by how his custom black suit, once exquisitely tailored, hangs on his thinning body, while his yellow tie appears rather enormous.

"There's been a change of plans, Ms. Stevens. One of the key players can't come here. I'm meeting him and the others at an off-site location."

I almost laugh at the insanity of this moment. The master player isn't such a master if Shane can predict his actions this closely.

"Understood," I say. "Do you need the handouts?"

"I do," he says, "and I need you to walk with me to the car. I have a document I'd like you to give Shane that I forgot to bring up this morning. I assume you'll be seeing him?"

I'm reminded that our living circumstances haven't been disclosed, but more so, I am aware that he is digging into how close I am to Shane. "I can have Jessica ensure he gets it."

His lips quirk ever so slightly. "Of course. Jessica."

"Let me grab your materials," I say, hurrying to the table and quickly gathering up the bound documents and placing them inside the canvas bag the copy center had used to deliver them. "I'm ready."

He gives me a nod and we head to the elevator, where I'm nervous about the conversation we might have once inside. Fortunately for me, several staff members join us, and I am saved from whatever he's intended to chat with me about. Not that "chat" is a word I typically use in conjunction with my boss. Another bit of luck, and it doesn't take long before we're on the executive floor of the parking garage and he's popped the trunk of a shiny black Rolls-Royce.

"Beautiful car," I comment, placing the bag inside, discreetly aware that Shane's Bentley is missing.

"I've had it parked in my garage for a while," he says, opening the back door and then shutting it, returning with an envelope in his hand. "But you only live once, I hear."

The joke amuses him, stirring a chuckle that turns into a cough he can't seem to beat, one or two hacks turning into an eruption. "Door," he says, pointing, and I open the driver's side for him, allowing him to sit, while he begins to cough up blood, which he blots with tissues he grabs from his pocket.

I kneel beside him, spying glimpses of Shane in him even now, and it hurts my heart. He's a part of Shane, a deep part of his soul, no matter how dark that stain might be. "Mr. Brandon. What can I do?"

"Stop looking at me like I'm helpless," he snaps, scowling at me as he straightens and seems to gain more control. "See that Shane gets that document," he says, handing me the folder, before he rotates to sit fully behind the wheel of the car and I have to scramble to get up before he slams the door shut.

The engine hums to life, and I back up, watching as he drives away. Brandon Senior is not even close to a nice person, but he's Shane's father, and it will hurt when he loses him. *You won't have to tolerate it for long. I'll be dead soon,* he'd said last night. I believe him. I wonder if Shane has really, truly prepared himself for this, and my gut says no. He has not. Deciding I need to talk to him about it tonight, I head for the elevator. I'm almost to the doors when they open, and to my dismay, Derek steps out.

"Well, well," he says, closing the small space between us. "Don't I have exceptional timing today. Always running into you at just the right moment."

He's mocking my pizza incident but I don't give him the satisfaction of noticing, and I have bigger things on my mind, as should he. "I walked your father down. He was bad, Derek. He was coughing up blood and he just . . . he wasn't good."

Derek's chest expands on a breath he holds for several beats and then lets out. "I guess we know why he's set the board meeting then."

"Right," I say, intentional condemnation in my voice. "The board meeting. Unbelievable. That's what matters when your father is dying." It's not even a question.

His lips quirk. "Righteous like my brother. No wonder he's fucking you."

"Apparently being an asshole runs in your family," I say, trying to step around him, but he grabs my arm, his grip a little too tight, his touch uncomfortable in about a million ways. But I don't pull away. I don't give him that satisfaction of rattling me.

"Are you referring to my brother or my father?"

"Both," I say, because it's part of me playing the used and abused lover. "You know. You and Shane are brothers. I don't understand the hate between you. Siblings have a bond that is supposed to last a lifetime."

"I wasn't aware you had a sibling to make that assessment."

"I don't," I say, not missing a beat. "But I wish I did. I wish there would have been that kind of bond to fall back on when my parents died."

"That's right," he says, and then proving he's already been looking into my background, he adds, "They died in a plane crash, didn't they?"

There is something about the narrowing of his eyes, the sharpness to his tone, that tells me he is suspicious of my story. Or maybe I'm paranoid, but then I have reason to be, but I don't get time to find out.

"Let go of her," I hear Shane say from just behind me.

There is a beat that turns into three and suddenly my arm is free. I whirl around to find Shane facing off with Derek. Neither man is looking at me. I am frozen.

Suddenly Shane is standing beside me. "Go upstairs, Emily."

I inhale and force myself to calm down before I do exactly what I'm told. I walk when I want to run. Slow. Steady. I reach the elevator and I punch the button to call the car, thankful it opens immediately. From there I barely remember entering or exiting to the main elevators, but once I'm on the ride up, my heart is racing, my knees rubbery. I said nothing wrong, but I didn't have to. Derek has been checking into me, but I tell myself that he still can't know who I am. He still can't trigger the Geminis' attention because they aren't looking for me. Unless my brother hasn't told me something. I flash back once again to the night of my stepfather's death and the moment my brother had said *What the hell are you doing here?* and for the first time I remember the look in his eyes. There was no fear or remorse for what he'd done. No regret. There was anger, at me.

SHANE

I stand toe-to-toe with my brother, and the fact that I haven't shoved him against the wall like the last time we stood in almost this same spot is a testament to my willpower.

"Protecting your woman?" Derek asks.

"You're just pissed I fucked her first, but then, I hear random fucks are off the table for you, since you're basically engaged to Adrian Martina's sister."

"What can I say? She's a good fuck."

"You don't just fuck the daughter of a kingpin, or the sister of the heir to their dynasty. Because when you stop, you end up dead."

"Adrian Martina cares about money, not me fucking his sister."

"Is that why he came to see me today? About money?"

"Because you're standing between him and his money."

"So you knew he was coming?"

"He wanted to know what was holding up further expansion of our relationship. You are the holdup."

"What part of 'he will take our company away from us' do you not understand?"

"Not if I'm in control, which is how this ends."

"This ends with you in a grave because he finds out you're fucking his sister to get close to him."

His lips quirk, as if I've amused him. "I guess we'll see, now won't we?" he says, stepping around me, and walking away.

I let the bastard go, but my suspicion that he threw me to the proverbial wolves with Adrian is now confirmed. He's willing to do more than lie and cheat to win the company. He's willing to shed blood, and that changes the rules. I walk to the elevator, my journey back to the Brandon Enterprise offices focused on two things: Emily and my plan to cage Derek.

Entering the lobby, I start toward my father's office, and Emily's desk, when the receptionist says, "She went toward your office."

I give her a nod, and stride down the hallway, cutting left to bring Jessica into view. "In your office," she says, motioning to the door.

I open the door to find Emily standing just inside the room, and I shut us inside. "He's been looking into my background," she blurts out. "He made a reference to my parents dying and it was sarcastic. He knows my file doesn't add up."

"Easy, sweetheart," I say, my hands settling on her arms. "Most likely he's looking at your company interview notes, but even if he has looked closer, a few holes do not lead him to your past."

"I know. In theory, I know, but he's turning over stones. He could find the right one. I hate this. I hate that I can't control what is happening. I hate that for the rest of my life, I will have to worry about the monster around the corner."

"I'm not going to let that happen. You will be hidden. Well hidden and safe." My hands go to her face. "I'll call Seth and make sure your records are done tonight, as he promised."

"Yes. Please. Thank you, Shane."

"Let's go home, get naked, and order room service after we work up an appetite."

"I have work—"

I kiss her, a long slide of tongue against tongue before I say, "Let's go home. Okay?"

"Yes. Okay. I need to get my purse."

"Actually, give me fifteen minutes to call Seth and wrap up a few things."

"Yes. That's good." She walks to the door, pausing as she's about to exit. "I put an envelope on your desk that your father wanted you to have." She exits and shuts the door behind her, while I remove my cell phone from my pocket and walk to my desk, where I sit down and dial Seth, who answers in one ring. "That documentation you said you'd have ready tonight? Where are we on it?"

"It's done. I plan to bring it to you in a few hours."

"Bring it to the apartment. We need to talk about a few new developments, but nothing that requires your immediate attention."

"Understood."

I end the call and grab the envelope my father sent to me, removing a document. My eyes narrow at a proposal to invest in the basketball stadium, which is actually a good investment, but something tells me this is a request from Mike, maybe even a payoff of some sort. It's time Mike and I have a chat. I reseal the envelope and reach into my pocket to remove the digital recorder I'd used for my conversation with Derek, hitting play and fast-forwarding to the part about Martina's sister that I plan to use to force Derek back to our side.

"You're just pissed I fucked her first," I say of Emily, *"but then,*

I hear random fucks are off the table for you, since you're basically engaged to Adrian Martina's sister."

"What can I say? She's a good fuck."

"You don't just fuck the daughter of a kingpin, or the sister of the heir to their dynasty. Because when you stop, you end up dead."

"Adrian Martina cares about money, not me fucking his sister."

I punch the off button and curse. It's not enough. I need the kind of ammunition that makes Adrian want to kill my brother.

CHAPTER THIRTEEN

EMILY

I sit at my desk and close my eyes, willing myself to get a grip. Shane was right. Derek is not going to lead the Geminis to me or Shane. Even Seth and his people couldn't find out who I really was until I told them. Inhaling, I open my drawer and grab the phone I'd used to talk to my brother, and go to throw it in the trash, and then kick myself for even considering such a thing in an office where everyone is in everyone's business. Instead, I stick it and its battery in my purse. For reasons I can't explain, Derek really got to me. I press my fingers to my temples.

Why is he getting to me?

Unbidden, my brother's words come to my mind: *What the hell are you doing here?* And then, Derek's words: *Righteous like my brother.*

It's then that my mind goes back to the night of my stepfather's death.

I gape at my brother in disbelief, a streak of blood down his cheek, trying not to look down at my stepfather.

"What the hell am I doing here? Why are you not calling an ambulance?"

"He's dead. I checked his pulse."

I start to shake. "Call the police."

"I killed him. If I call the police—"

"Call the fucking police!" I reach for my purse and suddenly, Rick's hand is on mine and I can feel the wet stickiness on my skin.

"We are not calling the police or we will end up dead."

"We? We didn't do this."

"He stole money. We fought. I was protecting myself."

"Tell the police that."

"If we go to the police, we become a liability to the Geminis. We die."

I am trembling inside and out. "The Geminis that I've been try-ing to get you to get out of for years?"

"Don't turn on the righteous bitch routine, Reagan. I'm the only person who's going to keep you alive."

My cell phone buzzes, snapping me back to the present. I grab it and pull up a text from Shane: *Meet me at the Bentley. You go first.*

Because we're trying, and failing, to keep our relationship a secret, which fits about everything else in my life. It bothers me, but I'm self-analytical enough to know my reaction is not about Shane. It's just me trying to get to that acceptance stage about the loss of my brother, and a girl named Reagan. I type a return text message: *Wait 5 to leave. I need to give the receptionist my number to reach me if necessary.*

His reply is instant: *See you soon.*

Considering my mood, I have no idea why, but that reply makes me smile, and the tension in my spine noticeably lessens. Standing, I survey my desk for anything that needs to be attended to, and walk to Brandon Senior's office to flip out the light. Then with my coat over my arm, I start for the front office, some of that tension returning with the prospect of running into Derek. Steeling myself for the possibility, I enter the lobby to find the receptionist juggling several calls.

Grabbing a piece of paper and writing down my number, I wait until she pauses between calls, almost ready to leave, when she finally looks up.

"This is my number. If anyone needs me or Mr. Brandon, call me. Do not call him. He's in a very important meeting."

She takes the piece of paper. "Got it. Call you." She points to her mouth. "No gum."

I laugh at her easygoing reference to my reprimand. "Very good choice."

She grins and then immediately answers another line and I waste no time darting for the door, and as far away from another encounter with Derek as possible. I start to dash for the door, and then force myself to go slow and easy. I am not going to cower before that man. What will that solve? In fact, if anything, he will be a wolf that smells blood. I am not prey. I am not a coward. I hold my head up high and I step on the elevator with my calm restored. I might not be Reagan anymore, but I am still me, and I am a survivor.

I exit into the parking garage and dig out the Bentley's key, unlocking the doors, and round the trunk to open the passenger's side door, where I set my purse and coat in the backseat, but I don't get in. Control is something I value and own too little of right now. I won't cower from anyone again, but I do think it's time I take every step I can to see what's coming my way, rather than hiding and hoping nothing finds me.

I've just reached the tail end of the car when the elevator doors open, revealing Shane as they part. He steps forward, his coat missing, his briefcase slung over his shoulder, his stride long and confident, and I am spellbound.

He is power. He is confidence. He is sex. He is everything that my history tells me is wrong for me, and yet, never before has anyone been those things and still managed to be comfort, pride, and friendship.

Suddenly, he is in front of me, and I haven't looked away, or even tried to hide how I've tracked his every step. "What are you thinking?" he asks, a lean away from touching me, but he does not.

"I don't even know where to begin," I confess.

"Anywhere you like," he says, "and only when you're ready."

It is exactly what I need and want him to say, though I didn't know it until now.

He motions to the car. "But preferably anywhere but here."

"I like that idea."

He walks me to the passenger door and opens it for me, and I'm about to get in when a memory flashes in my mind of the first time we'd met and he'd done the same. The urge to turn and face him hits me, but so do words I don't want to say with a potential audience. Instead, I sink into the soft tan leather seats and Shane seals me inside, and like that night, my gaze lands on the Bentley emblem; the spread wings with the "B" in the center. I reach out and touch it, years of goal-setting and studies replaying in my mind. My dream car, and I drove it today, on my own.

"Why do you love this car so much?"

I glance up in surprise to find Shane has joined me and I never heard the door open or shut. "My stepfather, of all people, made us keep dream boards. He even took us shopping to see fancy houses and cars. In hindsight, he was just luring us into the Geminis' web."

"But it didn't work on you."

"No," I say, letting my fingers fall from the emblem. "My

father was a law professor. I think I told you that, I'm not sure. Actually, I didn't. I just wanted to tell you." I don't give him time to reply. "He made me love the law."

"We have that in common."

"And somehow neither one of us are practicing." I shift in the seat to face him. "Do you miss it?"

"I did."

My brows knit. "Did?"

"I had to let it go to really be here and do this right."

Let it go. Those words speak to me, stirring memories of how I finally coped with my father's suicide and the loss of my mother. Now, it's the loss of a dream. "Do you remember the first night I rode in this car?"

"The night we met," he supplies.

"Yes. Do you remember what I asked you?"

His gray eyes darken, memory in their depths. "You told me I was driving your dream car after attending your dream school, therefore you weren't sure if I was your kiss good-bye to your dreams or your promise they aren't over."

"And you told me not to let the universe decide what those things meant. Not to let it have that power. But the universe didn't take my dream. My brother did, and we both know that means I can never go back to law school without the fear the Geminis will find me and consider me a risk."

"Emily—"

"Please don't try to make me feel better. You just said yourself that you had to accept the change you faced to really move forward. That's about claiming control, and I admire that in you. I want to admire that in me too."

"Acceptance is a bumpy journey."

"Maybe," I say, "but thanks to you I have a chance to ensure the Geminis never find me. I'm not going to screw that up by foolishly heading back to law school, even five years from now; I can't risk the Geminis finding me and considering me a liability they want to eliminate."

"I want to tell you that risk doesn't exist," he says. "But it does."

"Thank you for not giving me the candy-and-chocolate answer. I still want my Bentley, though. Not yours that I drive here and there. One I earn on my own and deserve."

"I know you well enough to know that if that's what you want, you'll get it." He leans closer, his arm on the console between us. "Do you remember what else I told you that night?"

"I remember everything from that night. Which part do you mean?"

"The part where I told you I wanted to fuck you so right and well you'd never forget me."

Heat rushes through me. "You did."

His eyes darken, then light with amber and blue. "I'm going to do it again."

"Promise?"

He laughs, low and deep, then settles back in his seat and turns on the engine. "I promise, and I never break a promise." And those words are the biggest seduction of all. A promise that is a promise. Someone I can really trust.

We pull out of the garage with a debate over pizza or Chinese, settling on Chinese, and Shane hands me his phone with the number for his favorite place in his directory.

"You must really love it," I say to him.

"I do and so will you." He winks. "I promise."

I laugh, hitting the auto-dial, and oh how that wink from Shane manages to have my belly doing a flip-flop. He turns us on the road and I place our order, finishing up as we reach the door of the Four Seasons. Tai, my favorite doorman, greets us, eager to brag about his daughter's restaurant making the food section of the newspaper.

"Emily has moved in with me," Shane announces, wrapping his arm around me. "So take good care of her."

Tai beams with this news. "Always. And just let me know when, I'd love to bring you dinner from my daughter's restaurant to celebrate this weekend."

Celebrate living with Shane. Who would have ever believed that my leaving Texas, and saying yes to a one-night stand with Shane, would lead here. "That would be amazing," I say with approval, and Shane is quick to agree. It's a good twenty minutes later when Shane and I step onto the elevator and he settles me in front of him, those wonderful hands of his resting on my hips, while his eyes promise me they will be many other places, soon. I'm pretty much melting by the time we exit and enter the apartment, Shane at my heels.

Before I can even turn, his hands are at my waist and he's turning me, backing me against the wall in that dominant way of his, his powerful thighs framing mine. "I want that taste of you I didn't get in that coffee shop." And then he is on his knees, and my skirt is already at my waist. "Shane. The food."

"I'll make it fast, I promise." He closes his hand around my panties and yanks. "Good thing you have on thigh-highs."

"I was cold, actually," I pant out for some silly reason.

His hands bracket my upper thighs. "I'll warm you up." He lifts my leg to his shoulder, and his thumb strokes my clit.

I pant again, my nipples tightening as if they were where he's touching. He strokes two fingers across the seam of my sex, and there is no time for me to prepare myself before his tongue flicks my clit. I rest my head on the wall, hands pressed there as well, every muscle in my body waiting for what comes next, until it's there. He's there and his mouth is on me, sucking, licking, teasing. His fingers slide inside me and I moan, biting my lip in the process, shocked at how fast that familiar deep ache in my sex begins.

"Oh," I rasp out. "Oh." I grab his head, steeping my fingers into the long, thick locks of his dark hair that give me plenty to hold on to. My nipples tighten painfully beneath my bra, that deep ache radiates through me until I can't move or breathe, seconds ticking by before I tumble into an explosion of desire. There is nothing but pleasure spiraling through me, and his mouth on my body, his fingers stroking all the right places. Time passes, yet stands still. I don't know, but I don't want it to end, but too soon the intensity fades, and that tight knot in my sex relaxes, the leg that is holding me up turning rubbery.

Shane seems to know; he always seems to understand what I need, even though the two men I knew before him were selfish, focused on themselves. It's a thought that comes from nowhere, but he drives home that point by wrapping his arm around my waist before easing my leg down. Then he is shoving up my blouse, his lips are on my belly, a rush of emotions crashing over me. I didn't want to care about anyone the way I do him, ever again.

The doorbell rings and Shane slides my skirt down my legs, calling out, "Just a minute," before pushing to his feet, cupping my face and kissing me, the taste of me on his lips. "Just in time." He smiles and strokes my cheek before reaching for the door, and my gaze lands on my panties smack in the middle of the floor, and in full view of the hotel staff person bringing our food.

I scramble forward, my knees wobbling, as I bend down to scoop up my panties at the same moment Shane opens the door.

The result is not good. I fall flat on my ass but fortunately Shane's big body is blocking me from view, and my panties would never have been seen. Shane shuts the door and turns to find me sprawled on the floor. He sets the bag down by the door and kneels beside me.

"What happened?"

I hold up my panties. "They were in front of the door and my knees were still recovering from ah . . . what you did to me."

He laughs, and snatches my panties, stuffing them in his pocket, and helping me to my feet. "Let's eat dinner and I'll have you for dessert."

"Promise?" I ask again.

"Oh yes," he assures me. "I promise."

Shane sheds his tie and jacket, while I lose my shoes as fast as I had my panties, and we set up our dinner on the coffee table. I choose a spot on the soft rug beneath it while Shane appears with not one, not two, but three bottles of wine, before claiming a spot for himself on the couch.

"I'm never going to make it past one bottle, let alone three," I warn him.

"This gives you a chance to pick one you like." He opens one of the bottles and fills my glass.

"I'm not going to waste wine," I say, lifting my glass. "This one will be fine." I take a sip and the woodsy, bitter taste takes me off guard and I grimace.

Shane laughs, downs my wine, and then opens another bottle. It's bottle number three that my taste buds finally enjoy, along with the meal, which we eat while watching the news and just enjoying our time together. And for once, we talk about politics and current events, finding we are in sync in all the ways that ensure we won't later want to kill each other. It's this normal kind of couple's thing that is not forced, but amazingly natural.

Once the food is gone, and we've cleaned up, Shane turns off the television and sits on the edge of the couch right in front of me, those gray eyes studying me. "What?" I ask.

"I don't remember the last time I just talked with anyone," he says, and it's clear in the way he says it that he's a little taken off guard.

"Well, since I live with you," I say, "I think you'd better get used to a lot more talking."

"The unexplainable thing is that I'm already used to it."

"You are?" I ask, sipping my wine.

"Yes. I am. I told you. I've never lived with a woman, because frankly, I didn't want a relationship."

"Me either," I confess. "I haven't lived with anyone."

"Did you ever come close?"

"No," I say. "My relationships have been——" I laugh again but this time without humor and amend, "My train wrecks are kind of embarrassing."

"There's nothing to be embarrassed about. Experiences make us who we are, and sometimes the bad ones are the best at making us grow."

"Experiences," I repeat. "Yes well, I've certainly had those."

"Tell me," he presses softly, those two words becoming his familiar way to push me to expose some part of me I never thought to show anyone, and yet, I'm about to now.

"Train wreck number one," I say. "That affair I mentioned with a professor before, was actually a *much* older law professor. Not my law professor because I wasn't in law school. I was a freshman and still living at home to protect my brother."

"How much older?"

"Twenty years and one of my father's friends. Obviously he was some kind of screwed-up daddy issue I was working through. Feel free to judge now."

"I'm not judging you, sweetheart."

"I do and the worst part . . . When my mother died——"

"How did she die?"

"A car accident, so it was a real shock. We'd fought over my stepfather the night before as well. It was misery, guilt, and pain." I am reminded of his father's coughing attack. "Things I promise you are coming with your father, despite how you feel about him. Are you ready for that?"

"No. I am not ready for that and right now, I'd rather talk about you. You were telling me what happened when your mother died, in relation to this professor."

"Right," I say, because he knows I'm here for him, and he has to deal with this his way. "I went to the funeral with my brother, and that led to us fighting over him and his Gemini connections. I was a mess afterwards. I showed up at the professor's house, and that's when I found out he was still married. I lost it and made a scene and so did she." I shake my head. "Why would I make a scene over a man that was clearly an asshole? That is not even the person I know myself to be."

"You were in pain and it sounds like I was right. That moment helped define who you are."

"You'd think, but I wasn't done self-destructing. I barely dated for the rest of my undergraduate years and then I started law school. It was some kind of trigger, and I went off the ledge, like a really late rebound with the complete opposite type of man. A tattoo artist who was into hard rock, hard sex, and not a lot of anything else. I guess the appeal with him was that I knew what I was getting and I didn't want more. There could be no heartache to come because there was no emotional attachment for either of us."

"How long ago was that?"

"We dated for six months and it ended about a year ago."

"And since then?"

"School took over and I lost myself in my studies."

"Which explains your LSAT score Seth mentioned."

"I'm very competitive," I say, "which fed an obsession with winning every challenge presented and snagged me an internship at a top firm."

"Which firm?"

"Norton, Mash, and Company."

He whistles. "That is not a spot that's easy to come by, but I can see why they chose you. And speaking of challenges: Let's talk about my proposition." He reaches under the table and produces a stack of files I didn't know were there and sets them on the coffee table before reclaiming a spot on the couch.

"What is all of that?" I ask.

"Potential acquisitions," he explains. "I want a clean slate for Brandon Enterprises, free of the often questionable ethics of my father. The acquisition of Brandon Pharmaceuticals was meant to produce large sums of money, thus allowing the painless shedding of those other divisions."

"Has it?"

"It's getting there, but it's come with high risk and liability. We need to balance that out with a lower-risk, high-profit addition to our brand. That's where you come into play."

"Me?"

"You," he confirms. "I don't have time to look for that next venture. You're smart and I trust you. I'd like you to help me nar-

row down the prospects to two or three, and then we'll run numbers and do the due diligence." He pats the folders. "These are the
companies I looked into with my notes, but we're not limited to
these choices. They're simply where I've begun looking."

"I'd love to help," I say, both thrilled and honored he wants
me to do this.

"I have a private CPA to help with the back end. If there's
something you have a question about, and need answered, he'll
help." He flips open a folder and indicates a card stapled in the
front. "This is him and I'll make sure he is accommodating."

"Are you going to get rid of the financial division your father
runs?"

"Everything that exists now will be replaced, but that knowledge is to stay with a small group of insiders, which includes Seth,
Jessica, and the CPA."

"Because people are going to be upset."

"Yes. They will."

My mind flickers to our morning and his abrupt handing
off of the Bentley. "Did that black Escalade that showed up in the
garage have anything to do with your plans to exit any of these
divisions?"

"It was about exiting a bad business deal Derek got us into."

"Since I'm looking for replacement investments, can you tell
me what it was and why it was bad, so I don't make the same
mistake?"

"You are not Derek," he says. "You would not have made this
deal."

"What was it?"

His hands come down on my legs. "Nothing you need to worry
about."

"But I'm curious. I want to do a good job."

"You will do a good job."

"You don't want to tell me," I say, confused by his mixed messages. "Is it a trust issue?"

"I trust you. You know I do."

"But obviously there are boundaries to what you feel comfortable sharing."

"Don't do this. Don't put a wall between us that doesn't exist."

"I'm not trying to put a wall between us. I just want to know that there will be a point when we're closer—"

"You are closer to me than anyone has ever been. I repeat. This isn't about trust. I can't say that enough times."

"Then what is it about?"

"You are too good to be a part of Derek's creations. That's what it's about. You're the future, not the past. You're the good that I need while I get rid of the bad."

"You're protecting me."

"You're damn right I'm protecting you."

"Like I was protecting you, but I ended up telling you everything. You insisted."

"And now I can keep you safe from everything."

"Who keeps you safe?"

"I don't need to be protected."

"But you decide when I do?"

"In this? Yes."

I have a flashback of my mother questioning my stepfather and him saying something similar. Only she accepted the answer. I won't. "I don't like secrets. My life has had too many secrets."

"This isn't a secret. You know this is about Derek's bad business."

The doorbell rings. "That's going to be Seth. He's bringing

you the details on all the holes he plugged in your background. We'll finish talking when he leaves. We'll figure this out." He stands up and walks away. I sink back onto the floor, pick up my wine, and instead of drinking, watch the red liquid swirl in my glass. Secrets. Lies. Trust. Love. Hate. Family. Sex. I guess I'd rather have silence than lies. Wouldn't I? I down my wine and reach for the bottle, refilling my glass before opening the first file, which ironically appears to be a winery. This intrigues me, but is it low liability? Maybe, if we aren't the ones doing the retail sales.

Footsteps sound behind me, and I shut the file. Shane reappears, and I twist around as he sits on the couch, placing a file on the table. "This has all the details about your past filled in. You'll want to study it."

"Of course." I narrow my gaze, noting the hardening lines of his expression. "What's wrong?"

"I need to head to a meeting with Seth and Nick, the person running much of our private security."

"Is there a problem?"

"We're working on a solution to last night's security breach at BP."

"Oh right. I forgot about that. What happened?"

"We don't know and that's unacceptable. I'm not sure how long I'll be gone."

"Any word on my security guard Randy?"

"I'm sure I'll get an update on that at this meeting, but no one has mentioned it to me since Seth started looking into it." He pushes to his feet and offers me his hand. "I have something to show you upstairs before I leave."

Curious, I let him help me to my feet and lead me forward. "What is it?" I ask as we start up the stairs.

"A surprise I arranged today."

Extra curious now, I'm excited to see whatever this might be. We enter the bedroom and he flips on the light, and then guides me to the closet. "Ready?"

"Yes. I'm dying to see whatever it is."

He opens the door and I walk inside while he flips on this light as well. I gape then, at the rows of women's shoes and clothes lining the closet. "Oh my God. Oh my God."

"You can take anything you want back and I'll get you a credit card tomorrow."

I whirl on him. "No. No, I don't need a credit card and Shane, this is too much. I don't need all of this."

"But I want you to have it. I want to take care of you." He snags my hips and walks me to him. "Please look at it and enjoy it. I need to go, but tell me how we did when I get home."

"Shane—"

He kisses me and then says, "You're beautiful," and then he's gone, leaving me standing in the closet. I stare after him, a tight ball of emotions beginning as a pebble in my chest, my body frozen in place as that pebble grows and expands. I squeeze my eyes shut and replay the past. I was fourteen and my stepfather had come home after being gone for several days without a call. He'd greeted my mother by going down on one knee and handing her a blue Tiffany box. Flash forward, to the moment he'd put the necklace on her neck, and then cupped her face and said, "You're beautiful."

My eyes snap open and I face the row of clothes, tags from expensive brands dangling from several sleeves. This would be the fantasy for many women, but it is not mine. Shane has secrets. Shane has money and power and I am enthralled. I am in love. Have I become my mother?

CHAPTER FOURTEEN

SHANE

With Seth by my side, I pull on my suit jacket as we exit into the public portion of the Four Seasons garage, where no one expects us to depart. One of Nick's men waits for us there, and we quickly exit the hotel facilities and hit the highway. Our destination is Nick's private facility, which I readily agree to visit if it means a solution to get Martina out of my company and life, especially with Emily asking questions I can't answer. We make a fast exit to downtown, but it turns out Nick's facility is on the other side of town, so we get stuck in one of Denver's many traffic jams; a twenty-minute drive transforms into forty-five. Considering I don't know the driver from Adam, Seth and I ride in virtual silence, and my mind lingers on my need to kill Emily's curiosity over my morning visitor. I'm not giving her a drug cartel to fear on top of the Geminis. I'm going to make this go away and she never has to know about it.

When finally we pull into the parking lot at our destination, the sight of an old warehouse does little to instill my confidence in Nick and his team. The private state-of-the-art garage we enter begins to sway me in the other direction. The building houses a half-dozen motorcycles and a classic Mustang, and a massive cobra painting on one wall.

Seth shrugs into his suit jacket that he'd abandoned somewhere along the way, and steps to my side. "Nick calls his team the Cobras."

"Calculating and lethal," I say. "Let's hope that proves true in what he has to say tonight."

"It does and it will," Seth assures me, motioning me toward a door, where our driver swipes a badge and then keys in a code.

We follow him into an enclosed area where he presses his fingers against a panel and another door pops open, and my skepticism over Nick's operations begins to fade, at least a little further. Nick is waiting for us when we finally enter the warehouse, wearing a navy-blue FBI T-shirt, a piece of his past that he keeps trying to drag into my future.

"This way to the conference room," he says, his stocky build and hard stare speaking of skill and confidence, while his graying blond hair speaks of experience, which I remind myself is valuable.

Seth and I fall into step behind him, moving through a surprisingly high-tech facility. The main room we're presently occupying is split into three parts: a boxing cage, a firing range, and a cluster of computer terminals.

"It's an impressive facility," Seth comments. "One of the selling points when I contracted Nick for Brandon Enterprises."

"I'll be impressed after I hear what you brought me here to hear," I say dryly.

"We have options to present," he assures me. "Good ones, in my opinion."

I cut him a look. "You keep saying that and you usually don't repeat yourself. It makes me wonder, who are you trying to convince? Me or you?"

"Just offering reassurance."

"Another thing you never do," I remind him at the same moment that Nick stops at a towering, steel-framed door and waves me forward.

Stepping into the next room, I discover a massive round stone table, as well as an aquarium against the far wall. I claim one of the twelve gray leather chairs around the table, my gaze flicking over a stack of files a few feet away, and then lifting and landing on a framed *Godfather* movie scene covering almost the entire wall in front of me.

Nick claims the chair to my right, following my gaze. "Badass, isn't it?"

"I'm not sure how to feel about you idolizing a gangster," I comment, while Seth claims the seat to my left.

"It's Pacino I love," Nick explains. "The man's a chameleon; he becomes whatever he want to be whenever he wants to be, like many of our adversaries. Something that picture never lets me forget. It keeps me sharp."

My respect for Nick ticks up a notch, but with caution. "I hope sharp enough to give me a solution to Martina that doesn't include me going to the FBI."

"We have a plan," Nick confirms. "It's now a matter of your approval."

"First things first though," Seth says, sliding one of the folders from the center of the table to him. "We pulled the security feed from the night Emily met her guard Randy." He opens the folder and sets a photo clearly captured by elevator footage. "That's Randy. Real name José Garcia." He sets another picture down, this one of José with Adrian Martina. "He is to Adrian what I am to you."

I look up and between Seth and Nick. "What the hell was he doing in my offices and near Emily?"

Nick answers. "It's not immediately clear if the contact with Emily was intentional or by chance. And since Derek was not in the building, his purpose for being there is also unclear."

"In other words," I say. "I have no way of knowing if Emily is a target."

"In my professional opinion," he replies, "she isn't a target. Not yet."

I arch a brow. "Not yet? What the hell does that mean?"

"It means," Seth says, "that we believe Martina's visit this morning was about him trying to draw you into his circle."

"The man has a god complex," Nick adds. "He believes he can mend all, and do all, including your resistance to this partnership. Emily won't be in danger until he decides you're a problem he can't solve by simply including you, where Derek has excluded you."

My jaw sets hard. "Then, as I've already stated, we need to get him the hell out of my company before that happens."

"I agree one hundred percent," Nick quickly says, "which is what we want to talk about today."

"Let me summarize what we've done thus far," Seth interjects, sliding a folder to me. "This is all inside the file if you want to follow along."

"Just get to it," I say, eager to hear solutions, not problems.

"We have a paid informant inside the locker rooms at Mike's ball club, as well as for the one associated with Brody Matthews. We also pulled records on Ridel, the drug that we assume is being used to package an illegal performance-enhancing drug. We've found prescriptions have doubled since last year's records, with a concentration in Colorado."

My lips thin. "A drug that is all but retired has doubled in usage. Were the users athletes?"

"We're still working on that," Seth replies. "As well as looking closely at the doctors and medical clinics involved."

"And while doubling in numbers sounds big," Nick adds, "the numbers are still extremely low. This is good news, as I doubt Martina would be involving you if he planned to localize Sub-Zero. He'll plan a wider release, which we have no reason to believe has happened as of now."

I think of the video Seth obtained of after-hours packages being moved out of our Boulder division. "What about the transportation division?"

"They may be testing it out," he replies. "Using it to supply these doctors, or for other substances."

"That is way too deep into our operation for comfort," I say. "What if one of those trucks gets stopped?"

"Which is all the more reason to shake things up now, not later," Nick says. "Adrian wants to rule the world. He's power hungry, savvy, and smart, which makes him dangerous, but it also means he doesn't make stupid mistakes. If we can give him cold feet, I'm of the opinion Adrian will be forced to pull out. If he doesn't, and his father gets word of what's happening, he'll yank him out of here himself. And believe you me, Adrian doesn't want that to happen."

"Cut to the chase," I say. "What's the proposed plan?"

Nick and Seth exchange a look, with Seth delivering my answer. "We stage a raid of both the main BP facility and the Boulder warehouse in unison. We'll do them late at night when there are limited employees present."

Nick quickly adds, "We believe that this is the kind of heat that will get Adrian's attention, especially this early in the Martina-Brandon relationship. Will that be enough to get him to pull out?

We can't promise it will be, but this is only step one of a two-part plan."

I am not ready to move away from step one. "Who would do these raids?"

"Obviously we need it to appear official," Nick says, "but we have to tread cautiously. Pretending to be an agent when you aren't is a federal offense."

"But I have a solution to that problem," Nick quickly offers. "And his name is Ted Michaels. He's an active agent that contracts for me."

I flick a hard look between them. "Are we really going down this path again? I told you both no Feds."

"He'll run the raid off the books, and after hours," Nick assures me. "He's a good man, and we can trust him."

"Define 'off the books,'" I say, far from ready to say yes. "And if he's trustworthy, why is he operating off the books at all?"

"Tragedy and necessity," he replies. "His sister had a DUI accident and ended up paralyzed."

I narrow my eyes on Nick, looking for where this goes south. "What about insurance?"

"She was the drunk driver and her own victim. Insurance isn't covering anywhere near the special care she needs. In other words, Ted needs money, and since this is not something he'd normally do, it's going to cost you."

"How much?"

"Fifty thousand," he says.

I whistle. "That's a big number for a one-hour operation with no guaranteed outcome."

"I've checked out Ted," Seth says, sliding a thumb drive in front of me. "That includes my notes, his personal history, as well as my live interview with him earlier today. He gets my thumbs-up."

"Even if I agree," I say cautiously, slipping the drive into my jacket pocket, "aren't there repercussions to Ted for doing this off the record, and still using his badge?"

"There could be," Nick agrees, "thus the price tag, but we have a plan if this ever surfaces to cover his ass."

He stops there, as if I'd actually let him get away with telling me nothing more. "Go on," I press. "Because if he's busted, the FBI is then linked to my facility."

"We're covered and so are you," Nick says firmly. "We're contracted by the Feds on several Most Wanted List cases. It's known he works for me on a contract basis because of his sister's situation. We're going to tell them we were on a case that led us to your facility. With reasonable cause, Ted made the decision to lead my team inside. That story also covers any press that might arise out of this."

I shake my head. "No. I don't like the Feds being involved at all. And I'm damn sure not paying fifty thousand dollars to invite them into my facility."

Seth leans in closer. "Think about this, Shane. You need to shake Martina loose, and it's better to do this on your terms, not someone else's."

I bite back another rejection, reminding myself Martina is a problem we might not survive, quite literally. "You said you want to do the raids here and in Boulder, in unison. Ted's one man. He can't be in two places at once and this Most Wanted List idea won't hold water for multiple locations. He can't chase someone into two of my locations. Not without implying we're sheltering fugitives."

"That's where I come into play," Seth says. "I'll go to Boulder, report an insider tip about a raid that never materializes, but everyone will scramble and I'll get a bird's-eye view."

My mind goes back to this morning. "Martina assured me there is nothing to find in my buildings."

"It's not about what we find," Nick responds. "It's about him thinking the FBI is looking into you, which leads to him."

I lean back in my chair, considering all they've said, but not ready to make a decision. "I'll think about it. What else?"

Nick studies me for a few beats, and I have the distinct impression he wants to argue but apparently decides better. "Mike Rogers," he says instead. "He's rich, powerful, and has a lot to lose by way of a drug scandal. I have nothing to support this theory, but my gut is that Martina has forced his involvement with some sort of threat or leverage."

"If that's the case," I say, "then he's voting to give my brother control and we can assume that the head of the transportation division is as well." I consider that possibility, thinking back on my brother's recent behavior, and my own gut regarding Mike, whose silence, and my father's file, has made me question. "No," I say firmly. "Derek is still too afraid of me for that to be the case. Mike must not know what's going on. He's a target they want to own, just like me. I'll talk to him, and feel him out."

"He's shut you out, Shane," Seth reminds me. "That doesn't speak of innocence."

"Based on Mike's file, he's hiding money with my father," I say, thoughtful again. "In fact, he has to know Derek isn't the man to protect his money. I am."

Seth arches a brow. "Are you suggesting you take over your father's efforts on his behalf?"

"I'm suggesting I either convince him to let me handle it legally, or that we move his affairs before my father is no longer capable of handling them."

"You need to tread cautiously here," Nick warns. "If you're wrong, and you say anything about Sub-Zero to Mike, he could alert Martina that you've become a problem."

I cut him a hard look. "I can handle Mike. You handle Martina."

My cell phone beeps with a text and I grab it from my pocket and find a message from Jessica: *Brody wants you to call him.* And then the number. I glance between Seth and Nick. "Brody Matthews sidestepped his management team and made direct contact with Jessica. He wants me to call him."

Seth arches a brow. "Really? That's unexpected."

I key in the number and it rings once before I hear a voice. "Shane Brandon?"

"That's me," I confirm. "I assume your team told you I wanted to chat."

"Yeah, man, but we both know it's not about an endorsement deal."

Yet something else I don't expect and I eye Seth. "No. It's not about an endorsement deal." Seth tilts his chin slightly and I add, "It's time we talk."

"In person," Brody agrees. "Tonight."

"That works for me. When and where?"

"There's a bar downtown called Majors. I'll meet you in the basement level."

"I know it. When?"

"Thirty minutes."

"An hour and I'm bringing my right-hand man with me."

"An hour," he agrees and hangs up.

I replace my phone in my pocket. "We're meeting at Majors downtown in an hour and he knows what I want to talk about." I stand and Seth and Nick follow.

"What's your read on him?" Nick asks. "Is it a warning or a solution?"

"Brody isn't the kind of guy you send to deliver a warning." And a solution sounds really damn good right now.

• • •

An hour and a half later, Seth and I sit in the dimly lit lower bar area of Majors, sitting against the wall, and watching the door, while Brody is nowhere in sight, nor is he answering his calls. I punch in his number one more time, with the same direct-to-voice-mail response. Frustrated, I set my phone down and reach for my freshly filled cup of coffee. "Why call me at all if he was going to do this?"

"He got spooked," Seth says, flagging down the waiter and pointing at his cup. "The question is by who? Your brother, or the middle man, who's most likely the supplier he would have given up tonight."

The bartender, who's serving as the only waiter on this level, appears, warming up my cup and refilling Seth's. "We're inside his team locker room now," Seth says as soon as we're alone again, tearing open sugar packets. "We're going to find out how he's getting his drugs."

I lift my cup, my gaze catching on Nick as he strides across the room toward us. "Looks like Nick gave up on being our front-door guard."

Seth's gaze lifts and catches on the other man. "Walking with a purpose. That's never good. I need the real drink I can't ever afford to take."

"Right there with you," I say, and we both lift our cups, taking drinks and setting them down at the same moment Nick claims the seat across from Seth and to my left, setting an iPad down on the table.

"I've got another man on the door," he announces, as if we've asked. "And we've had someone watching his house for days. He hasn't shown up there, either."

"And yet you're sitting here, for a reason," I say. "Why?"

"My man has been on the ground in Austin for the past six

hours, and it's been eventful. We haven't located Emily's brother, but we've confirmed her story with physical evidence." He keys his iPad to life. "He went to the stepfather's house, which was dark, and invited himself inside. Everything appeared in place, until he found this." He turns the iPad in our direction and the image is of a floor and wall splattered with blue color.

My brow furrows. "What is that?"

"Blood," Seth answers. "Emily's brother wiped up but didn't know how to get rid of the residual blood."

"My man cleaned it up, to keep it from leading back to Emily," Nick says. "The brother's house is dark, and there were papers stacked up. If he told Emily the truth and he's out of the country, he didn't leave on his own passport."

"I can't believe these words are coming out of my mouth," I say, "but where is the body?"

"That's my question," Seth agrees. "Because considering the way he handled the blood cleanup, I don't have a lot of faith about how he handled the body."

Nick's phone buzzes where he's set it on the table and he grabs it, reading his screen before he curses softly. "We didn't find Brody, but he found us. He's been in a car accident. It's all over the news."

Hating where this is leading me, I bite out the question I'm needing answered. "Are we sure it's an accident?"

"My question exactly," Seth agrees.

"I know as much as you two do," Nick replies, rotating in his chair to look around the room, and then stands to make a beeline for the television.

Seth and I quickly follow, all three of us lining up at the bar, while the bartender flips channels. "There," Nick says, as the news flashes with an image of what I think used to be a sports car, and at the sight my hands land on the bar, my head sinking low. He's dead and somehow, some way, it's related to me and my family. As if confirming my assessment, or driving it home with vicious precision, the reporter's voice lifts in the air. "I repeat," a female voice states, "Brody Matthews, star pitcher for the Denver Eagles, is dead at the young age of twenty-eight, and at the height of his career."

That tightness in my chest is now full-blown anger, an emotion only Derek has stirred in me in my adult life. I push off the bar and walk toward the stairs and I don't stop until I'm on the street, where I am blasted with freezing cold wind that didn't exist thirty minutes ago, because that's the fucked-up way of Colorado. And fucking up everyone else's life is the way of my family. My hands go to my hips and I look skyward, letting the wet flakes of snow hit my face, the cold doing nothing to soothe the burn inside me. I inhale a chilly wet breath, fighting down anger that wants to go to Derek right now and handle this like we did as kids. Gloves off, balls to the wall. But we are no longer those people and I don't let anyone force my hand or my temper.

Seth and Nick step to my side, and I lower my head, my voice steady, my mood leveled off. "We all know this isn't an accident, be it that he was murdered because he was going to talk to me or he was driving under the influence of a drug that traveled a path through my company."

"It won't show up on drug tests," Nick says as if that actually makes this any better. "And I have a man on scene who I'm heading to meet now, though I doubt we'll know much tonight."

"I'm headed to Brody's wife place," Seth adds. "She's going to be shaken and I'd prefer she take comfort from me, than the press or the police."

In other words, her silence is all that matters, not her loss, not the murder of her husband. "Murder" is the word that replays in my mind and I face them both. "I want Emily here, by my side, where I know her brother can't somehow throw out a web and catch her, which I believe will give her the same ending as Brody. But I need to know if she's safe here. Can you protect her?"

"We can and will," Seth assures me, his suit jacket now covered in white flakes. "And I agree. She needs to stay here, under our net, and with the people I trust to protect her. I trust me, and our people, to know if anything shifts with her brother, or the Geminis, that puts her in danger."

"We also have several safe houses we can move her to if necessary," Nick adds, "but I do have to urge you to approve the raids. She's not on Adrian's radar right now, but that could change."

"Hire Ted," I say. "I'll have my CPA handle the money transfer." I shift my attention between both men. "But I'm not sitting back and risking this failing. I'm going to go to Adrian right after the raid happens and convince him he has to get out."

"You do not want to open the door to that relationship," Nick warns. "It will seal your fate with him."

"You're right," I say. "It will because I am in control of my destiny, not him. And I am going to ensure he sees the writing on the wall, which is me saving him from the jail cell my brother will ensure he ends up inside. I set that stage with him this morning."

Seth jumps on the warning bandwagon. "This is dangerous territory," he says, and I don't miss the edge to his voice that he rarely allows to surface. "The kind you hire me to tread for you."

"And you do so exceptionally well," I tell him, true respect for him beneath those words. "But some things need to come from me. How soon can the raids happen?"

Both of them look like they want to argue, the fall of snowflakes now as heavy as the seconds that tick by, before Seth replies. "We need a few days, logistically. I need to get Brody's wife out of town, which means after the funeral and the processing of her money, which we need to do now, not later."

The poor fucking woman can't even grieve for a man who shared part of her life without us shoving her into a hole. "I'll expedite it in the morning."

A black sedan pulls up in front of us. "My car," Nick says. "I'll drive you both wherever you want to go."

"I'll walk," I say.

"It's snowing, man," Seth argues, but I'm already moving, putting space between me and them, but not enough between me and my brother to suit me. I start for the apartment, where Emily calls to me, where she would be my escape, when I rarely need one. But I'm not so sure she isn't the one who needs an escape, and not from her brother or the Geminis. I turn the corner, leaving the men who are supposed to be a layer between me and pretty much everything behind. I intend to walk off this clawing guilt that Brody's death stirs in me but I make it a block, and my jacket is sticking to me thanks to the damp snow, my mind on Emily, who I suddenly justneed to know is in our apartment, safe and warm, when I am fucking cold to the bone.

I cover the next few blocks quickly, cutting through the garage to avoid attention, and then I am on our floor, and then our door, in a matter of minutes. Opening the door, I see the apartment is dark. The idea that Emily might have gone out and somehow is now in danger is not a feeling I ever thought to feel or want to feel again. I start for the stairs, perhaps never before in my life needing to know another human being is safe in the way I do with Emily now.

CHAPTER FIFTEEN

SHANE

I cross the foyer, traveling the stairs two at a time, to reach the bedroom door, darkness beyond. Pausing in the doorway, relief washes over me hard and fast, with the instant awareness of Emily in the room, not by sight, but a feeling. That is how much I am in tune with this woman, how much I feel her, like I have never felt another human being in my life. There has only been family, and they have always been a mix of love and hate that was impossible to reconcile. That made me leave and put distance between us. Love from afar was somehow easier and better. But with Emily, I don't want her from afar at all. I don't want to lose her and for reasons I can't explain, tonight I feel like I will. Like it's destiny, bound to happen.

"Shane."

The sound of her soft feminine voice cuts through the empty space between us, and I swear, I can finally breathe when I wasn't a moment ago.

I don't immediately speak, my eyes adjusting to the room,

shadows replacing darkness, allowing me to trace the outline of her silhouette where she sits in bed, allowing me to see her more clearly, when tonight, I'm questioning if I ever want her to see me the same way.

"Shane?" she asks again, but I know she knows it's me. I know that she feels me just as I do her.

"I'm here," I say, and there is a rough quality to my voice that I know speaks of things I do not want to exist, but I don't seem to be able to escape tonight.

"Why are you just standing there?" she asks, throwing the blankets off.

Hearing the confusion in her voice, I close the space between us, reaching her as she twists around to face me on her side of the bed. Some small slip of gown I can barely make out is all that covers her. I don't immediately reach for her, or her for me, and I was right about what I sensed in her. She is uncertain. But still I stand over her, and she seems to hold her breath, or maybe I hold mine, waiting for what comes next. For me, those seconds are about controlling that edge that is inside me. For her, I suspect it's trying to understand what is happening with me, and us. What it is between us, yet isn't about us. But guilt won't stop clawing at me, and she is the only answer I know to silence it.

I lean over her, my hand on her waist, my body pressing her into the mattress, my forehead finding hers. "My God, Shane. You're soaking wet."

There's concern in her voice, and it hits me that I don't know what it's like to have someone care about anything I do. It feels remarkably good, something I oddly did not think I needed, until it was her who cared. Her offering it. Giving it freely. "It's snowing," I say. "I walked home in the snow."

"You have to be freezing," she says, her soft palm warm on my face. "You are freezing. Why did you walk?"

"It's a long story, but I was meeting someone about a corporate sponsorship a few miles from here and—"

"Brody Matthews," she says. "I heard you talk about him."

"Yes," I say. "I waited a long time for him but he didn't show up."

"That's crazy. Why would he do that?"

"He was in a car accident."

"Oh God. Oh no. Is he okay?"

"No. He's not." The next words are lead on my tongue. "He's dead."

She gasps. "Oh my God." Her hand flattens on my chest, gently pushing me back as she tries to see my face through the darkness. "I'm beyond words. When. How?"

"Beyond words is good," I say, my palm sliding under her backside, finding her warm skin beneath her silk gown. "Because talking isn't what I have on my mind." My free hand frames her face and my mouth slants over hers; the rise of something dark and hungry inside me, dark and out of control, is hard and fast, a fire burning through me. That same something I didn't want to feel, nor do I want her to taste. I tear my mouth from hers, and the sound of her panting breath is soft, and sexy, and my cock thickens, stretching my zipper.

"I'm making you wet in all the wrong ways," I say. "I need to go shower." I try to move, and she grabs my jacket.

"Don't go."

"I need to go shower," I repeat, but what I need is to get my fucking control back or to be inside her, which won't go hand in hand right now.

She hesitates, holding on to me, as if she will refuse to let me go, but her fingers slowly slip away. I waste no time pushing away from her, putting space between us, and crossing to the bathroom. I flip on the light, shutting the door behind me, but I do not look in the mirror. I walk to the shower and turn on the water, then strip off my shoes and clothes before pressing my hands on the glass. I came here to save my family, but I haven't saved them, and I damn sure didn't save Brody. I played my brother's games. I tried to save him when he is the one who doesn't deserve to be saved. And because of that, I haven't done enough, and others could die that might have lived.

A tight knot forms in my gut and I walk to the mirror and I don't know what happens. I take one look at myself, an emotion I cannot name explodes inside me, and I punch my reflection, glass splintering, but not shattering, and a line forming across my image.

"Shane!"

"Fuck," I breathe out with the realization Emily has entered the room, that I've done this, and she has seen a side of me I barely recognize as who I am. I grab the sink, pain splintering through my hand, stickiness clinging to my skin. "I need you to get out until I get—"

It's too late. She's already by my side, and the minute her hand comes down on my back, I have even less control than a moment before. I need her. To touch her. To taste her. To be inside her, and I grab her, pulling her in front of me, not giving her or me a chance to change our minds. My fingers tangle roughly in her hair, while my free hand cups her backside, and then the next moment, my mouth is on hers, my tongue licking into her mouth, and this time, I don't hold back. I let her taste everything that was on my lips in the bedroom, and more. I let her taste my hunger. I let her taste the betrayal I feel from my brother, father, maybe even my fucking mother. I let her taste what I only realize now, in this moment: that Brody's death was preventable, whereas my father's is not. I can't save either of them, and I have given up on saving my brother. They are lost, but she is here and I will not lose her. I will not let anyone hurt her.

She moans into my mouth, and the sound is fire in my veins, my cock thickening where it now rests at her hip. Wanting, needing, skin against skin, I reach down, and grab the top of the silk gown she is wearing, yanking it, the material ripping down the front. She gasps, and my gaze rakes over her high, full breasts, her rosy pebbled nipples. And then I am kissing her again, my hand on her breast, fingers tugging at her nipple, nothing gentle in my kiss or my touch. There is just this deep need that has only one answer and that is her, and she is right there with me, as if she is as desperate for some unknown answer that we can only find with the unobtainable pleasure. Touching me, pressing against me, cupping my hand over her breasts.

I lift her to the sink, spreading her legs and yanking away her panties. She grips my shoulders while I grip my cock, sliding it along the slick seam of her body. She pants, holding onto my shoulders. "Shane." My name is a plea, and I need no further encouragement. I press inside her, cupping her backside and lifting her to pull her fully down my shaft, the fullness of her breasts pressing against my chest. I thrust, pulling her down against me, and the pulse of pleasure that follows leaves room for nothing else but Emily, and that is exactly what I need.

"I have you," I say, sliding my arms to her back. "Lean back."

She doesn't hesitate to trust me, immediately letting her weight fall against my hands, the angle driving my cock deeper into her, and giving me a view of her gorgeous breasts bouncing with every thrust. And I do thrust. Harder. Faster. She pants, arching her back and letting her head fall back between her shoulders, her body stiffening a moment before her sex clenches around my shaft. Holy fuck, it's good. So fucking good, and I grind her against me, pumping as I do, and then I am right there with her, my body shaking, my release coming with a deep ache that is there and gone too soon.

She edges forward and sinks against my chest, and my legs are suddenly exhausted. I walk to the sink, now several feet away, and sit her on the top. In no hurry to pull out of her, I linger there, our foreheads pressed together, our breathing in unison, that edge I'd been fighting sliding away. It's because of her, and I have no explainable reason for that, except that she is the light in the darkness that is everything about the name Brandon I've tried to reject.

I cup her cheek. "Not exactly the way to make love to your woman."

She inches back to look at me. "Make love? You've never said that before."

"Right after I fucked you like there's no tomorrow isn't the right time to start," I say, pretty sure I've just confessed something to both of us that I'm not ready to say. Not with my fucked-up family in control.

"Fucking like there's no tomorrow was pretty great."

Maybe she knows I want off the hook. Or maybe she just hits all the right buttons for me, because it's the right answer for here and now. I reach up and stroke her cheek, and I grimace with the throb in my knuckle. She must notice, grabbing my hand to inspect it.

"It's bad, Shane," she says, inspecting the swollen knuckle that has at least stopped bleeding. "Did you break it?"

I flex my hand. "I can move it. It's not broken." I glance up and behind her. "The mirror didn't fare so well though." Disliking that I was capable of so little control, I grab a towel off the sink and pull out of her, pressing it between her legs. "I need to turn off the shower." I turn away from her, doing as I've indicated, before snagging another towel, which I wrap around my waist. Her gown is ripped and dangling from her body, her knees pulled to her chest. The sight of blood on her leg sends me across the room again to inspect it, only to find it's my blood on her. Not hers.

"I'm okay," she says, obviously reading my concern. "Are you?"

"I didn't want you to see me like that."

"That's not an answer," she says, but rather than pushing for more, she makes a case for why I should offer it freely by adding, "And if I'm going to live with you, you can't hide a part of yourself."

"That's not a part of me. That is not something I do."

"I know that," she says. "You have to trust me enough to know that. You have to trust me enough to talk to me, Shane. To believe I can see whatever is there, no matter how difficult, and that I can handle it."

"I don't want you to handle it," I say. "And you can argue all you want but you're my woman, and I have a right to protect you."

"Your woman."

"Yes. My woman. And if you don't like that title, I think it's pretty important we talk about that right now." My cell phone rings. "I have to take that and you need to think about your answer." I push off the counter and grab my jacket, removing my cell phone and glancing at the caller ID that registers Seth. I punch the answer button and walk into the bedroom, crossing to the closet. "What's the update?" I ask, flipping on the light and opening a drawer.

"Everyone is at the accident scene, including my person of interest." He means the wife, going on to add, "Nick has eyes on everything but there's not much to tell. I'm going to head that way, and if you don't hear from me again tonight, nothing has changed and all is well on all counts."

Again, he means the wife. "Understood." We end the call and I stick my phone in the pocket of my pajama pants, entering the bedroom to find Emily standing just outside the closet, a short lavender robe covering her slender curves.

I close the small space between us, my hands settling on her waist. "You look stunning in that color. I can't even imagine you blond."

"Shane." Her hand flattens on my chest. "About the clothes—"

"Don't tell me I can't buy you clothes. I want to take care of you. Don't tell me I can't do that for you, the woman who is the one good and right thing in my life."

"I am?"

"Yes," I say, backing her toward the bed. "You make me remember I need to be good and right in my choices."

"Do you ever question doing what is good and right?"

"There have been times when I felt like my hand was forced."

"When you were a lawyer?"

"No," I say. "I manipulated the law, as does every attorney, but I never broke it. I'm talking about when I'm with my family."

"Did you go where they lead?"

"Not so far."

"That sounds like you might."

"I don't want to be them."

"You aren't them. You don't have to be them."

"I know that," I say. "But you just keep telling me so I don't forget." Her legs hit the bed frame and she grips my arms.

I lean into a kiss and she pulls back, her hand pressing on my chest. "Wait. Now it's my turn to say talk to me. Are you okay?"

"Death happened. The one thing I can't control. It's not the night to push me to stop protecting you. Not tonight. Can you do that?"

"Yes. We can."

"We," I repeat, "and that word sounds as good on my tongue as I know you're going to taste. I'm going to make love to you properly. The way I plan to many times in our future." I reach down and untie her robe, letting it fall open; my fingers slide underneath just far enough to tease her nipples. They pucker beneath my touch, and her lashes flutter, settling on her cheeks. "But when it's over, I'm going to fuck you hard and fast again."

I tug gently on her nipples and she bites her lips. "Look at me," I order gently.

She opens her eyes, and there is desire in their depths, but there are shadows there too. I do not think she intends for me to see doubt or uncertainty that wasn't there before. That I do not like or wish to know ever again. I want it gone. Now. Tomorrow. Forever. I reach up and rip the silk tie from her robe, wrapping it around my hand, before I reach up and caress the robe off her shoulder, letting it tumble to the ground.

"Give me your hands," I order, but it's really a question: Does she still trust me?

She studies me for several beats, her eyes narrowing ever so slightly, and I do not know what she sees in mine, but she offers me her hands. I wrap the silk around her wrists then lean in close to her, my cheek against her cheek, my body touching her nowhere else. "Now you're at my mercy."

"Yes," she agrees. "I am."

"How do you feel about that?"

"Warm."

My lips curve with the answer that is every bit the combination of sweet, sexy honesty I've come to expect from her. "I'm going to make you warmer."

"Promise?"

I go still with that question, which on the surface is innocent, but I wonder if it truly is or if it's about those shadows in her eyes. "I promise," I say. "And you know, I never—"

"Make a promise you don't keep."

"Exactly," I say, and her reference to my previous words tells me that I am not the only one on a mission of trust, and I intend to deserve hers.

I bring my hands to just above her shoulders, letting them lightly touch her before beginning a slow caress downward. She makes a soft little sound that has my cock thickening and my blood running hot, but I won't rush this. My lips follow, tracing a line down one of her arms, then the other. I lean and caress my lips over hers, a feather light touch that teases me, if not her.

I take her hands in mine, pressing them behind her head. "Hold them there, for me, so I can see all of you. Understand?"

"You intend to tease me incessantly," she says, without so much as a hint of hesitation. "Yes. I understand."

I wrap my arm around her waist and pull her naked body against me, my free hand on hers above her head, our mouths a breath apart. "I intend to lick every part of you, and then do it again, so yes. If that's the definition of incessant teasing, then yes. I am going to tease you incessantly." I close my mouth down on hers, my tongue licking into her mouth, a deep, hungry tasting I force myself to end far too quickly. "That was the beginning. Should I could continue?"

"Yes. Please."

"Please," I say. "I like that."

"I think I might want to reverse this and make you say 'please.' "

"Sweetheart, there are many reasons I'll say 'please' to you." I drag my lips over her cheek, her jaw, back to her neck, and ear. "Please, can I touch your nipple? Please, can I lick it? Please tell me where you want me to lick you." I turn her to face the bed, my hands on her hips, leaning in close again, my hand on her belly, my cheek pressed to hers. "Where do you want me to lick you?"

"I'm not really picky."

I smile against her neck—no one would have convinced me I'd smile anytime this night, or anytime soon—the sweet feminine scent of her teasing my nostrils. "I love how you smell." It's all over the sheets. I want it all over me. My teeth scrape her neck. My hands slides to her breasts, cupping them. "Do you know what I'm going to do to you?"

"Fuck me?"

I go still with that answer and the realization that my quest for control has done exactly the opposite of what I'd intended. I've made this about me, not her. Not us. I turn her back around, pulling her arms between us. "No. I am not fucking you. In that bathroom I fucked you. Right now, I'm making love to you." I untie her arms and cup her face. "But I still want to kiss every part of you before this night is over." I kiss her now, a slow slide of tongue, and I don't rush it. I revel in the taste of her. In the soft little moan she makes. In the way her hands settle at my waist and press a little harder against me with every slide of my tongue, until finally I say, "Kissing you all over isn't about teasing you incessantly. It's about enjoying you and making that moment when I'm finally inside you feel better."

"Shane, I—"

"Just like that," I say, brushing my lips over hers. "Say my name again, not 'please.' Okay?"

"Yes," she whispers.

"Good," I approve, my hands settling at the sides of her breasts, fingers stroking the delicate skin, and slowly I lower myself to my knee, blowing warm air on one nipple, then the next. I repeat my attentions to her nipples but this time with my tongue. She lowers her hands and her fingers slide into my hair, and when I suck her nipple into my mouth, her grip tightens, I smile and drag deeper. My reward is her sexy little moan. I take my time, licking and sucking; waiting for that moment she finally gives me.

"Shane."

It's a plea, and the one I wanted. I stroke her nipples one last time and move lower, my mouth caressing a path to her belly button. But still I make her wait, and not because I really do want to tease her incessantly. Because kissing her, exploring her body, might make my body hard, but it softens another part of me, it unravels that "something" I fought in the bathroom. I want her to know she's mine and that means I cherish every part of her. My hand settles on one of her hips, my fingers slip between her legs, into the wet, slick heat that speaks of how aroused she is, but I want more.

I lap at her clit, and her fingers go to my hair. I do it again, and she grips me a little tighter. My mouth closes down over the swollen nub, and yet a little tighter. I sink my fingers inside her and she outright moans. "Shane." It's all the motivation I need to give her what she wants. To lick her all over, stroking her with my fingers and tongue with one goal: her pleasure, not my control. And when she comes, she is sweet honey on my tongue, addictive in every way. She trembles with her release, and I wrap her hips, holding her a moment before her knees give way.

Her body gives way, melting against me, and in that moment, I am struck by all she has been through, and how completely she gives herself to me. I didn't need to look for her trust. It is mine to lose, not find, a gift I do not think this woman gives easily, but even after witnessing one of my darkest moments in that bathroom, she gives it freely to me. I press my lips to her belly, lingering there a moment before I look up at her, her cheeks flushed.

"Why, when I know control is an issue for you, did you so readily offer me your arms?"

"Because it's you. You make me feel safe."

"Safe." It is a surreal word to hear, on a night when I feel as if a life has been lost that I could have saved.

"Yes," she says firmly. "Safe."

My lashes lower with her confirmation, and I try to revel in those words, to tell myself I deserve them, but that dark something I've fought since hearing the news report at Majors stirs inside me. Emily shocks me then, reaching down and cupping my face, our eyes meeting. "Shane," she says softly. "Wherever you just went, don't go there."

"I'm right here, where I want to be."

"No. You're back where you were, right before you punched that mirror."

I am baffled by how easily she has read me. "How do you know that?"

"I don't know how I know or why we connect, but we do. I can be safe for you too. If you let me."

"I did let you. You saw me in that bathroom in a way no one else ever has."

"Because I was worried enough about you to walk in even though you shut me out. I witnessed what was already happening. What you chose to show no one."

"What I didn't want to exist."

"But it does. It did. We all have those moments." Her fingers stroke my hair, tenderness in her touch I do not think I have felt from any other human being. "Even Shane Brandon," she adds.

I catch her hand and kiss it, standing as I do, and sit her on the edge of the bed, my lips brushing hers, our eyes lingering a moment, the air shifting and changing, something between us changing with it. Deepening in some way I cannot name. I step back from her and shove down my pants. Her gaze strokes boldly down my body, over my erection. It is sexy and bold, a reminder that she isn't timid. She isn't submissive by nature. Closing the space between us, I join her on the bed, laying us both down. Her hand flattens on my chest, and my fingers slide into her hair, our mouths coming together, my cock pressing into the slick sweet spot between her legs. There is that same tenderness to this kiss as I'd felt in her fingers in my hair.

I lift her leg over my hip, cupping her backside, and while our lips part, our breathing becomes one, our bodies with it as I press inside her, then pull her down my shaft. For several moments, we don't move, and as easy as it would be for me to take what I want right now, to take her body, that is not what she needs right now. It's not what I need, either. I roll to my back and pull her on top of me, her chest molded to mine. "Now you have control," I declare.

She sits up, every curve, every sweet spot on her body, displayed for my viewing, and says, "We both know that's not true, Shane Brandon."

I sit up with her now, one hand settling between her shoulder blades, fingers splayed. "I don't think you understand the power you have over me. And that's big for me, sweetheart. To let you have that and to do so willingly."

"Then why won't you let me understand what really happened tonight?"

"I told you the part that matters. The part that won't let go of me, and therefore it affects you."

"Death," she says, repeating what I've told her.

"Yes. Death. That is the honest truth I would tell no one else."

"I guess I'm selfish with you because I need you to share more."

"It's okay to be selfish about wanting more from me. I'm damn sure selfish about wanting more from you."

"And yet you're not saying more."

I open my mouth to shut her down, but I know it's a mistake I don't want to make with her. "I will. Not now. Not tonight. But I will."

"When?" she presses.

"Soon."

She leans back and holds my shoulders, searching my face. "Promise."

That my promise matters to her is everything, and to give it to her and not mean it is a betrayal I know we would not overcome. "Emily," I breathe out, not wanting to see the fear in her eyes that I myself fear that this part of my family, of me, will stir in her.

"You aren't really going to tell me, are you?"

There is defeat in her voice that I am certain will turn to withdrawal if I let it, so I cup her face. "Damn it, woman, you're stubborn. I will soon. I promise." My mouth comes down on hers. One stroke of my tongue against hers, and we can't get enough of each other, some sense of needing to hang on, between us. She can't get enough of me, and I can't get enough of her. Our bodies sway and rock and I forget the promise. I forget everything but her touch, her taste. But when finally we are sated, her body in front of mine, her back to my chest, I hold her close, listening to her steady breathing. And then, I think about that promise I cannot betray. I have to tell her about Martina and it has to be soon. But I will not put fear in her eyes. I will end this before I tell her, no matter what I have to do to make it happen.

CHAPTER SIXTEEN

EMILY

I wake to a shadowy room, with the light of a new day peeking through the curtains hiding the wall of windows in the bedroom, the scent of Shane lacing the air, the sheets, and my skin, but he is not here. I know this even before I roll to my back, and I am not surprised at his absence. He is troubled. He is fighting a war against not just his family, but also himself. I know that now, and it makes his silence on some matters easier to swallow. I glance at the clock, noting the seven A.M. hour, proof I've slept later than I should have, and that the shadowy room must mean that the snow Shane walked through last night is still with us.

Stretching briefly, I climb out of bed, the chill of the room unfriendly to my naked body, sending me scrambling for my robe. Finding it on the floor on the opposite side of the bed, I pull it on, and grab the sash from the floor. I inhale, staring at it, the memory of Shane ordering me to give him my hands coming back to me. But it really wasn't an order. It was a question, timed on a night

I'd spent worrying about him, and questioning myself. I waited for hesitation to come to me, but there had been none. His admitting to me that he was tempted to the dark side was a confession my stepfather would have never made. Shane is a good man in a bad situation and I'm not sure how to help. I just know I have to try. He also blames himself for Brody's death, which is very confusing. How could he be to blame for a car accident? I don't let myself go where that might lead me. Shane promised to tell me what's going on. I believe he will.

I walk to the closet, flip on the light, and look at the row of clothes Shane bought me, his words replaying in my mind: *Don't tell me I can't do that for you, the woman who is the one good and right thing in my life.* He'd shut down my objections with a statement that says much to me about where his head is now. The world of law had been right and good for him. Brandon Enterprises isn't even close to his passion, but it will be if he can run it the way he believes it should be run. I refocus on the clothes, and while it's hard to shake that feeling of being a kept woman, as I believed my mother was, in my heart I do not think that was Shane's intention. I also believe the last thing he needs right now is for me to reject a gift that my instincts say was from his heart. And I haven't even thanked him, a situation I need to remedy.

Allowing some excitement to rise in my belly, I start looking through my options, which are insanely wonderful. I can't even choose what to wear and I start trying things on, loving almost everything. Finally, I have a long-sleeved pale pink Chanel dress picked out and I kneel on the floor to dig through a bag, where I find ribbed black tights.

"Do you like the clothes?"

At the sound of Shane's voice, I turn to find him leaning against the doorway. He is the picture of tall, dark, and handsome in a charcoal-gray suit, perfectly fitted, the pinstripe a pale gray that matches his shirt and tie, not to mention his eyes. He is refined masculinity, with dark, neatly styled hair, but something about it looks different today. "Is your hair wavy?"

"More than I like. It was curly when I was a kid."

"Curly? Really?"

"Oh yes. I hated it. You didn't answer my question: Do you like the clothes?"

"Yes. I do. Very much. Jessica has amazing taste, and she, and you, spent way too much money. Thank you."

"I'm glad they please you. I would have sent you yourself but you wouldn't have gotten what you need."

I grab a tag. "I don't need a fifteen-hundred-dollar dress."

"You do if it pleases you."

"Shane, I don't need you to do this. I need you. Not clothes, but I don't want to sound unappreciative. You doing this is special, but I don't need you to take care of me."

"No," he agrees. "You don't. And somehow that only makes me want to take care of you more. I've never had anyone I wanted to take care of until you."

My hand balls at my chest and my eyes actually pinch. "Okay. That just took me off guard and made me get emotional."

He closes the space between us, his warm hand sliding under my hair to my neck. "Why did that make you emotional?"

"Because no one has ever really tried to take care of me and to tell you the truth, letting you do this scares me."

"Why does it scare you?"

"What if I forget how to be on my own? What if it changes me?"

"Nothing will change you that you don't allow to happen. Of that I am sure. And I don't want you to remember how to be alone.

But since we're talking about money." He reaches into his pocket and produces a credit card.

"No," I say, shaking my head. "I'm not taking that."

"I have made a lot of money and I invest it well. How much? I'm going to tell you so you won't be afraid to spend when you need or want to spend. Millions. I've made millions. Money that has nothing to do with my family or their business. It's blood and sweat and I have never wanted anyone to share it with me, until you. Take the card."

"Millions? You've made millions?"

"Yes. I have. Does that make you feel better?"

"No. Not at all. I mean, I'm amazed and impressed at every- thing you are, but it's not my money. I still want to make my money."

"You can make your own. I'll support you any way you want, even if that means you only let me cheer you on when you buy your Bentley with your money. But you're still sharing mine." His lips curve. "And I'll share yours."

"Could anything be more perfect?"

"I'm glad it's perfect. Take the card, woman."

I reach up and take it. "I'm not going to—"

"You will," he says. "Because you'll have to if you're a part of my life."

A part of his life. It is exactly what I want him to say, and still it terrifies me. "What if we decide this isn't going to work?"

"I'm going to make sure that doesn't happen."

"What if I snore?"

"You don't."

"What if I start?"

"I'm quite sure it will be sexy when you do." He changes the subject. "We had an early dinner last night. I'm starving. Are you hungry?"

"I'm starving too."

"Your normal omelet?"

"Yes," I say. "My normal omelet."

He kisses me. "I'll wait twenty minutes and then order." He releases me but I catch his arm, inspecting his hand, which is now black and blue.

"Does it hurt?"

"The memory of doing something that ridiculous is what hurts. It's fine. And when Jessica asks you how I did it—"

"I'll tell her an alligator jumped out at us on the way to the car, and you were the hero that fought it off and saved me from it."

His lips curve. "Where did that come from?"

"Random stuff just pops into my head. It was actually very helpful in law school."

He laughs and kisses my forehead before walking to the door, but before he leaves he turns and faces me. "Do you know what I love about you?" He doesn't wait for a reply. "Aside from the alligator story, which was adorable, before that you told me exactly what you feel and want. The only games you play with me are in the bedroom, and those I welcome." He turns and disappears into the bedroom.

I stare after him, and I want to be pleased with those words, but all I can focus on is his use of the word "games." He's used that to reference his father often and it tells me where his head is this morning. Death is still on his mind and it will guide every action he takes today, and my gut tells me that is a reason to worry.

Eager to get downstairs and try to have some time to talk to Shane, I quickly shower, allowing myself only a few minutes of excitement over the huge makeup selection I find at my disposal in the bathroom. I choose Urban Decay shades of pink for my eyes, a gorgeous pink stay-on lipstick from Chanel, which I dab on my cheeks as well, and I finish everything off with powder and Chanel mascara. Even my new flatiron is amazing, and between it and new shower products, my hair is a rich, shiny brown that almost makes me forget how much I liked being blond. The memory of law school slips into my mind and I shove it aside, thinking instead of the stack of files downstairs filled with ventures Brandon Enterprises might undertake. I'm about to exit the bathroom, when I pick up the eye shadow palette again. Makeup. Yes. Makeup. An investment that's low risk, high reward. Every woman wants it, and some men.

Feeling excited about exploring this idea, I hurry to the closet to dress. Bypassing the ribbed tights for sexy thigh-highs, which I think Shane will prefer, I slip on my fitted pink Chanel suit dress, and now I'm thinking about high fashion. Makeup or clothing, or both, could be an amazing part of the Brandon empire, but I need to evaluate the potential and find an opportunity before I say anything. Focusing on finishing up, and getting down to breakfast, I slip on a pair of amazing strappy black Versace heels and complete the look with my new black and gray purse that has an adorable buckle. I stroke the leather, thinking about a purse line for Brandon Enterprises, but my mind goes elsewhere. Suddenly, I am remembering the day I'd walked into a pawnshop several weeks ago, after no contact from my brother for weeks, and given up my Hermès. I'd been alone and scared, upset over the loss of law school, and now I'm wearing Chanel and Versace, thinking about investments, and about to go have breakfast with a man I absolutely love.

The doorbell rings, no doubt with our food. I grab my new black Versace trench coat, which I adore, hurry back to the bathroom, and spray myself with the Chanel No. 5 on the counter before heading downstairs. Once I'm in the foyer, I hang my coat and purse on the rack, and walk through the archway to find Shane standing at the island facing me, talking on the phone with his head bent. As if he senses my entry, he looks up, his eyes traveling my body and warming with appreciation.

"I'll have the check cut by noon," he says, motioning me forward. I walk toward him, and he rounds the counter to meet me. "I'll call you back," he says to his caller, ending the conversation and setting his phone on the counter.

His hands settle at my waist. "You look beautiful, sweetheart. Do you like it?"

"I love it, Shane. Thank you. I feel spoiled."

"Stop saying 'thank you.' It's not a gift. It's our life and it's not about being spoiled." He doesn't give me time to argue that point. "I wasn't sure how long you'd be. I put the food in the oven to keep it warm. You ready to eat?"

"Very," I confirm, and together we sit at the island, talking about the food and the snowstorm that's coming down outside, and we even plan a weekend movie escape. Everything is great, including our food. It's a good morning, a prelude to what feels like many to follow. But even so, there are random shadows in Shane's eyes. A glimpse of what the man who punched that mirror faces this morning.

We head to the door, and Shane pulls on a long gray trench coat before helping me with mine, his hands lingering on my lapels, and that feeling that he is battling some internal war hits me again. "You're very stressed," I say, cupping his cheek.

He covers my hand with his and pulls it between us. "Why do you say that?"

"I see it in your eyes."

"Impossible. I could beat a world champion poker player with my courtroom face."

"I'm not a world champion poker player and this isn't a court-room, Shane. It's me and you, and I'm the woman in your bed."

"My mother did warn me about the woman in my bed."

"She warned you about me?"

"She warned me in general." He smiles. "And I'm teasing you. Apparently, my delivery is lacking today. You're right. I'm on edge."

"It's Brody, right?" I ask, relieved that he's willing to talk to me. "Did you know him well?"

"I didn't know him well, but I know that he had the world in his palm, and based on the press he's gotten in the last few days, it seems he ended up on the wrong path. Like my brother has gone down the wrong path."

"And you've tried to right him," I say, understanding completely. "Like I did my brother, but you see where that ended. I think it's right that I tried to save him, just as it is that you've tried to save Derek, but don't hold on too long like I did."

"I'm done holding on to Derek." There is a finality to his voice and a hardness in his eyes that delivers relief and sadness, as I know what it's like to be betrayed by a brother.

"Acceptance," I say, remembering what he'd told me about knowing versus accepting. "That's where you're at."

"Yes. That's where I'm at." He strokes hair from my eyes, and seeming to guess where my mind is headed, he promises, "You'll get there too, and believe it or not, it's a relief."

"Is it?"

"I didn't say you'd celebrate, just that you'll find some peace when you get to this place." He motions to the door. "Ready?"

I nod, and we head to the door, and then onward to the elevator, where we ride in silence, his thoughts a heavy weight between us, but so are mine with thoughts of my brother. It's kind of surreal to realize that the idea of talking to my brother again comes with dread. I don't feel like he's my blood. Now, he feels more like the enemy.

I blink and we've exited to the garage, and Shane breaks the silence. "Look out for alligators."

I laugh, and he drapes his arm over my shoulder. The memory of yesterday and the black Escalade pops into my mind, and I open my mouth to ask about it, but think better. He's letting go of a brother, and dealing with the upcoming loss of his father, two things I understand more than many would. He said he'd tell me and I have to give him room to do so on his terms. I have to let go of my past to have a future here, and judge Shane by Shane. I have to trust him or we are nothing before we are ever something.

Shane parks the Bentley in the private section of the office building garage and kills the engine, rounding the car to help me out, then popping the trunk. "Why don't you leave your coat down here with mine?" he offers, shrugging out of his and sticking it inside.

I let him help me remove it, and he shuts both inside, offering me the key to the car. "This is the extra for you to keep."

"I'm not going to just drive the Bentley, Shane."

"Yes, you are," he says, firmly.

"What if you need it?"

"I have another Bentley in New York that I'm going to have shipped to us. One I bought myself so believe you me, I'd rather drive *it*."

"Your father gave you this one."

"And I hate it."

"Shane—"

He presses the key into my hand. "You can still buy your own. Until then, we'll make do with the two at our disposal. Agreed?"

A car pulls up nearby and I give a reluctant nod, slipping the key into my purse.

"Good," he approves, and we walk toward the elevator.

"So there's a Bentley just sitting in a garage?"

"For a year, which is insanity, but proof I wasn't committed to staying here."

"You have an apartment there too?"

"Yes and I'm keeping it." He punches the button to the elevator. "In fact, why don't we plan a trip? I have this family meeting my father wants to have Sunday, but we can go next weekend. We can have that talk I promised then as well."

I think he's buying time but he's still planned a time and place to talk, and I can happily live with that. "That would be wonderful. I'm excited to see what a place you picked and decorated looks like."

Once inside the elevator for the short hop to the lobby, he adds, "We still need to decorate this one." His eyes meet mine, jagged emotions in their depths. "I think I need to do it now."

Before his father dies, I supply mentally, and quickly agree. "I think that might be a good idea."

We exit to the lobby and soon we're on the main car, headed to Brandon Enterprises' corporate level, and almost to our floor when I suddenly remember Randy. "Any word on the security guard?"

"He's not on our staff," he says, "but we think he's connected to Derek. I'll let you know when I have confirmation."

That news makes my stomach somersault. "I tried to get into Derek's office that night. He could have so easily caught me in there."

The elevator dings. "You shouldn't have been trying to get into his office," he warns. "Don't put yourself at risk."

The doors open. "I thought I was alone and I didn't get caught," I say, stepping into the hallway and he quickly joins me, catching my arm and turning me to face him.

"Don't take risks with Derek. Now it's your turn to promise me." I open my mouth to argue and he doesn't give me the chance. "Promise, Emily."

"Yes, okay. I promise."

He studies me a moment, as if confirming my agreement, before releasing me, and we continue to the offices, where the glass walls allow confirmation that the receptionist is not yet in and has not witnessed our encounter. "I'm going to have a chat with my father before I go to my office," he says, holding the door for me.

"I'm actually going to go thank Jessica for shopping for me."

He gives me a quick nod and turns away, while I head down the hallway toward his office. Derek's secretary is already at her desk, but as usual she doesn't bother to even glance up at me, which suits me just fine. Cutting left, I bring Jessica into view and her eyes go wide. "Oh my God," she says, standing up, her prim navy suit jacket with white trim proving the woman knows how to shop. "I knew that dress would look amazing on you."

I stop in front of her desk. "I love it. Thank you, but I have a bone to pick with you."

"He's my boss. I have to do what he says."

"You didn't have to spend that much money."

"He wanted me to do it and he said you wouldn't do it for yourself."

"I wouldn't have. I wish he wouldn't have."

"He wanted to do it. Honey, he cares about you. I've never seen him like this with anyone."

"You've known him a year."

"But I know him better than most. Now. Forget the money. Did I do well? Do you like everything? Because we can return things."

"What is not to love? You have exquisite taste." Footsteps sound and I look up to find Shane approaching, the flutter in my stomach at the sight of him impossible to ignore. He's just so perfect, at least to me.

He stops between me and his door, his hand settling at my back, warming me all over, his head tilting low. "Let me know when my father gets in, sweetheart."

"Of course," I say, and he disappears into his office, shutting the door.

Jessica's eyes light. "You two are so sexy together. I'm jealous."

I blush and a prickling sensation on my neck has my head turning to the right where I find Derek's secretary, whose name I can't even remember, sitting at her desk, and giving me a *You tramp* kind of knowing look. Embarrassed, and appalled at how unprofessional I look, I turn away, and grab Jessica's phone, punching in Shane's number. "Shane," I say, over the intercom.

He picks up immediately. "Is my father here?"

"I don't know, but—" I shut my eyes, not sure what I'm going to say. "Never mind." I hang up.

Jessica's brows furrow. "What was that?"

Shane's door opens but I don't face him. "Come here, Emily," he commands.

Now, I turn to him. "I need to go to my desk."

"That wasn't a request."

Not a request. I do not like that, but for the moment, I comply with his demand. I march to him and he backs into his office, shutting the door behind me the minute I enter, but I take control.

"Don't order me around with the pretense of work, when it's personal."

"How would I know that call was personal?"

"It was. You can't touch me like you just did at Jessica's desk here at work. Derek's assistant just looked at me like I'm a slut."

I barely get the words out before I'm pressed to the door I just entered. "You mean, don't touch you like this?" He pulls my dress up to my waist.

"What are you doing?" I demand, grabbing his arms.

"We aren't at Jessica's desk anymore," he says, cupping my sex. "We're behind closed doors."

I press my hand to his chest. "This can't—"

His finger slips under the lace of my pink panties. "Are you sure about that?" He strokes over the seam of my body that is instantly wet, sending a shiver of pure pleasure through me.

"This is so not right," I say, but I can't seem to ask him to stop. He yanks down my panties and tears them off of me. "Damn it," I gasp. "I loved those."

He shoves them in his pocket. "I'll buy you another pair," he promises, and already his fingers are back between my thighs, stroking, caressing, and I stop fighting the pleasure—as if I could anyway. A tight knot is already forming in my sex, spiraling to a peak way too fast.

My head rests on the wooden surface behind me, and he leans close, his breath warm on my neck, his free hand at my waist. "I only wish I could get to your nipples so I could lick them like I did last night."

Every part of me feels those words and in combination with his fingers, I am panting out, "Oh God. Oh . . . I'm going to. . . ." And I do. I come so hard and so fast that it shakes my entire body and I end up leaning forward, gripping his arms.

When I finally blink back to the present, his sexy mouth is curved, and his fingers slide from inside me, and he brings them to his mouth and licks them. "Now, that's a memory to get me through the day." He reaches down and pulls my dress down over my hips. "You may go to work now, Ms. Stevens."

He actually begins to step away and I have no idea what comes over me, but it's both fierce and daring. I grab his lapels. "Not so fast, Mr. Brandon." He arches a brow and says, "My turn or yours, depending on how you look at it." I start to lower myself to the ground, dragging my hands down his body as I do, and once I'm on the floor, my palms flatten on either side of his zipper.

"What are you doing, woman?"

"I'm pretty sure you know what I'm doing, Mr. Brandon." I stroke over his zipper, and he is harder, but not as hard as I plan to make him before I'm done.

"Emily," he breathes out, his voice a soft rasp, his expression darker now, but that too, can, and will, be even darker.

I kiss him through his pants and then unhook his belt. "This looks too tight."

"You don't—"

"Have to?" I ask, dealing with his button and then unzipping him. "If I had to, I wouldn't want to. But I do want to." I push aside his clothes, freeing him, and his cock juts forward. I wrap my palm around him, stroking down the length and I am aroused all over again. "Why haven't I done this before? You're just so overwhelmingly dominant, I never get the chance, but I'm going to change that." I lean down and lick the salty sweetness pooling at the tip. His intercom buzzes.

"Shane—" Jessica calls out, and he says, "Not now, Jessica," in a deep command that not even she would ignore.

The room goes silent. "I wish we had more time," I say, "but

I'll make it fast." I draw him into my mouth, just the head at first, sucking it, and then swirling my tongue around it.

His hand comes down on my head, encouraging me, and my gaze lifts to his, and the dark passion and desire etched in his stare does all kinds of wonderful things to my body. I want him, but more so I want to be the woman who makes him look like that over and over and over again. I draw him deeper, watching him as I slowly take him inch by inch, pleasure sliding over his handsome face.

My lashes lower, my lips touching my fingers where they hold him, and he is not small. He is long and thick, and he pulses in my mouth, another thing I like. I like it a lot. I drag my mouth up and down him, my tongue in action, my grip at the base of his cock tightening. His breathing is heavier now, his grip just a little tighter. I begin a pumping action, using my hand and my mouth, and gradually getting faster. His hips begin to move with me, and I reach around him, cupping his amazing backside. It seems to arouse him, a soft sound escaping his lips, and it's a powerful feeling to make a man like Shane Brandon want like I sense he wants. I suck harder, grip harder, lick faster.

"Emily," he pants, his grip softening, urgency in his voice. "Emily, stop or—"

I don't consider stopping or slowing down. I hold on. I pleasure him. I take his pleasure and it is mere moments before his grip tightens again and he is shaking, shuddering, and the salty taste of his release touches my tongue. Now I slow, becoming gentle as his body seems to ease into that sated aftermath he'd given me first. When I am certain he is through, I slide my mouth away from him and stand up, scooting my dress into place.

He quickly adjusts himself, looking at me with this kind of stunned appreciation that I pretty much love. "Now, you can go back to work, Mr. Brandon," I say, turning to the door, but right when I would open it, his hand comes down on the surface above my head.

"Don't ever do that to me here again."

Stunned, I face him and he laughs, those gray eyes filled with mischief. "That was the biggest joke I've ever told. Well delivered, if you believed it."

"I did and it wasn't funny."

"I'm sorry, sweetheart. I was sure you knew I couldn't be serious." He reaches down and runs his hand down the material of my dress. "One side was still halfway up your hip."

My eyes go wide. "Oh God. That would have been bad."

"Yes. It would have. And now, you can go to work, Ms. Stevens. But buzz me if my father is in."

"I will," I say, and this time when I turn, he flattens his hand on my belly, and says, "You are so damn sexy," before he releases me and steps away.

Smiling, I open the door and exit, while Jessica gives me an arched eyebrow, which turns into a huge grin. "How about lunch?" she asks.

"Yes I . . . ah no. I forgot I'm having lunch with Shane's mother." I lean on the desk. "I didn't tell him. Can you mention it? I don't want to go back in there."

"Of course, and be careful. She's——"

"I know. You warned me and you were right. I can handle her."

Approval lights her pretty blue eyes. "Yes. I believe you can. I'll tell him. Coffee later though."

"Yes. Good."

I push off the desk and start toward the hallway at the same moment Derek appears in his doorway, his tie once again red, his eyes once again hard. They are also inappropriately honed in on me, following my every move in a far too intimate way, making it nearly impossible for me to keep a steady pace. Nearing him, I am forced to acknowledge him, and I wave. "Good morning." But just as I would turn to my escape, he stops me.

"Wait just one moment," he says, stopping me in my tracks, my heart suddenly thundering in my chest.

"Yes?"

"I'd like you to come join me in my office, Ms. Stevens."

My heart falls to my feet with the use of my formal name emphasized, when Shane just teased me with it. Shane's office must be bugged. "I really need to go check in with your father."

"You had time for my brother. Make time for me."

I am officially trapped but Shane's warning plays in my mind: *Don't take risks with Derek.* I cannot go in his office. I will not run to Shane for help. I need to just handle this man.

"Well, Ms. Stevens?" Derek presses. "Are you coming or not?"

"Get to your desk, Ms. Stevens."

At the sound of Brandon Senior's voice, I look right to find him standing in the hallway I wish I'd already traveled down. "Mr. Brandon," I say in shock.

"Get to work," he snaps, and when I don't immediately move, he adds, "Now, Ms. Stevens."

For once, his cranky commands are welcome, and I dart past him, all but running to the lobby, where I force myself to slow, and greet the receptionist. From there, I welcome the hallway leading to the private alcove that is my desk in front of Brandon Senior's office. Nearly collapsing into my chair, I feel as if I've run a marathon and the day is barely starting. I press my hand to my face, angry at myself for not having a comeback to manage Derek.

I knew he could pull a stunt like that. I should have worked through scenarios in my mind, like I had when preparing for mock trials in school, and been ready with solutions. I can't be this unprepared ever again because I saw the look in Derek's eyes. He has me in his sights. I am a target.

CHAPTER SEVENTEEN

SHANE

The minute my father heads for Derek's office, I follow, and the ways I want to get Derek the fuck out of this company, and Emily's life, are too many to count. Standing in my doorway and giving her room to deal with him, as I know she would want, rather than rescue her, had about killed me. But that would have also made her look weak and set her up as more of a target for brother dearest.

My father disappears into Derek's office and shuts the door. I pass Derek's secretary, wondering if she knows he's fucking Adrian's sister as well as her, probably in the same day. I don't look at her. I walk on by and open my brother's door and enter, shutting it behind me. Derek laughs. "Did I offend your little girlfriend? Are you here to protect her like my father?"

The surprise in his taunt isn't the taunt itself, but the reference to my father, who I look at now, arching a brow.

"I don't have time to hire a new secretary and Emily has a mind of her own," he snaps. "I'm not counting on your bedroom skills to keep my secretary." He cuts a look at Derek. "Leave her the fuck alone."

Derek gives me an amused look. "Your turn. Defend her honor. Get it over with."

"Actually, Emily's the kind of woman who'll grab you by the ball sack and get a hammer. Please. Keep agitating her. I want to watch."

"I do like it rough," he says, successfully making me want to punch him, but that would empower him, not me.

"We need to move past getting laid to staying out of jail," I say, leaning against the door and crossing my arms in front of me. "Not only did Brody Matthews die, but he did so with our pill bottles in his medicine chest."

"And you know this how?" Derek demands.

"Because I know a hell of a lot more than you think, Derek. Brody's ex ran her mouth at Eric's plastic surgery office. I did damage control, but it might not be enough. The Feds are looking into a connection between a drug they call Sub-Zero and professional athletes. If he has a bottle left over, with pills in it—"

"He won't," Derek says.

My gaze jerks to him. "Did you kill him?"

"He had a car accident."

"That you arranged?" I ask.

He leans on his credenza, arms folded in front of him. "No one made him drive his car into a tree."

"So Adrian Martina arranged it," I say. "Same thing."

My father says nothing, asks nothing, which tells me he's far more in the "know" on this than I had hoped. I look at him. "You know about all of this, don't you?"

"Be specific," he instructs, his noncommittal answer his

standard formula, but the fact that he sits down as if he can't stand, taking a submissive role, is not.

"All right," I say. "Let's be clear. I'll tell you what I know. I'll tell you what I expect."

"Save your breath," Derek says. "Because this endeavor is worth a lot of money."

I focus on my father, speaking to him, setting him up to remember this conversation when the raid takes place. "Our drug Ridel is being used to package Sub-Zero. The Feds are looking into a connection that led them to Brody's accident last night. Should they find Ridel bottles, they will test what's inside. Furthermore, Brody's wife was ready to tell the police he'd been using Ridel and acting weird. I paid her off, and it wasn't cheap, and she's agreed to leave the country. Now, I have to keep her silent throughout his funeral, when grief drives people to do things they wouldn't otherwise do."

My father shows no reaction. "Is this where you threaten to walk?" No denial. No concern. "Because considering what you've done to cover this up, I think it's too late to abandon ship and not go down if it sinks." The edges of his mouth quirk ever so slightly.

And there it is. My father, the master game player. I'm trying to set him up, and he's trying to turn the tables. "Actually, that's why I'm here. She hasn't been paid. You or Derek need to issue the payment off your employee account. Personally, I'd say you have the least risk."

Ridiculously, my father's look transforms to one of pride, and I'd be flattered, but I know him. I've simply extended the game he wants to play. "How much?"

"Three hundred and moving expenses," I say, "so make it four."

"Cut the check, Derek," my father says.

"I didn't make this deal," Derek says. "It could be a setup. I'm not cutting the check."

"He'll cut the check," my father assures me.

"We sidestep one problem with this," I say. "This will not end well for us if don't get out of business with Martina."

"This is where you threaten to get out," Derek says.

I push off the door and look at him. "No. This is where I threaten to get you out if you don't get Adrian Martina out."

"We were already in a war," he says.

"But I haven't drawn my blade. I let the word 'brother' matter. But one man is dead now. That changes everything. That makes you a murderer and no one I recognize or wish to call family."

"Am I supposed to be afraid?"

"I hope you aren't, because people who don't feel fear are always the first to fall."

I turn and reach for the door, and he says, "Then you're afraid."

I suck in air and let it out, turning to face him. "I felt fear in my gut before every trial and negotiation I ever won. And you know what I feared? Losing. Which is why I don't let down my guard and I always win."

I give him my back and exit his office, making my way past his secretary again without a look, my gaze going to my secretary's empty desk, which can mean only one thing. She's with Emily, which isn't a bad thing. I respect Jessica and I believe she's a friend to Emily and me, when Emily, I know, needs to feel a sense of family that mine doesn't even give me. Cutting down the hallway, I cross the lobby and take the path leading to Emily's desk. Rounding the corner, I bring her into view where she sits at her desk with Jessica squatting by her feet.

Emily whirls around to face me while Jessica pops to her feet, and I close the space between us, leaning forward to rest my hands on Emily's desk.

"Are you okay?"

"Of course, I'm fine. I'm no wimp but I'm pissed off at myself for not being more prepared for him."

"She blamed herself," Jessica supplies, going on to prove why I think she makes a good friend to Emily by adding, "I told her Derek's the problem, not her."

"Jessica's right," I agree, "and I know you know that."

"I should have been prepared for him. I knew he could have—" She pales and faces Jessica. "I need you to leave."

She gives a mock look of dismay. "That's just rude."

Emily grabs her arm. "Oh God. I'm sorry. That sounded horrible. I'll make it up to you, I promise."

"No worries," she says. "I'm no wimp, either." She gives me a wave and heads for the lobby, while Emily twists back around to face me.

"Derek called me Ms. Stevens," she says softly, "and he emphasized Ms. Stevens. Do you know where I'm going with this?"

"My office is wired. Considering I have it checked frequently, that's new and poorly timed." I soften my voice. "Sorry, sweetheart. What's between us should stay between us."

"It's not your fault, Shane, though what is also poorly timed is the lunch with your mother I forgot about. I'm going to be wondering if she knows, and considering this is your mother, she'll just tell me."

"You don't have to do the 'make nice with my mother' thing."

"Have you told your mother that?" She holds up a hand. "It's fine. Declining your mother's invitation will only ignite the chase with her."

"You figured her out pretty fast."

"She's not hard to figure out, but I should probably go get my coat."

"I'm going to go to the apartment to work for a little bit until I clean my office of bugs. What time are you leaving? I'll bring it to you before you leave."

"One, but I can walk down with you."

"I'll be back long before you leave." I study her for a few beats, amazed at how cool and collected she is, considering everything that has happened this past week. "But again, you don't have to play nice with my mother."

"You said that. And contrary to the example I just set, I can handle myself just fine. And I'll be ready for Derek next time."

I want to grab her and kiss her, but instead I say, "Call me if you need me."

"And you call me if you need me."

"Sweetheart, I was already needing you sixty seconds after you left my office." I wink and push off the desk at about the same moment my father rounds the corner, the two of us stand toe-to-toe.

"Did you look at the paperwork I had Emily bring you?" he asks, as if the encounter in Derek's office never happened.

"Is that a bribe or an offering to Mike?"

"In my office," he says, and he starts to walk around me.

"I'm not following anymore," I say. "Not to your office. Not to hell."

I suck in air and he levels me with a stare. "In my office, son." He turns and walks into his office, and that's when the hacking ensues. Deep, gut-wrenching hacking. I can feel Emily staring at me, willing me to follow him into the office. Damn it. I walk forward and find him standing almost in my face, anger burning in his bloodshot stare. I shut the door and he blasts me. "We don't talk this kind of business in front of others. Even if you're fuck-ing her."

He's volatile in a way I do not know him to be. Vile, yes. Rude, yes. But not volatile.

"That proposal," he continues, "offered you good, clean busi-ness the way you like it."

"But what you're using it for isn't good and clean, now is it?"

"Why will it matter once I'm gone?"

"That's not a no," I say. "And it matters because whatever deal you're using it for will still exist. Besides, a deal that big will take investors."

"Just sign the damn paper."

"Does Mike know about this?"

"No one knows about this but you, and it needs to stay that way."

"You think Mike won't approve."

"I don't care if he approves."

"You want to own him and his vote."

"Just sign the damn papers, Shane."

He walks to his desk and when he faces me again, I say, "I'm not doing anything to give you all of the power." I face the door, my hand going to the knob.

"I have investors to do this on my own. I will do it on my own."

The meeting with the bankers that never happened. He's bluffing and I'm done being a token in his game. I exit the office and shut the door. Emily looks at me, and the moment she sees my face, disappointment fills her. I think she's fallen into the same trap I always have. The one where I think my father will change but he never does. I give her a nod. The door behind me opens and I start walking, but right as I round the corner, I hear my father ask

Emily, "How much influence do you have over him?" and I stop dead in my tracks.

One hell of a lot, I think, but she replies, "Seriously?" as if he's crazy, before laughing and asking, "How much do I have over you?"

"Some," he says thoughtfully, "or I wouldn't drink that damn tea you bring me."

"You ask for that tea," she points out.

"Because you made me drink it the first time, and no one but Maggie makes me do anything. So I ask again: How much influence do you have over my son?"

"I couldn't make Shane drink the tea."

She knows damn well I'd drink the tea if she wanted me to try it, but her loyalty to me shown in this response is golden in ways no one else in my family is. And my father is no fool. He knows she's loyal to me, not just because she told him she is, but because it shows in her actions and words. And yet, curiously, he wants her by his door. I cut through the lobby and exit, quickly grabbing an elevator alone, repeating that thought. He wants Emily by his door. It speaks of him protecting me, but my father protects no one but himself. "What are you up to, Father?"

Exiting the elevator, I punch in Seth's number, and he answers on the first ring. "You need to sweep my office," I say.

"I swept it yesterday."

I enter the elevator to the garage. "Well then, it got bugged last night," I say, punching my floor.

"I won't ask how you know," he says. "But I can't get there anytime soon. Right now, I'm meeting with the team we discussed last night, but I have another situation. I don't have a certain woman under control. She's not taking my calls. I'm hoping she's sedated from the stress. Once I finish this meeting I'm headed there."

"Keep me posted." We end the call and I enter the garage, already dialing Mike's office, but I hang up before I get an answer. There is more to the story with Mike Rogers than meets the eye, though the man is a damn ghost as of late. That in itself is a signal of a bigger picture. I slide into the car, and dial my mother, who doesn't answer. I don't leave a message. I'm not sure why I don't leave a message. Something is bothering me that I can't quite nail, and when I get these feelings, there is always a winning play within reach.

EMILY

The energy Brandon Senior brings to the office when he's in poor health makes me wonder what this place must have been like when he was in his prime, and certainly explains how it became a big success. The morning plays out with him barking orders, and the phone ringing off the hook with what feels like a million questions about the board meeting, as well as me juggling yet more changing arrangements. Come noon, I try to get lunch for Brandon Senior, concerned that he refuses to eat considering his blue suit and yellow tie look like they were made for his big brother. The man is dying and I have gut-wrenching moments when I think about how soon he may be gone from this world, and Shane's life, that always seems to trigger memories of my own father.

It's almost time for Shane's mother to arrive for our lunch, and I dart into Senior's office despite him being on the phone and set the file he's been demanding on his desk. I'm about to head back to my desk when he ends the call, and surprises me. "Is that a new dress, Ms. Stevens?"

"It is," I say, feeling awkward about this leading to Shane, but instead he says, "About damn time. Funeral black does not suit me and that's all you ever wore."

He's wrong on my wardrobe, but I say, "No black. Duly noted. Are you sure you don't want some lunch before I leave?"

He leans back in his chair, ignoring my offer of food. "That's right. You're lunching with my wife today."

"I am. I hope that's okay?"

"As if I'd have a say in the matter. This is my Maggie we're talking about."

"I kind of like that she's the only person who can get her way with you. It's rather romantic."

"Do you get your way with my son, Ms. Stevens?" he asks, bringing us back to the earlier conversation about my influence on Shane. "Would he drink the tea because you told him to, as I did?"

"We're back to tea?" I ask, finding it such a weird analogy, but clearly it's some sort of head game.

"Yes," he confirms. "Tea. Would my son drink the tea if you told him to?"

"I don't even know if he likes tea," I say, trying to beat him at his own game.

"Assume he doesn't. I sure as hell don't."

"I fear I am going to disappoint you, but it's very doubtful he'd drink the tea."

He narrows his eyes on me. "What would you have done today with Derek had I not appeared?"

"Told him my boss is an asshole and that I had to get back to my desk."

He shocks me and laughs. "Shane would drink the tea." He waves me off. "Now go have your lunch and get it over with. I have work for you to do."

Really truly confused by the softer side of Brandon Senior, I wonder if it's part of his game. A way to reel me in? Shane does call him a master. "Shut the door behind you and tell my wife I'm in a meeting."

I exit into the exterior office to find Shane waiting on me. "I owe you this," he says, his gray eyes warm as he indicates my coat draped over his arm, and it looks way better on him than me.

"I all but forgot it. It's been a crazy, busy morning."

He leans in close, the heat of his body warming me. "I like how you smell today."

"I'll have to remember that."

"I like how you taste today too."

"Shane, honey!"

At the sound of Maggie's voice I all but jump with guilt, heat rushing to my cheeks, while Shane's eyes light with mischief. I glower at him and quickly right my expression before we both turn to greet his mother, who is as elegant as ever in a light blue pant-suit and boots.

"Tell me you aren't stealing my lunch date," she says, rushing to Shane and giving him a hug.

"I wouldn't dream of stealing your date or the time you intend to invest in scaring Emily."

My lips part in shock, while it's Maggie's turn to glower. "Don't be silly," she says. "I don't scare her in the least, which is part of what makes her interesting."

"I called you this morning," he says. "Did you forget to call me back?"

"I have no message."

"I'm in your missed calls."

"Oh please. No message means don't call back. You'll call me when you get time. Besides, I had a meeting at the Capitol this morning." She holds up all her fingers and waves them. "That's right. The Capitol. My interior design business is taking on a life of its own."

"How exciting," I say. "Are you redoing a specific part of the interior or is it a broader scale project?"

"One senator's office," she says, "but it's a start." She checks the time on her dainty diamond watch. "Shall we go? With the snow outside, we need to drive anyway, so I thought we'd go to a place a few miles away." She points to the office door. "I should say hello to my husband quickly first though."

I hold up a finger. "Oh he's——"

She goes into his office and I cringe. "I wasn't supposed to let her in."

Shane laughs. "It's my mother. You never had a chance to stop her and my father knows that." He holds up my coat to help me into it, and I slip my arms inside, only to have him lean in close, and murmur, "I'd drink the tea."

I whirl around. "You heard?"

"I did and you were protecting me."

"I was, but do you think——"

"All right then," Maggie says, reappearing. "We are off."

"I need to talk to you, Mother. Come see me when you get back."

She points at her watch. "I have meetings. I'm not coming back up. I'll call you."

Shane does not look pleased and I wonder what he thinks she's avoiding. Maggie laces her arm with mine and drags me forward, giving me no chance to even tell Shane good-bye. In fact, I have to wave at the receptionist and shout out, "Call me if there's any-thing urgent!" before we step into the hallway.

"Gorgeous coat, honey," Maggie says, punching the elevator button. "Did Shane buy it for you?"

And there it is. Her games and really, I think she is as much a master as her husband, because this is a subtle attempt to hit a nerve that sets me up to run my mouth later. I don't take the bait. "You do know I get paid extremely well for working for your husband, don't you?"

"Really?" she says. "How well?"

"Well enough that I was willing to take the title of secretary."

"You're a paralegal, right?"

"Yes," I say, choking on the lie I need to get used to telling, but lies just don't become me. "And I'm making more than I would in that role elsewhere."

We step onto the elevator and this time she punches the but-ton. "Well, you certainly earn it. He's difficult. He always has been, but the cancer has made it worse."

There is no grief in her voice, no torment like I feel in Shane when he speaks of his father. More like agitation, but then, he's sleeping around on her, even now. "How long have you been married?"

"Thirty-seven years. I was a teenager when I married. Young, in love, and pregnant."

"Oh. I had no idea. That must have been hard."

"Believe it or not, back then your cranky boss was a charmer like Shane."

"I see glimpses of that side of him."

She sighs. "Me too, but it's rare." She stares ahead and for a moment doesn't speak, and this time I do sense torment in her that she doesn't wish for me to see, several floors passing before she's back to chatter. "The restaurant is excellent and Mike Rogers, our stockholder, owns it, so we always get extra-special treatment."

"Mike Rogers," I say. "I hear his name all the time but have never seen him. I guess that will change at the board meeting next week."

"Ah yes," she says, the car stopping at the lobby level. "The board meeting." We exit the car and walk to the garage elevator. "My husband is going to announce his retirement to prevent news of his cancer from leaking and then set a vote for the head of the table."

"I figured as much but he's been very hush-hush," I say as we exit into the garage.

"Well, whatever you do"—she hits a clicker and a silver Mercedes I know is one of the most expensive they make, beeps— "don't tell him I told you. I'll never hear the end of it."

We climb into the car and she starts telling me all about the food at the restaurant, and in only a few blocks we're in the parking lot, with a flurry of snowflakes around us. She parks the car and her cell phone rings. She kills the engine and digs it out of her purse, glancing at the number. "The senator I'm working for. I have to take it."

"Of course," I say, removing my cell phone, with Shane on my mind.

I pull up my text messages and send him a note: *What was I thinking? I should have gone along with your father and let him think I could influence you. Then I could have found out what he is up to. I'm a horrible spy.*

His reply is instant: *I don't want you playing spy. You were perfect and I'll show you how perfect tonight.*

I type: *Promise?*

His response is exactly what I expect: *Promise. And I never break a promise.*

I smile and almost laugh.

"Is that my son you're talking to?" Maggie asks, clearly having ended her call.

I glance up to find her staring at me. "Yes. It's Shane. He's good at making me laugh, which is perhaps the reason I can't stay away from him."

She gets a rather distant look, several beats passing before she agrees. "It's certainly not a bad quality. Shall we go eat?"

"Yes. Please. I'm starving." We both pull up the hoods to our coats and exit the car into the cold, snowy day, meeting at the trunk and making a mad dash for the restaurant.

One of the staff opens the door for us, and we rush into the warmth, tugging our hoods back down. We are greeted warmly by a thirty-something pretty blonde in jeans and boots who clearly knows Maggie. "We have your regular table ready, Mrs. Brandon. This way."

"Mike's a rancher," Maggie explains, "so this place is all about that piece of culture."

Boy is it, I think, as we are led to the left, where neon signs and cowboy hats decorate the walls. There's even a jukebox by the pale wooden bar that matches the floors. We walk up several steps and claim one of only four booths that overlook rows of tables, with five big screens mounted on a wall above us. The waitress leaves us with menus, takes our drink order while we are still standing, and then both Maggie and I shed our coats before sitting down across from each other.

"Do you ride?" she asks, smoothing the collar of her silk blouse.

The Texas girl in me opens my mouth to say "yes" but I quickly amend my words, before I speak them. "Cali isn't big on horses. At least, not in L.A. It seems like fun, though."

"Oh it is. Shane loves to ride. We own the adjoining property to Mike's just outside of Denver. Much smaller than his, as ours is simply a pleasure spot, and his is big business, but we have horses. You should come out one weekend."

Shane and horses. Somehow, I have no idea why it fits him, but it's hard to see prim and proper Maggie riding. "Thank you," I say, but I'm confused as to why she's being so nice when I'm supposed to be Shane's one-minute woman, and therefore off Derek's radar. "I am not sure Shane would want me to join you."

She rests her elbows on the table and studies me. "Really? Because I saw how you two looked at each other."

I don't blink or look away. "What happened to warning me away so I don't get hurt instead of teasing me with what I can't have?"

"You already have him and from what I understand, it's driving Derek crazy."

"Okay, you're very confusing," I say. "In one breath, I have Shane, and in the other I'm the score sitting outside your husband's door."

"Whatever you started out being for my Shane, you're more now and we both know it."

"I don't know it."

"If you don't, you will. But I think you do, and I think it's lovely." She opens her menu. "So, do you want recommendations?"

I'd push again toward the one-minute girl agenda, but who am I kidding? She's made up her mind, and I have a feeling she's made her thoughts clear to Derek, thus his attention this morning. "Recommendations would be great." And from there, I am thankful for the reprieve from the darts being thrown at me, as the conversation turns to food, before we place our orders for overstuffed Texas baked potatoes that she swears are gourmet.

"Maggie Brandon."

At the sound of a deep male voice, I look up to find a linebacker of a man, who I can only describe as a gray fox, his white dress shirt stretched over broad shoulders and rolled up his powerful forearms, his light blue tie a perfect match for his eyes.

"Mike," Maggie says, accepting his hand, and oh wow. Her eyes warm the way I think mine do when I see Shane. "I had no idea you'd be here this afternoon."

"Lucky it worked out this way," he says, and he's still holding on to her, and I'm pretty sure I don't exist.

He releases her finally, though, and turns his attention to me. "You must be the Wonder Woman keeping David in line. Emily, isn't it?"

"Yes," I say. "Emily, and I assume 'David' is Mr. Brandon."

Maggie and Mike laugh. "Yes," Maggie confirms. "That's him."

The two of them then share another look that is a little too familiar, and seems to be some kind of silent communication before Mike refocuses on me and extends his hand. "Forgive me," he says, as I accept it. "I'm Mike——"

"Rogers," I supply, and already he's released me. No lingering grip for me. "I call your offices often."

"Indeed," he says. "And always urgently."

I have no idea why, but I feel a little protective of Shane's father, and I say, "He doesn't exactly have a lot of time."

"He never has," Mike agrees, and I'm reminded that Brandon Senior's retirement announcement is about hiding his cancer. Mike is close to Maggie, but I don't think he knows, or he's pretending not to quite well.

He glances at his Rolex and then back at Maggie. "You ladies enjoy your meal."

"We will," she says.

He gives her a nod, then turns one on me before disappearing into the main restaurant. Our food arrives at that moment, and Maggie is noticeably less talkative while being reserved on the eye contact. We chat about my dress but she doesn't ask if Shane bought it this time. Her phone beeps and she looks at it. "That would be the senator. I need to find a quiet spot and call him. I'll be right back."

"Of course," I say, removing my phone, texting Shane: *I met Mike Rogers.*

He doesn't reply. And doesn't reply. It's not like him, but he's a busy person, I know. I flag a waitress and ask for a bathroom. Once directed, I hurry through the bar and into another dining room, turning a corner to catch a glimpse of Mike with his hand on Maggie's waist. I duck back around the wall and flatten, my fist balling at my chest.

"I have to get back to Emily," she whispers, sounding breathless.

"But I want you more than she does, I promise you."

That's all I need to hear. I dash forward and back toward our seats; my mind is racing right along with my heart. Once I'm seated, looking like I've never left, it hits me then that Mike knew who I was without being told, so he had to know who Maggie was lunching with today. And Brandon Senior's reference to her being gone often the other night when I was with Shane. My God. Is Brandon Senior having an affair because Maggie's having one while he's dying? Or vice versa? My hand goes to my throat. Oh no. Maggie controls the vote if she controls Mike. Which son has she picked to run the company? And how am I going to tell Shane any of this? I dread the way it's going to hurt him.

"I'm back," Maggie says, "and I can't believe this, especially since our last lunch got interrupted, but I have to get to the Capitol now." She flags down a waitress. "Do you want to stay and take a taxi service, or get your food to go and ride back with me?"

She has to get naked with Mike before the Capitol is what she really means. "I'll get a taxi. You go on ahead."

"You're sure?"

"Of course."

"Okay then." She stands and puts on her coat. "The bill is paid and dessert is on the house." I blink and she's gone. Feeling like I have whiplash, and with a whole lot of dread at what my spying skills now require I tell Shane, I flag down our waitress and arrange a cab. Once I've tipped her well, she steps away and my gaze catches on the headlines on one of the TVs, my stomach falling. I can't be seeing what I think I see. I rush closer to the screen and read the headline: WIFE OF BRODY MATTHEWS COMMITS SUICIDE AFTER HIS TRAGIC DEATH IN A CAR ACCIDENT LAST NIGHT. This is insanity. I dial Shane and I get his voice mail. I head for the door and try again. My cab is waiting and I pull up my hood and rush forward, climbing inside, spouting out the address. Again, I get Shane's voice mail and I text him. And I wait, knowing there is more to this that meets the eye and knowing that somehow, some way, Shane is connected. That terrifies me.

CHAPTER EIGHTEEN

SHANE

After Emily leaves for lunch with my mother, I head to my office. No longer willing to wait on someone else to find answers, I busy myself going through every piece of data I can find on Mike Rogers. I'm an hour into my research when Jessica walks into my office unannounced and shuts the door, resting against it. "Brody's estranged wife committed suicide. Oh my God, Shane. It's tragic. I talked to that man on the phone and now he's dead and so is she."

I go still, ice splintering a path down my spine. "How do you know this?" I ask cautiously, aware that my office is bugged, and that Jessica has no real clue what is going on.

"I went downstairs to get lunch, and the TV was on. It's all over the news. She's dead."

"How?"

"They haven't said or I didn't hear."

My intercom goes off, and Seth's voice fills the air. "I'm at Jessica's desk. I need to see you."

"I'll go," Jessica says, opening the door to leave. Seth appears, shutting us inside, and without saying a word, he removes an electronic box with antennas from his jacket pocket and starts scanning the office. Almost instantly, a beeping sound leads him to a bookshelf where he removes a book, opens it, and then shows me a tiny chip. He continues his scan and ends up at my desk, focused on my stapler, which he proceeds to open and remove yet another chip. The final stop is at the bottom of my chair. I step back and watch as he removes yet another listening device, and then pulls a bottle of water from his jacket, unscrews the top, and sticks all the offending objects inside. He screws the top on and drops it in my trashcan, and the scanner goes quiet.

He rests his hands on the desk. "Did you hear about Brody's wife?"

"Yes," I confirm grimly. "I heard. How did she die?"

"A bottle of aspirin and slit wrists," he says. "Someone was making sure she didn't survive."

"Murder?"

"Murder that looks like suicide," he confirms. "I'd bet every ounce of trust you give me on it."

I face the window, snowflakes pummeling the glass, and that silence inside me begins to pool like oil in my gut, churning to anger. Seth steps next to me, his voice inflected with rare regret. "I should have left a man on her and I didn't."

"This is not on you," I say. "This is on my brother." I hesitate, thinking about my demand for a check to be cut this morning in Derek's office. "Or my father."

He turns to face me, both of us crossing our arms in front of our bodies. "You think Senior had a hand in this?"

"I demanded a check be cut to her this very morning, and not in my name. I didn't want the connection that could be used as blackmail. My father insisted Derek put his name on it, despite his situation making him the obvious choice."

"Interesting. Protecting his legacy or setting Derek up for a fall?"

"His motivation is more difficult to decipher now than usual."

"Derek had a visit with someone in a black Escalade about an hour ago."

"Adrian," I say, that name acid on my tongue.

"It was," Seth confirms. "We confirmed his plate."

"Where's Derek now?"

"His office, no doubt expecting your imminent explosion, which I'm guessing you won't give him."

"And my father?"

"He's at lunch with Wit Newman."

"The owner of the Denver Sports Center, where Mike Rogers's team plays." I supply. "My father wants to buy the Sports Center."

"To control Mike," Seth concludes.

"To control his vote," I amend. "He wants me to sign off on it or he claims to have the resources together to do it on his own. Where was he later in the afternoon yesterday?"

"The Omni tower for about three hours, in the offices of Huffman Investments. Sounds like he might be trying to make good on that claim to use his own money to buy the Sports Center."

"And while this is important, getting Adrian Martina the fuck out of my company comes first."

His cell phone rings and he removes it from his pocket. "Nick," he says, taking the call and listening before he speaks a few clipped words, and then says, "I'll tell him and we'll get there." He ends the call. "Nick says he needs to see us at his facility now and we need to make sure we aren't followed. He's sending a car to the private garage again. It'll be here in fifteen minutes."

My intercom buzzes. "Emily needs to see you," Jessica announces. "She says it's urgent."

"Give me a minute." I eye Seth. "She must have heard and she's connecting dots."

"I'll step outside." He walks to the door and exits, with Emily appearing in his place, and she pulls the door shut behind her.

Her skin is pale, her eyes worried. "You know about Brody's wife?"

"Yes," I say, pressing my fingers to my desk, and putting it between us. I can't have a conversation with her about this now. "I know."

She takes several steps forward. "You're connected to this."

"I had nothing to do with this."

"You're *connected* to this," she repeats.

"Emily," I say softly. "I can't do this right now."

"Was she murdered? Was she?"

"Don't do this right now."

"That's a yes." She crosses to stand in front of my desk. "How bad is this for you?"

I lean on the desk and study her. "You know I'm not responsible for their deaths."

"That doesn't mean you won't be blamed."

She's right and the idea that this could be a setup is not one I can ignore. "You need to stay out of this. Don't talk about it. Don't ask anyone about this. Do not touch this."

"You have no intention of ever telling me what's really going on, do you?"

"I told you I'd tell you everything and I will."

"When?"

"I'm not doing this now." My voice is sharper and harder with the pressing need to fix this before I end up in jail and take her with me. "I need you to go back to your desk and let me handle what I need to handle."

"Go back to my desk," she repeats. "Right. I'll do that." She marches toward the door, but not before I see hurt and doubt in her eyes that I'd hoped to never see directed at me. I pursue her, reaching her as her hand comes down on the doorknob, my palm flattening on the door above her, my hand at her waist.

"Don't go like this," I say, lowering my voice to add, *"Please."*

"You told me to go."

"Not angry. Not doubting me."

"You all but dared me to feel those things."

"Not by intent. I'm focused on solving problems and keeping everyone safe. The idea of you feeling either of those things will mess with my head, and I can't have anything messing with my head right now."

She faces me, folding her arms defensively in front of her. "So that's what I've become? Someone to mess with your head? To distract you?"

"Sweetheart," I say, my hands settling at her waist, "that *is not* what I said."

"You don't have to." Her hands close around my wrists. "And I don't want to be that to you. I want to be helpful. I want to be a partner."

"You are the best damn thing that's ever happened to me. I'm trying to make sure my family doesn't destroy us."

"They can't destroy us, but secrets can. If I'm a distraction—"

"Emily—"

"You *can't* end up like Brody," she says. "If I'm a distraction, you need to send me away, even if it's for a few weeks."

"I'm not sending you away."

"Then you need—"

"Tonight," I say. "We'll figure this out tonight, but I'll likely be late coming home. And I need you to promise me you'll go home right after work and stay there so I won't worry about you, but I'm going to have security monitoring you."

"This is that bad?"

"Do you want the real answer?"

"I need the real answer."

"Then yes. It's that bad."

She studies me for several long beats. "You really expect me to just walk out of here in the dark, don't you?"

"Yes, because you're smart enough to know that this isn't the right time or place to have this conversation."

"No. It's not. The right time and place would have existed before right now, but bottom line, I'm in the dark, which means I'm flying blind when it comes to evaluating what's important, therefore, I have to tell you something I found out about Mike Rogers today." She hesitates. "And I really didn't want to share it like this."

"That doesn't sound good but I need to know."

"This is not how I wanted to tell you this," she repeats, which only sets me more on edge.

"*Tell* me."

"Fine. Tell you. Right."

"Emily—"

"Your mother and Mike are having an affair."

I feel those words like a punch in the chest, the idea of my mother being the one sane person in my family I've clung to, is shattering moment by moment. "How do you know?"

"He showed up at the restaurant, and it was pretty obvious between them but I wasn't going to jump to conclusions. But then, your mother went to take a call, and I went to the bathroom. I rounded the corner and they were very intimate, his hands on her, the things they were saying——"

"I don't want to know," I say roughly. "Did they see you?"

"No. They did not."

I release her waist and press my hands to the door above her head, my lashes lowering. My mind races and lands on the Sports Center, which takes on a new twist. Maybe my father wants to ruin Mike, not just control his vote. "Can my family get any more fucked-up?"

"Shane, I'm sorry," Emily says, her hand flattening on my chest, over my racing heart. "Maybe your father's cheating hurt her or maybe she's coping with him dying."

I open my eyes. "Or maybe she's trying to control the vote."

"Is that in your favor?"

"I have no idea anymore." My hand covers hers. "Thank you. I needed to know. It pieces things together that now make sense."

"What things?"

"Emily——"

"You aren't going to tell me."

"I need to do damage control. When it's done——"

"Right. Because why would we do this together." She turns for the door.

My hand flattens on her belly, my body arching around hers, and I press my cheek to her cheek. "Emily," I say, and this time her name is roughened with the torment I feel over shutting her out and keeping her close at the same time that I know can't continue. "I'm asking you to give me until tonight. Please. Just give me until tonight."

She doesn't immediately respond, and the seconds tick by until she finally says, "Just come home safely, Shane."

I hold her for several more beats, looking for an answer, but there isn't one I can give. I push off the door and she waits for me to speak, willing me to say what she wants to hear, what I don't give her. She abruptly moves, opening the door and leaving without the promise that I will come home safely. Because that might not happen and I will not ever lie to her.

An hour later, I'm back at Nick's warehouse, in the conference room with Nick and Seth on either side of me.

"Do I believe Brody and his wife were murdered?" Nick asks. "Yes. Is there proof?" He pauses, sipping from the black FBI mug he's holding that matches his black FBI shirt, which is too much fucking FBI to suit me right now. As if he doesn't agree, he decides to give me a little more. "So far, no, but the FBI is looking into it. This case is on their radar."

"I don't believe there is any way they will connect the dots to you at this point," Seth says.

"The wife was the one connecting point," Nick says, "and we can assume Adrian, and your brother, came to that same conclusion."

"Or my father," I say. "He knew about Brody's wife, and not long after finding out—I'm paraphrasing here—he told me neither Mike, nor Martina, are going to control his company."

"You think he had Brody's wife killed?" Nick asks.

"No," I say. "The only thing my father likes dirty is his money. Never his hands. I think he might have urged my brother to make the problem disappear. How Derek did it is on Derek. He also wants to buy the Sports Center Mike's team plays in, and I don't think it's just about controlling Mike's vote. Emily went to lunch with my mother today, and Mike showed up. She believes they're sleeping together, and if my father knows, this just got personal for him."

"Emily's right," Seth confirms. "We've been watching them. She visits frequently under the guise of redecorating for him."

I cut him a look. "You knew it was more and didn't tell me?"

"Apparently Mike and Maggie have suddenly gotten careless," Nick supplies. "It tends to happen when people go undetected for a while, and feel invincible." He slides a folder to me. "Those are photos we took of them early this morning. She stayed at his house last night, which has not been the case, in the past."

I don't even think about opening that folder. It's enough to have to see my father's mistress in my own building. "Other than pictures, what do you have for me?"

"We still can't tell you whose side he's on," Seth says. "His only connection is your father."

"My father is a man of many double standards. He might fuck around on my mother, but he doesn't want her fucking around on him. Or maybe he does and she does. I have no clue, but Mike and my father have a long history, and that changes everything." My teeth grind together. "Whoever's side Mike is on, my father is against it."

Seth narrows his eyes on me. "What are you thinking?"

"The same thing I'm sure my father is thinking. That my mother is far more of an opportunist than I gave her credit for being. She sees Mike and/or Derek running the company in the future, and she wants to be right there with them."

"That puts your father on your side, and you at the head of the table."

"Unless Mike plans a hostile takeover, which could come at us framed in any number of ways."

"And you think your mother knows about it?" Seth asks, though it's more of a statement of understanding.

My lips thin. "Like I said. She's an opportunist and my eyes are open to the problems he could represent. If he's in with Derek, he's after control. If he's not, he could use Derek's stupidity to force that hostile takeover. Whatever the case, while I was trying to prove Mike was dirty, my father was just looking for the juggler, proving he's a brilliant bastard, and controlling that sports stadium is exactly what we have to do."

"Are you willing to trust your father with that kind of control?"

"Never," I say, "which is why I need to insert myself into the negotiations now, today, and ensure I personally become a key stockholder, which translates to me getting well funded just as quickly."

Seth gives me a deadpan look that I know as his version of *Are you fucking crazy?* before saying, "That's a big undertaking for a small window of time."

"New York is a river of money I know well and I plan to take a deep, dark swim. In the meantime, I need to simplify my problems to a place that the Sports Center solves everything." I look between both men. "Do the raid tonight," I say. "If I have to pay extra, I'll pay it. I want to look in Adrian's eyes and know this is over." I look at Seth. "Get on a plane and go to Boulder now."

"That's fast," Seth warns. "We need time to plan this out."

"I'm going to disagree, Seth," Nick says. "I think tonight is the right move. It presents the heat level from the FBI as high."

"Exactly my thought," I say. "And since my brother went to Adrian the minute he heard about me paying off Brody's wife, you can bet he'll go straight to him when he finds out about this. I want them together. I want Derek to know he has no moves left. And I want to be the one to deliver the news to him about the raid."

"Understood," Nick confirms.

"I'm the voice of reason here obviously," Seth interjects. "Making this happen and doing it right are two different things. Can we do it right?"

"We can and we will," Nick says. "I've already talked to Ted about making it happen." He looks at me. "No extra charge. The sooner we exit the alignment with Martina, the safer the exit, for all of us."

My respect for Nick is officially given freely. "What time?"

"Ten o'clock," Nick says. "We've already started preliminary arrangements, and preparing for this we simply need to expedite it. We'll report to you on your brother's location by nine and we'll have men watching you; blink for assistance if needed."

"I wish like hell one of those men was me," Seth says.

"We'll take good care of everyone," Nick assures him, glancing at his watch. "But it's five o'clock and I have a lot of prep work to pull this together."

"And I have a flight to arrange," Seth says, eyeing me. "Are you staying here or going back to the office?"

"I'll stay here and make sure I avoid any collision with Derek that could throw off our plan, but I'll need to borrow a car or to get a ride to mine at some point."

"I'll have a driver take you to your car," Nick offers. "You'll want to appear as normal tonight as possible, and that means your own car."

"Normal," I say. "There's a concept I barely comprehend." I dismiss my own words, and add, "Emily will drive my car home tonight, so I'll need that ride to be to the Four Seasons."

"Not a problem," Nick says, and both men head for the door,

but while Nick disappears, Seth pauses in the archway. "I don't like you going to see Martina without me."

"He won't kill me," I say. "He needs me. You're another story. I'll see you on the other side of this."

Respect and friendship I value from this man more than any other, perhaps because he gives it rarely, fills his eyes. "Be safe, Shane," he orders, giving me a mock salute before disappearing. I stare at the empty space he no longer occupies, my mind choosing to be just as empty, a brief, but needed, reprieve from the black sludge my brother has created for me. The problem is, he's in it too, and doesn't even see it, and I've accepted he can't be saved. That doesn't mean I have to like it.

Shaking myself, I immediately remove my phone from my jacket and dial my father, who answers quickly and gets right to the point. "Unless this is about the deal we discussed—"

"It is. How much is it going to cost?"

"Four hundred and fifty million."

"And you have the cash."

"I'm short two hundred, but close to getting it."

"I'll give you the cash and the signature you need, but I'll have terms."

"You wouldn't be my son if you didn't, but I wouldn't be your father if I just accepted them. And Shane. Make it fast. I'm on a deadline." He ends the call and I suck in a bitter breath on the words referencing his death. The one thing worse than a lie. Only with Emily . . . I find myself worried about the truth.

I spend hours in Nick's conference room, working to put together a group of interested investors I can use to buy into the Sports Center, and while I have interest, I also have a long list of questions I need to answer for them, and me. By nine o'clock, Derek's location is revealed and it's almost comical to discover he's at Martina's sister's house, fucking himself into a jail cell or a grave, whichever comes first. Nick ends up loaning me a car, and I head in that direction, stopping at the private garage of the Four Seasons and parking next to the Bentley. Wasting no time switching cars, I climb inside my vehicle, my senses instantly filled with the sweet scent of Emily that's permeated the car. The smell softens a part of me I know has become hard, reminding me of everything right about holding her in my arms, that Adrian Martina makes wrong.

My cell phone buzzes with a text message from Nick: *We're a go.*

Translation: Ted's team has entered the BP plant and now I have to wait on the guard to call me to confront Derek. Things are about to get crazy and I dial Emily. "Shane," she says, answering immediately and sounding anxious. "Where are you?"

Close and yet so far away, I think. "Still problem solving. It's going to be a few more hours. Midnight or later."

"Oh. Okay."

"You don't sound like it's okay."

"I'm worried about you."

She's worried about me. Not about the magnitude of the problems she discovered today, but about me. As an adult, I've never thought I needed, or wanted, anyone to worry about me, and yet, Emily caring matters. It calms and soothes the many rough spots inside me, which I am not sure I even knew existed.

"Shane?"

I blink and realize I've lost myself, and her, inside my own head. "It's me who's worried about you."

"I'm safe in the apartment with a trusty guard protecting me."

Her voice is strained, her attempt at lightness failing. She's captive to my hell and her own, and I have to fix it all, starting with Martina, tonight. "A few more hours," I say softly, when my phone beeps. "I have to take that. I'll see you soon."

"Shane, I——"

"Soon, sweetheart."

I end the call and sure enough, it's security at the BP plant. "I'll be there as soon as I can," I say, ending the call, and putting the Bentley in drive. Only ten minutes later, and a few miles away, I park in front of Teresa Martina's little white cottage of a house that runs about half a million——hard to afford on a waitress's pay. I grab the tape recorder from my pocket and turn it on before exiting the vehicle and charge up the walkway, pounding on the door. The curtain moves and then there is silence before Derek steps outside, his shirt hanging out of his pants.

"What the fuck are you doing here?" he demands.

"The FBI is inside the BP facility."

"Fuck." He scrubs the stubble on his jaw. "Right now?"

"Right now."

He inhales and straightens. "They're not going to find anything."

"You better be damn sure of that or we're in a world of hurt right now."

"I am."

"What about in Boulder? Because I just put Seth on a plane in that direction, and I need to warn him if there is anything there."

"It's clean."

"You better be fucking sure, Derek."

"I'm sure, *Shane.*"

"I'm not exactly confident in a man sticking his dick in Adrian Martina's sister. You're really an idiot with a death wish."

"Or really damn smart, but then, you get the friends in the right places thing, or you wouldn't be fucking Emily. Fine piece of ass, man. I hate you beat me to her, but I'm up for the challenge of turning her from your cock to mine."

I want to hurt Derek, and I want to hurt him badly, but this is a test, a way to discover any feelings I have for Emily, which works in my favor in ways Derek can't begin to understand. Not yet but he will. My lips quirk. "You can try," I say, intentionally goading him for a reaction, "but I've always been better than you at everything, and you can't stand it. I, on the other hand, quite enjoy it. I'm going to BP to ensure we don't all end up in jail."

His anger is instant, darkening his features, and crackling in the air around us, but I don't stay to enjoy it. I turn and start walking, his stare following me, a hot beam that feels downright violent, my spine stiff as I wait for an attack that doesn't come. I climb inside my car, and he's no longer on the doorstep. I start the engine, and pull around the corner but still able to see the house, to wait for what I am certain will follow. And sure enough, five minutes later, my brother's Porsche pulls out of the garage, turning toward downtown.

I follow, and in all of ten minutes, we're at Martina's restaurant. I park a block down and watch my brother enter, but I don't alert Nick's people I know are following me. They're here. They're watching, but we all know they can't go inside with me. This one is on me. I grab the tape recorder that's still running and turn it off, and not about to risk Adrian finding it, I leave it in the car. Stepping out of the Bentley, remnants of the snow crunching under my feet, I leave my coat behind. I start walking, the cold air welcome, its biting viciousness reminding me that I am alive and plan to stay that way. Emily's voice plays in my head: *Just come home safely, Shane.* I shove it aside, facing the truth. You don't win in a courtroom by fearing a loss. You enter the room confident, even arrogant, about the preparations you've made up to that point. And that's the person I have to be right now. That's the person *I am.*

I reach the entrance to the restaurant and I don't hesitate even a moment. I pull open the door and enter.

CHAPTER NINETEEN

SHANE

"Table for one?" a hostess asks at the same moment my gaze lands on a rounded booth in the back where my brother now sits with Adrian.

I step around the woman I've barely glanced at and make a beeline for my targets, neither looking up until I'm already sitting down with them. "I think it's time we talk," I say, noting that even in a UFC T-shirt, Adrian has this edge of arrogant money about him that reminds me of my father, who I'd once aspired to be, and perhaps resemble far more than I'd like.

"Holy fuck, Shane," Derek growls. "What are you thinking?"

Adrian arches a brow. "I'd be curious to know the same, since I don't typically take uninvited guests."

"I assume my brother told you the FBI is at the BP facility."

"He did," Adrian confirms, "and since you're understandably concerned, I'll excuse your intrusion. This is uneventful. I told you. Your facilities are clear."

"We are on their radar," I say. "An insider told me the FBI

is looking at sports players as users of a drug they're calling Sub-Zero."

"Because I call it Sub-Zero," he says. "And they've been looking into it for a while. It doesn't show up in tests."

"We have a stockholder that's in sports," I say. "We hold a drug company in our portfolio. Don't you think that makes us dangerously visible?"

"There's a reason we left Mike Rogers out of this," Adrian says, and I see the irritation flash in Derek's face, as if his hand has been shown before the vote. And it has been. I was right about Mike. He's too cautious, with too much to lose, to land in dangerous waters by choice. Adrian sips his whiskey. "He's the perfect cover, don't you think?"

"That's nothing shy of insanity," I say, treading cautiously so as to not get Mike killed. "He's a magnet for attention just like BP is as a pharmaceutical company. Made worse by Derek's careless actions."

"Spoken by the brother afraid to ever take a damn risk," Derek bites out.

I reach into my pocket and grab a sheet of paper, which I unfold and set in front of Adrian. "That's my brother paying off a federal official to get drug approval. The FBI found out."

Adrian inhales a slow, calculated breath and looks at Derek. "Is this true?"

"It was necessary," my brother says, and what comes next is so fast, so unexpected, I don't have time to prepare myself.

Adrian picks up a steak knife, and stabs it through my brother's hand, all the way to the table.

Holy fuck.

Derek cries out in horrific pain and the brother in me wants to rescue him, but Adrian isn't looking at him. He's looking at me. "What the hell?" Derek demands. "Get it out! Shane, get it out!"

I don't move, my gaze locked with Adrian's cold, brutal stare, as he says, "Shut up," to Derek, "or you will not like the results."

I discreetly slide my knee to Derek's, giving him a silent warning, and he sucks in a trembling breath, saying nothing else.

"Where were we?" Adrian asks, his hand leaving the knife, which he doesn't even attempt to remove from my brother's hand. "Oh yes, where Mike Rogers fits in. If our answer is that he doesn't, let's buy him out. Whatever the price, I'll pay it."

And there it is. Adrian is now exactly where he wants to be, setting himself up to own a piece of Brandon Enterprises. "I'm not selling you any part of my company."

"Then I'll go to him directly."

"My father was never an overly honest man," I say. "He got away with a lot of things, and recently I saw him in action, and was reminded that he is a king for a reason. Much like your father. Let's not be the two dead brothers."

He narrows his gaze on me. "You know about my brother."

"And you now know about mine. This is going nowhere good. This will destroy us both."

"We'll take a three-month breather," Adrian says. "We'll let things cool off."

"Three months is nothing to the FBI and don't you think they will look at what prescriptions Brody was taking? That's going to tie back to us."

"He had a legitimate prescription."

"So will others who end up dead."

"No one has died," he insists.

"Brody."

"That was a car accident."

"You and I both know that's not true and this is death number two the FBI is looking into. Real drugs covering for illegal drugs have a trail you can't avoid. In premise, this was a good idea, until you find out where it leads, and that's to you, then your father."

He considers me for several long seconds, his expression unreadable, while Derek's heavy breathing fills the air. "You've become far more profitable to me than you know."

I feel those words like a punch in the chest. "And far more of a liability than you know."

"We'll rotate drugs."

"They still lead back to you and me."

"We'll find a way around it."

"We won't."

"I'm not walking away from the money. You're smart. You'll find a way to protect us, like your father always protected your business before you."

I lean forward. "Like our fathers protected our businesses," I say, making sure he gets the point. "And they survived, and continue to do so, by knowing when to stay out of something, or when to get out, when they were already in."

"Find a way to redirect my sales, and I'll get out, but not until then."

My lips thin. This is not the solution I wanted, but it's at least an option. "I need to know what you're doing, and how you're doing it, in order to do that."

"If you can't figure it out, then neither can the FBI. Figure it out. Get me out with money in my pocket, and we'll be passing friends. And control your bloodline or I will." He rips the knife from Derek's hand, sliding out of the booth, and leaves us with blood everywhere.

I grab a napkin and steady my brother's arm, holding it when it trembles, wrapping his hand, before grabbing another napkin. He doesn't stop me. He hardly moves and is clearly in shock, blood already seeping through the napkins. I grab my tie, loosen it and pull it free, to create a tourniquet around his arm.

"Don't move," I say, standing and walking to the hostess booth, where the woman behind the counter gladly supplies me with more napkins and the scissors she has at the stand. Derek still isn't moving or speaking, and I cut cloth and wrap it around his palm, tying it off this time.

Derek's gaze meets mine, his eyes pure bloodshot hate. He stands up and takes two steps before he sways. I am there before he falls, catching him. Still, he doesn't speak, and I focus on getting him the hell out of here before Adrian makes a further example of him. I manage to get him out the door, and when he shoves away from me and starts walking, he falls again. His weakness and pain, no matter how we've grown apart, guts me, and I drop to a knee by his side. My hand goes to his back, and he arches forward, managing to push to a knee. "Get the fuck away from me, Shane. This isn't over. In fact, it's just begun. He doesn't want out. He's not getting out."

"Derek! Oh God. Derek!"

I look up to find Teresa, Adrian's pretty brunette sister, rushing forward, and she's on her knees in a heartbeat. "Please tell me my brother didn't do this to you." Her hands are on his face, and it's clear she cares about my brother and will take care of him.

"He needs to get to the hospital," I say.

She looks at me. "Yes. Of course. Can you help me get him——"

"No," Derek growls. "No help."

I inhale and let it out, pushing to my feet, and walking to my car, my legs weak from the rush of adrenaline surging through me. Digging out my keys, I click the locks and slide into the driver's seat, staring forward, the sweet scent of Emily fading into that of blood and betrayal. I don't let myself think about it just yet, needing to get past a visit to the BP facility that will be expected to uphold this failure of a façade. I start the engine and drive to the facility. I barely make it in the front door before Lana has thrown herself into my arms, hugging me.

"Oh God. I can't believe this is happening."

Irritated that I'll now have to explain to Emily why I smell like a woman she knows I once fucked, I grab her arms and pull her off me. "Why are you even here at this hour?"

"I've been auditing records later at night, checking up on that problem you and I discussed. The problem that brought the FBI here." Her eyes go wide. "Oh my God. Why are you bleeding?"

I don't blink. "It's not me. My brother cut his hand and at this point, I have no idea why the FBI is here, but you keep your mouth shut."

She gives me big puppy-dog eyes. "You know I would never betray you."

In other words, she would. "We'll talk tomorrow."

"Okay," she says, all innocent when she is not. "Tomorrow."

Regretting any involvement she has, despite her figuring out Ridel is the hiding spot for Sub-Zero, I walk toward the security booth. Ted, a tall, dark-haired man in jeans and T-shirt, a gun at his hip, presents his badge and we head into a private office, where I update him on the failure of this operation. As my contact man he's not any more pleased than I am, but full of assurances they'll come up with another plan.

It's an hour later when I finally pull into the Four Seasons hotel, having decided I've played too nice and too straight up. I can't win that way, but I'll find an answer that gets Adrian out of my company, and I have one thing my brother does not: My father is on my side now, and ironically, I guess I have my mother to thank for that. I might be farther from an answer to my Adrian Martina problem than I thought, but I'm closer to the head of the table.

But right now, my biggest challenge is facing Emily. The easiest thing to explain will be the blood and perfume on my shirt. The hardest will be that I'm now committed to working for a drug cartel, while my brother is committed to making sure the next knife is in my hand.

Lies destroy, but I fear the truth is worse. Maybe lies are better. Or maybe they aren't.

EMILY

Somehow, I end up in black sweats and a tank top rather than pajamas, sitting in the middle of the floor of Shane's office, leaning against the couch to the far left of the door, a laptop on the coffee table, and files all around it. I'm obsessing about a Brandon clothing and cosmetics line, loving the idea, and I try to focus on every way this is a good move, in order to present the plan to Shane. But my gaze keeps going to the time on the laptop, where I'm putting together spreadsheets on companies, historical profits, and success stories. It's midnight, the moment the pumpkin is no longer a carriage and I feel a bit like Cinderella, dreading the loss of her prince, and I don't like how it feels.

Twelve thirty comes and the door opens and closes, sending a rush of relief through me, but I force myself not to move. He's home. He's safe. We can talk, but rushing at him and demanding answers won't help us as a couple at all. And I don't want to be this nagging, demanding woman, who says *Now, now, now.* I want to be his partner in life, and that means he has to invite me into it.

That means I might have to accept that he's not ready to talk and that my need for immediacy is, at least in part, about me and my past, not him.

He appears in the doorway, oddly wearing a T-shirt with his dress pants. "Hey sweetheart," he says, eyeing my work. "What are you working on so late?"

I move to sit on the edge of the couch. "I have this idea for Brandon Enterprises that I'm pretty excited about. I'm trying to make sure I give you reason to be as well."

He leans on the door frame as if he isn't overly anxious to come near me, and I'm not sure why or how to feel about that. "Cosmetics and clothing. Ties. Shoes. Purses. We could buy stock in a big company, but there are several growing brands with potential we could take over. It's really not corruptible and we could have brands within the brand to hit price points, and ensure economic stability."

"I like it," he says quickly. "And I really like that you're so excited about it."

"I am," I reply, and the silence that follows beats like my heart—unbearably heavy—and I blurt out. "Why are you dressed like that?"

"I was with Derek when he had a hand injury. He bled all over me."

"Oh God. Is he okay?"

"He didn't exactly invite me to the hospital with him." He hesitates. "There's another reason. There was an ordeal at the facility tonight. I went there, and Lana greeted me at the door by flinging her arms around me. There were witnesses. A camera, and I can—"

"I don't need a camera or witnesses," I say, no hesitation in my response. "I want to not feel what I feel right now. I want to stop thinking I'm my mother, with a rich man buying me things and keeping secrets."

I've barely gotten the words out and Shane is in front of me, shoving back the coffee table and bringing me to my feet, his hands cupping my face. "Don't do that to you, me, or us. Don't make us them when we are not. I worked my ass off for my money that has no connection to my family and I invested it well. I won't apologize for my money or finally having someone I want to spend it with or on." He doesn't give me time to digest that before he moves on. "As for secrets, I have none. I simply have things I wanted to fix before they scared you away."

My heart squeezes with the emotion etched in his confessions and I flatten my hand on his chest, his heart thundering beneath my palm, telling a story of worry and trepidation. "This is me you're talking to. You know my past. You can't scare me away."

He takes my hands in his. "We're about to find out."

More relief washes over me with those words and he sits, taking me to the couch with him, his hands settling on mine where they rest on my knees. "Let me cut to the chase. Tonight was all about a major effort that should have let me tell you what I'm about to tell you, and that I could have prefaced by saying that it's over. It failed. It's not over."

"What isn't over?"

"Derek got involved with a drug cartel who wanted to infiltrate a legal pharmaceutical company."

"Oh God. That's bad. Really bad."

"Yes. It is. That Escalade belongs to Adrian Martina, the son of the kingpin, who is proving his value through us."

"How are they using BP for illegal drugs?"

"There's a new stimulant that isn't detectable in testing, and they're packaging it as one of our near defunct drugs. The story is long, but I hired men to stage an FBI raid that was intended to spook Adrian. It didn't. He says if I want him out, I have to find a way to replace the profits for him."

I study him for several beats. "And you agreed."

"I didn't agree, but it's that or go to the FBI, which would ensure my brother goes to jail, and our company is tainted in a way we might not recover from. I bought a drug company, a corruptible entity, with my brother, who is corruptible. It was, perhaps, the biggest mistake of my life."

"It's not a mistake, Shane," I insist. "This is not your fault. It's your brother's and he has to be stopped before he destroys us all. What happened to his hand?"

"Adrian put a knife in it."

My eyes go wide. "Did it at least scare him?"

"No. It did not scare him."

"Of course not," I say. "It's Derek. Can you sell BP?"

"Not without Adrian coming after me. Unless . . ."

His brow furrows and I press for more. "Unless?"

He refocuses on me. "You might have sparked an idea I need to work through, but not right now." He softens his voice. "I can send you away until this is over. I can—"

I lean in and press my lips to his, my hand curling at his jaw. "Why would I leave you now, when you're going through hell? Why would anyone who cares about someone else do that?"

He takes my hand in his again, and leans back to look at me. "It's a drug cartel. They're vicious. They're dangerous."

"And you have me guarded around the clock. I do think this makes the idea of this new clothing and makeup line all the more important. It's—"

I blink and I'm on my back with him on top of me. "I want to hear about it, but not now. Right now is about us. I almost lied to you. I walked down the hallway to the apartment, thinking of things I could tell you that you'd believe."

"Why didn't you?

"Because your honesty about your feelings, about your mother and stepfather, unraveled what might have been my lies. We aren't them. I won't let us become them. And I have never needed anyone the way I do you right now."

"I need you too," I whisper, and a frenzy of undressing follows until we are naked on the couch, me straddling him, his hand in my hair, dragging my mouth a breath from his.

"I need to taste like you, and smell like you, and feel your skin everywhere against mine," he declares, his voice roughened with passion.

Heat rushes through me, my sex clenching his cock, his name whispering from my lips. "Shane, I—"

He kisses me, a deep ravishing, hungry kiss that borders on desperation. I do not believe I fully understand it, but some part of me knows that it's telling a story that is dark, hard, and passionate, in ways I need to reveal. And while yes, those things are about us, I believe they are more about him, and where he feels he is being pulled, and that I cannot, under any circumstances, let him go.

SHANE

Saturday proves to be typical of Colorado, with the snowstorm gone, temperatures in the sixties, and plenty of time for Emily and me to try to put the last seventy-two hours out of our minds. We walk the city, shop, talk, and buy furniture. In between it all, we stop for coffee, and I tell her all about Mike, my father, and the win of having him on my side, despite the way it's come about. It's news she celebrates with me, and hours later, we order takeout, settle onto the couch in my office, and get lost in developing a new fashion brand for Brandon Enterprises. When we've finished our takeout, I pull her beneath me on the couch.

"This is a brilliant idea."

"You really think so?"

"Yes. I do. And I should have thought of it myself. I want you to run this division."

"Shane—"

"I really want you to run it. You thought of it. I've listened to all of your ideas. This is your baby and you deserve the credit and the creative control."

"Can we do it together?"

"We can do everything together as far as I'm concerned. You know everything now, Emily. I wasn't trying to shut you out. I was just trying to protect you. I'll get you the name of an analyst to contact about reviewing the companies you'd like to look into acquiring."

I kiss her then, and it's a long time before we start back to work. And for the rest of the day I make sure I tell her she's beautiful. I tell her she's mine. Before, after, and during moments I have her naked. What I don't tell her is that I love her. It's there. It's between us and I know she feels the unspoken words as I do, but I need to deserve her when I say them. And right now, there is a war raging not just with my family, but within me, between good and evil. I have to end Adrian Martina's control of my family, and I've learned a lesson. I can't think like me, like the way I used to. I have to think like my father. I have to think like Martina himself. I have to do whatever it takes to win, and in the process, I have to keep from lying to Emily about what that means. Because lies do destroy.

Come Sunday morning, I wake with her pressed to my side,

and I lie there, staring at the ceiling as the sun comes up, thinking of the loss of my law career, the loss of her schooling that somehow led us to each other. "Penny for your thoughts," she says, proving she's as awake as me.

Having no desire to start her day thinking about law school, I reply with my belly, not my brain. "I'm thinking I want pancakes, then you," I say, rolling her to her back. "Actually, amend that to you, pancakes, and then you again."

My cell phone rings and we ignore it, which is easily done considering we're both already naked. A good hour later, we split my pajamas between us—her in my shirt, while I slip into my pants—and head to the kitchen, where we dive into the job of pancake making. Emily is managing the batter on the stove, and I'm making us both coffee when the doorbell rings.

Emily abandons the stove and faces me. "Seth?" she asks, hugging herself, already looking worried, and I hate that I can't take away her fear that the Geminis will one day find her, no matter how hard I try. It will always be there in the back of her mind.

I step to her and cup her face. "Stop fretting. Seth wouldn't show up on a Sunday unannounced. Housekeeping stops by on the weekends." I kiss her and my nose twitches. "I smell burning pancakes."

"Oh dang it." She turns to the stove and murmurs something not very ladylike that still manages to be adorable coming from her, and I'm laughing as I reach the door, only to have the bell ring again.

"Shane!" she calls out. "You have no shirt on!"

"Because you're wearing it!" I call back, opening the door, taken aback to find my father standing there in yesterday's suit, his tie in his pocket. He eyes my chest, his lips quirking with surprisingly good humor, before he says, "I smell pancakes."

His nose twitches. "Burnt pancakes. That's no way to keep a woman, son."

Now, it's my lips that quirk, and I can't remember the last time I shared a moment of amusement with my father. "Would you like some burnt pancakes, Father?" I ask, unable to judge him anymore for his woman on the side, considering my mother has Mike on the side, and I have no idea who came first. "Obviously you've been in the building working up an appetite."

"I ate," he assures me. "Just reminding you about dinner tonight."

"I'll be there."

"Bring Emily. That's not a request. It's mandatory." He turns and starts walking away.

I inhale and shut the door, returning to find Emily throwing out the pancakes. "I'm starting a new batch," she says, then asks, "Was that your father?"

I rest my hands on the island and she turns to look at me. "He wants you at dinner tonight."

She studies me a moment and then leans on the counter. "Do you want me to go? Because Shane, there's no pressure from me."

"I always want you by my side, Emily. Tonight is no exception, but of course, my father is playing a game."

"I can handle your father's games. You know that and I want to be by your side, Shane, but my concern is Derek. You said we were keeping a low profile with Derek."

"I also thought I was ending this Martina problem last night. That didn't happen. You're in my life. Derek is going to figure that out."

"Actually, your mother referenced the way we look at each other and made it pretty clear she thought we were more than a fling."

I round the counter and snag her hips, pulling her to me. "It's time we make it clear we're a couple."

Her hand flattens on my chest. "What about Derek?"

"We've filled in the holes in your past, which was what I wanted handled before he had a reason to look any closer at you."

"He is looking closer at me as of yesterday," she says. "I saw that in his eyes. I'm a target."

My mind goes to the recording I'd made outside Teresa's house last night; I should have already played it back. If it's as perfect as I think it is, I own my brother. "He can't touch you," I say, cupping her backside. "Just me, sweetheart, which is how I plan to keep it."

"I like how you touch me," she says, and despite her daring, her cheeks flush, a contradiction of qualities I find sexy as hell.

"Screw the pancakes," I say, setting her on a barstool, and going down on one leg in front of her, my hands settling on her bare thighs. "It's you I want."

She smiles, and sighs follow, but pancakes do not. We order room service. I think Emily and I will be ordering a lot of room service, and that suits me just fine.

Despite the early six o'clock hour, it's already dark outside when we arrive at my parents' house. I park the Bentley at the rear of the house, next to Derek's Porsche.

"I'm suddenly nervous," Emily says, as I open her door and help her to her feet, the dim glow of outdoor lighting surrounding us, a light breeze lifting her long, dark hair.

"Don't be," I say, draping a black cashmere wrap over her navy blouse, which I've matched with my tie, skipping a jacket. "You know my family and you were right. You do handle their games well."

"I hate that the word 'family' means games to you."

I gather her hand in mine and kiss her fingers. "Family means you to me now, Emily."

Her expression softens. "That is the best thing you've ever said to me. You're that to me too. You really are and it's kind of scary."

"Then we'll be scared together."

"You? Scared? Never, Shane Brandon."

"I don't want to lose you," I admit. "Alone is safe. There is no fear of losing anything. You can't get hurt."

"Then you've never truly felt alone, because alone is a cold, empty place."

I cup her face. "You will never feel that again. And before you ask, I promise." I lean in and kiss her, my tongue doing one slow, caress against hers, followed by her shiver. "Let's get you inside." I drape my arm over her shoulder, and we enter the open foyer with towering ceilings I always take for granted, but Emily is amazed, walking to the center of the tiled room, and staring up at the domed ceiling.

"I love this so much," she declares as my mother enters from the kitchen, and laughs.

"I still do and say that sometimes," she declares, looking lovely as ever in black pants and a matching blouse, and while I'd love to just be proud of my mother, I can't. The son in me is thinking of her nabbing Mike, a younger, powerful man, and how that might be related to positioning herself for the future.

"Come to the library," my mother says. "Our chef says he needs another thirty minutes to serve and your father has a pre-dinner announcement that even I've been kept in the dark about. Frankly, I'm eager to find out what it is."

Emily and I share a curious look, and I close the space between us, taking her wrap and hanging it by the door before lacing the fingers of one of her hands with mine. Together, we walk ahead of my mother and under the winding stairwell to the right, passing through the towering arched wooden door. Once over the threshold, we find my brother and father standing at the fireplace against the far wall, in deep conversation.

"It's gorgeous," Emily murmurs beside me, while my gaze lands on Derek's hand, which is now well bandaged. I am struck by how alike my father and brother are tonight, both dressed in starched white shirts, both tall and striking in similar ways.

Shaking off the idea that I too am like them, I turn my gaze on Emily, to find her taking in the walls, lined with bookshelves, and topped with another domed ceiling that is painted to look like a globe, and the fireplace burning in the center of the far wall.

"My parents do have good taste," I agree. "And I wonder how my brother explained that bandage on his hand."

"I was wondering the same," she replies softly.

"I have the champagne," my mother announces, breezing past us, and toward my father and brother, while I guide Emily that direction and inside the square formed by the dark brown leather couch framed by chairs.

My father motions to Derek. "Give it to him." He eyes Derek. "Open the bottle, son."

Derek lifts his hand and my father grimaces. "Right. The attack of the steak knife your date somehow landed in your hand." He looks at me. "Get it done, Shane."

Derek's expression darkens with the irony of the moment that says I always have to come to the rescue, and the look he gives me is pure hate. I open the champagne while my mother holds out glasses, which I fill as she passes them out. Finally, I set the bottle on the ledge above the bar and step to Emily's side.

That's when Derek's eyes land on Emily. "Had I known we were bringing dates, I could have brought one myself."

"If your date is Teresa Martina," I say, "we're all better off with you leaving her at home."

"And yet Emily is welcomed?"

"Emily won't get us all killed," I say, while my father adds, "I invited Emily."

"And I want her here," I add, "because she's now family. She lives with me."

"Oh my," my mother says. "That's amazing." She smiles at Emily. "I knew there was more to you two."

"Interesting," Derek says, his eyes glinting with a purpose I don't like and will shut down.

"Let's move on," my father says. "Originally, this was going to be a dinner to announce the vote for head of the table. New events have occurred and I'm canceling the board meeting."

It's not a completely unexpected move, considering my father is now looking to control Mike before that vote, but it does seem to indicate his desire to do so is newfound.

"What new events?" Derek demands, his voice cutting with irritation.

He holds up his glass. "Seems I shouldn't drink my way through chemo, and to my grave, after all. This drink is for show tonight, at least, for me. There's a new experimental cancer treatment I've been approved to take part in. Of course, a generous donation to the right people helped."

My mother's eyes go wide, relief filling her face. "What treatment? How successful is it? When can you start?"

Her response pleases me, but I've researched these experimental treatments and fear she is simply headed for more pain.

"What matters here," my father says, "is they've had patients

enter remission that otherwise were thought to be imminently terminal. I won't be giving up control of the company as quickly as I
thought might be necessary."

My mother hands me her glass and embraces my father. Emily moves forward and takes my father's glass as well, and he wraps
my mother in his arms. Derek's gaze meets mine and he eyes the
chess table sitting on the far left wall. "Let's play, shall we?"

The last thing I want is to join Derek in a game of chess, but
it's better than standing here, looking at each other. I down my
champagne and set both glasses on the coffee table. "Game on," I
say, giving him my back, my hands coming down on Emily's shoulders, softening my voice. "You okay?"

"Of course. I'm not fragile."

My lips quirk. "No. No, you are not."

"But please kick his ass in chess."

"I will," I promise, releasing her to claim the leather chair
across the table from my brother. "How long has this game been
set up and going?"

"Seven years," he supplies, "but I say we end it tonight."

"Yes," I agree. "Let's end it tonight."

We start playing, and the game is quickly intense. I lose track
of time. My father pulls a chair up to sit between us. My mother
tries to get us to break for dinner. But Derek and I stare at the
board and soon I am backed into a corner. Derek's gaze meets mine.
"You could always sacrifice your queen and let her die a royal
death. Would it—would she—be worth it to win?"

My blood runs cold, the threat against Emily clear. I am about
to reach in my pocket and remove the tape I made of him at Teresa's house the other night when my father leans in close and says,
"If anything happens to Emily, Derek, I will disinherit you. And
I mean *anything*, so you damn sure better hope a natural disaster

doesn't happen." He reaches into his pocket and sets a piece of paper on the board. "There's the amended page. It's done. She's one of us now and we protect her."

"Why do you care about Emily?"

I might be shocked at my father's actions, obviously planned to be a part of this night, but his motivation is clear to me. He wants my support to take down Mike, which means he'll protect what is mine. His answer, however, is more simply his own, typical of who he is, and always has been. "Because only pussies use their women to fight their wars. Real men, Brandon men, fight one-on-one."

Derek stands up and so do I, but my gaze lands on the empty spot where Emily no longer sits. I forget about my brother and my father, cutting around them to find Emily is not in the room. Nor is she with my mother, who is standing by the fireplace. She lifts a finger to point toward the door, the look on her face warning me that Emily had reacted to the exchange that just took place. Exiting the library, I search the foyer and the kitchen, my gut telling me she's outside. Sure enough, she's standing under a tree in the center of the yard, and she hasn't even bothered with her wrap. Concerned, I walk to her but she doesn't turn when I know she must hear my steps.

"Emily," I say, stepping in front of her, my hands settling against her neck, under her hair. "What's wrong?"

"Your brother threatened to kill me."

"I don't think that's what he meant."

"Your father did. What are we doing here? What is happening?"

I press my forehead to hers. "We're okay. You're okay."

"I think I need you to promise that right now."

"I promise."

In that moment, I know I should offer to send her away again, but I can't find the words. I can't send her away. No matter how selfish it makes me, I need her too much to let her go. And if I have to use the tape I made to protect her, even at the expense of Derek's life, I will. Without question and for the first time, I can say it without guilt. I know that means that this war has changed me. I know that winning it—which I must—will change me even more. But I am also certain that I won't lose myself, as long as I don't lose Emily.

ABOUT THE AUTHOR

New York Times and *USA Today* bestselling author LISA RENEE JONES is the author of the highly acclaimed Inside Out series, which is now in development for a cable television show to be produced by Suzanne Todd (*Alice in Wonderland*). In addition, her Tall, Dark, and Deadly series and The Secret Life of Amy Bensen series both spent several months on the *New York Times* and *USA Today* lists. Since beginning her publishing career in 2007, Lisa has published more than forty books translated around the world.